Gravity s Whisper
By Ben Winter

Gravity s Whisper
By Ben Winter

Published by Success Improv, Colorado, USA

ISBN: 979-8-9895476-8-5

For inquiries and other work by Ben Winter, contact:
https://mrimprov.com

Author's Notes

This book is the third to emerge from a five-book challenge I set for myself—to write five novels at the same time. Ambitious? Definitely. Smart? Not so much. I've since learned that I write best when I focus on one story at a time. Sure, hopping between books helped me sidestep writer's block, but it also left each story paused in limbo while I wrapped up the one before it.

If you're looking for writing advice, I don't recommend that kind of challenge. But I do recommend finding support. Having friends or a group to bounce ideas off is invaluable.

I owe a big thanks to John Osborn—an aspiring author himself—who gave me the nudge I needed when I was stuck. John, you'll recognize your suggestion in the book immediately. Thank you.

And of course, I must thank my rocks:

- Chris Hagon, a brilliant author and one of my most trusted creative minds.
- My mom, a brilliant author as well, whose talent and encouragement continue to inspire e.
- The love of my life, for supporting me during my oddest writing hours.
- And my son, who doesn't read my books but still asks about them. That alone means everything.

I truly enjoyed writing this story—if I hadn't, it wouldn't be finished. And is it finished? Honestly… I'm not sure. A sequel has started tugging at my brainstem. Will it happen? Time will tell. In the meantime, another book from the challenge is well underway, and it's time I turned my attention there.

Finally, to anyone reading this who's ever thought about writing: do it. Start. Don't worry if anyone else reads it—just enjoy the journey.

Chapter 1

"Fuck!" Doug snaps, slamming his palm down on the control panel. "Not again."

He's strapped into the pilot seat of his busted, overused single-rider personal skimmer, frantically pressing buttons and flipping switches like a madman trying to wake the dead. Nothing responds. The console lights stay dark. The hum of the engine? Silent. The onboard diagnostics? Useless—because he can't afford a real one.

"Stranded again," he mutters. "This broke-ass bullshit is going to end me."

Doug kicks the console in frustration. "Can't afford repairs. Can't afford diagnostics. Can't afford a ship smart enough to scream before something breaks instead of after."

He pounds a side panel. "What am I even doing out here? Can't keep scraping parts off dead junkers forever. Rent's past due. Food cubes running low. If I don't get to this gig, I'm toast."

The spiral begins.

"No backup generator. No nav system. No ship system monitoring computer. Just me and this tin can playing dead again in the middle of nowhere. Fuck!"

Doug exhales a sigh and flips the one switch he knows will work: his distress beacon. It clicks on with a tired pulse. At least that part of the ship isn't garbage—he checks it before every flight like it's his religion.

He unbuckles himself and floats out of his chair, arms crossed, seething. "And now I can't even make the credits to fix this hunk of trash… because I can't get to work. This is a perfect circle of failure. What an unlucky and fucked up life."

Doug isn't exactly intimidating. He's in his late twenties, with a wiry frame and lean arms from years of hauling tools and crawling through cramped service corridors. His short brown hair is perpetually disheveled, not because he tries to look a certain way—but because even when he does try, it just ends up that way. His coveralls are old and faded, stitched in too many places to count.

Growling, he pushes himself beneath the console, knees knocking against floating panels as he starts tearing open access points. Wires spill out like guts. He yanks a few more panels, throwing them across the room in frustration. They bounce off walls and drift back toward him like taunting debris. With the imitation gravity out because the ship is down, placing things nearby isn't an option.

"Stupid floating shit," he grumbles, swatting one of the panels out of the air only to have it collide gently with his knee.

He flings it again out of frustration, then slams his fist into the pilot's chair. The rebound launches him backward, and his head smacks into a sharp edge near a cluster of wires.

"Fuck!" Doug shouts in anger.

Pain blooms behind his eyes. He swears again, louder this time, and then—blip—a small tone echoes from the nearby scanner panel.

Doug groans, pushing off the floor. He floats toward the sound, already spotting a few crimson droplets of blood hanging in the air. He touches the back of his head—yep, bleeding.

"Perfect," he mutters, snatching the wound kit from the wall. He applies gel, feeling the blood clot and harden around the wound.

He looks at the scanner. "Well, something's working."

It's faint. A signal spike, brief and odd. No ship ID, no transponder signature. Just a fleeting presence. Doug narrows his eyes and starts tapping at the controls to isolate the signal.

"Where's the ship?" he asks aloud.

He cycles filters. Asteroids, comets, radiation—none of it matches. The blip's gone, like it was never there.

"Maybe I hit my head harder than I thought…"

Still rubbing his head, he opens the logs. The scanner did record something—a raw, low-frequency burst that registers like... thunder. A short rumble, a static crunch that tapers off like a dying quake. But thunder doesn't happen in a vacuum.

Doug stares at it for a while. "No way that's a ship. That's got to be a malfunction. Just what I need."

He pulls himself back under the console, trying not to overthink the strange reading or spiral further into what it means if it is a malfunction. "Whatever. Doesn't matter unless it comes back."

The next couple hours are a blur of digging and swearing. Doug checks wiring harnesses, coolant lines, power junctions—anything that might cause a system-wide blackout. In the process, he finds exactly two things: dust, and a very dead flerp.

The flerp— a little rodent shaped lizard that eats insects, smaller animals, and really any scraps of food left around, just like an Earth rat—floats stiff and curled like a scaley hairball with teeth.

"Guess you picked the wrong ship to hide on," Doug mutters. "I barely eat myself. You must've starved months ago."

He flicks the flerp aside. It tumbles end-over-end before settling against a vent grille.

Doug stares at his suit locker. His EVA suit hangs there like a cruel joke, crusty with time and wear. He opens the locker and inspects it. One boot is warped, one glove's pressurization seal is cracked, and the oxygen tank has a stress fracture from his last near-death excursion.

"Yeah… last resort," he tells himself. "More like first step to dying."

I need a nap, Doug finally says to himself. Naps, his easy escape from worrying.

He floats back into the cockpit and straps into the chair. The scanner volume? Maxed. Eyes? Closed. Doug? Asleep in thirty seconds. He's always been good at that. Probably because his life requires a lot of escaping.

BLIP!

The alert punches through the silence and jerks Doug awake. "Shit—too loud," he mutters, blinking rapidly.

He unstraps, drifts over to the scanner. Another seismic-style reading—like the first one. But this one originates from a different direction.

"That can't be right..."

He compares the data. Location markers, timestamp, wave pattern—nope, it's not the same origin point. Just another random rumble from deep space.

"What the hell is that?" Doug mutters, gripping the console.

Then a new tone. A third blip. This one's different—clean. Ship-class signal. Someone's out there.

Doug checks the data. "Finally," he sighs. "Something real."

He looks toward the flerp. "Cross your claws, buddy. Let's hope they're not pirates."

This new ship draws near, then docks with a magnetic clunk. The corridor pressurizes. A few seconds later—knock knock—someone raps on the door.

Doug floats to the hatch and checks his sidearm. His laser bolt sits in its holster: compact, short-range, and set to stun. But it can definitely kill at the right setting. He adjusts it out of instinct, takes a breath, and opens the door.

Standing there is a woman coated in grease, grime, and confidence. Her jumpsuit is shredded at the knees, and there's a spanner wrench strapped to her thigh. Her face is smudged, but behind all the dirt, her skin is smooth, her eyes sharp and amused. Her bright red hair—almost crimson—is tied back under a cap, but strands escape wildly like she couldn't care less. She looks like she's been elbow-deep in starship guts for a year straight, and she wears that look like armor and pride.

"Hella place ta break down," she says casually.

Doug raises an eyebrow and says with a smile. "Anywhere in space is a bad place to break down."

"Ain't dat right," she smirks, peeking past him.

"Doug," he says, extending a hand.

"Clutch," she replies, gripping it with a mechanic's strength.

"That's a weird—"

"Weird name?" she interrupts. "E'ryone says dat 'til dey getta know me."

"Fair enough," Doug shrugs. "What's your real name?"

"Dat's kinda personal, dontcha tink?" she says, winking. "Let's getcha ta a station."

Doug lets out a dry chuckle. "Sure. Let's call it that. More like you drop me off and I rot while my job fires me for not showing up, leaving me stranded forever."

"Whatcha mean?"

"I'm broke. Was on my way to work. If I don't get there, I don't eat. If I don't eat, I don't survive. You know the cycle."

Clutch pauses, then shrugs. "I could take a look. See whatcha got busted. Got a suit?"

Doug laughs. "If I get in that suit, I'll end up an ice sculpture."

Clutch grins. "Well, ain't you jus' all kinds of fucked? Follow me."

She turns and walks back into her ship. Doug hesitates, then pushes after her. As soon as he crosses into her airlock, he hits gravity induction panels and stumbles.

Clutch chuckles, watching him wobble. "Grav ain't workin' needer?"

"Nope," Doug replies, catching his footing.

"Yup. Fucked," she says with a grin.

Doug smiles despite himself and follows. He fights the urge to ask if she's alone—better not to seem like a threat. Instead:

"So… what brings you to this back-end of nowhere? Nobody comes here unless they're desperate or hiding."

"'Splorin'," Clutch says.

"Sounds fun," Doug replies, unsure what she means.

"Treasure huntin', aksh'ly. Ain't found nutin' yet."

Doug snorts. "Takes a crew, a bankroll, and luck to find anything of value these days."

"Nah. Just willpower 'n desire," Clutch replies, her confidence undeterred.

"What kind of treasure? If you don't mine me asking," Doug asks, just to keep the conversation going.

"Anytin' new 'n diff'ren'. Old aileen shit, idee'ly."

Doug raises an eyebrow. "We've never met aliens. Nor has there ever been any proof they exist."

"I'm gonna be da first ta fine sometin'," Clutch replies.

That pretty much confirms she's alone, Doug thinks to himself.

"How do you afford this lifestyle?" Doug asks.

"Ain't ya a nosey fella," she laughs.

"Just curious. I would love to be in your position. Finding something of significance would be a dream come true," Doug shares. "Plus, if there is a better way for me to make a living, I want to know about it."

She doesn't respond, instead, she leads him into the galley—cramped but functional. Clutch points to a chair. Doug sits, scanning the ship's interior for clues about her background.

Clutch pulls food packs from a cabinet and drops one in front of him.

"Eat."

"Yes ma'am," Doug says out of habit.

Clutch's face turns cold. "Ain't no need ta be rude," her voice stern.

"What? Calling you ma'am is rude?" Doug asks, concerned he upset the one person who showed up to help.

"Yeah it is. I ain't no ma'am."

Doug lifts his hands, surrendering. "Alright. Clutch it is. No offense meant."

She nods. "Dat's better. Now eat up. Den we'ill getcha fixed up."

Chapter 2

Doug finishes the last bite and leans back, patting his stomach. "Thanks for the food, Clutch. I haven't had a good meal in… I don't even know how long."

"Yer welcome," Clutch says through a mouthful, crumbs dusting her chin as she chews. She washes it down with a long gulp from a dented water canister, then lets out a sharp, unapologetic burp.

Doug chuckles, appreciating how normal Clutch seems. "Are you seriously going to help me with my ship?"

"Karma," she says bluntly, wiping her mouth with her sleeve.

Doug raises an eyebrow. "Karma?"

"I ain't one ta fuck wif karma," she says, tilting back in her chair. "If I can keep da balance by helpin' some'un driffin' in space, I'ill do it. Keeps da 'verse from bitch-slappin' me layder."

Doug smiles at her logic. It's crude, but somehow comforting. "I like it."

Clutch stands, brushing off her hands and motioning for Doug to follow. "Come on. Let's see if I got a suit yer size."

They head out of the galley, her boots clanking softly on the floor panels as Doug trails behind. He glances around, noting the layout of her ship. It's more spacious than he expected—cleaner too, despite the grease stains and clutter. Practical. Lived-in.

When they reach the cargo bay, Doug whistles. "Wow! I think I could park my entire ship in here."

"Nope," Clutch replies without missing a beat. "Ya got an Awop77. Jus' a meter too wide. Ain't matter how ya twist it. She ain't fittin'."

"Figures. That'd be my luck," Doug says, rolling his eyes.

"Ya don't like walkin'?" Clutch asks.

"You mean space-walks?" Doug asks, just making sure he heard her correctly.

"Yup."

Doug exhales slowly. "Not really. Almost died once. Lost my grip. Drifted for twenty minutes before someone snagged me."

Clutch winces. "No tedder? Ain't ya got no backup?"

"No money. Remember? Tethers might be essential, but so is food," Doug replies, reserving his self-hatred for when he has time to himself.

She snorts. "Boy, ya could do wit' some karma fixin'."

"You ain't lyin'," Doug says with a chuckle.

"Ya makin' fun?" she asks, stopping to eye him sharply.

Doug puts his hands up. "No, ma'—uh, Clutch, not at all. Just something I heard a lot growing up."

She squints at him for a second, then grins and keeps walking. "Mmm hmm."

She stops at a row of lockers and pops one open. Inside hangs a space suit, clean, organized, and clearly maintained.

Doug wipes the back of his neck, relieved she didn't bite his head off. "Looks like it might fit."

"Prolly will. Go 'head n' suit up. I'ill grab mine."

She disappears down the corridor while Doug pulls the suit out and inspects it like protocol taught him. He checks the seals, flex points, filtration ports—everything. It's pristine. Better than anything he's ever worn.

A few minutes later, Clutch rounds the corner already half-suited. "Ya ain't ready yet?"

"I was doing a suit check," Doug justifies.

She tilts her head. "Ya ain't trus' me?"

Doug shrugs. "Don't really know you. And it's habit. Drilled into us since we were kids."

She smirks. "Good habit. Jus' s'upid when I'm 'round. I keep my s'uff good."

"I believe you," Doug says, sliding into the suit. "But this thing looks brand new."

"'Cause I keep it dat way."

Once they're both geared up, she leads him to an exterior airlock. She moves like she's done this a thousand times—efficient, unbothered. Doug follows, his nerves rising the closer they get to open space.

Clutch opens the inner hatch and steps inside the lock, motioning for Doug to follow. She tethers him to her belt, then clips herself to the ship. When the inner hatch closes and everything is secure, she opens the outer hatch.

A rush of silence and starlight pours in. Black space yawns around them—cold, infinite, merciless.

They push off. Clutch leads confidently, one hand securing a second tether from her belt to Doug's ship before unclipping from her own.

"Tedders," she says with a smug grin.

Doug groans. "Sure. Just rub it in."

Clutch smiles and moves on.

They float toward his ship, grabbing external grasp points as they reach the hull. Clutch immediately starts inspecting the exterior with a practiced eye.

Doug watches for a few moments, then speaks up. "Hey— are you good with scanners?"

Clutch doesn't look up. "Course. Why?"

"Mine picked up two weird readings before you showed up. Didn't make sense. Thought maybe the scanner was broken."

"Wurf a look," she says casually. "But ya saw me comin', didn' ya? Cain't be dat broke. We'ill check it after."

Doug nods, still unsure what to make of the strange signals.

They drift around the hull until Clutch stops abruptly and opens a couple of panels near the engines.

"Well, der's yer prob'em."

Doug squints. "What am I looking at?"

"Ya got shit fuck'd in here," she declares flatly.

"Very technical," Doug says, doing his best not to be overly sarcastic.

"Yup," she says, already pulling components free. "Buncha cross-link wirin', co'sion on da coolin' ducs… and what da fuck?"

She pulls out a stiff, shriveled flerp and tosses it into space. The little thing tumbles in slow motion, its scaly body twisting with each turn.

Doug flinches. "Could've warned me! I thought you were throwing out part of my ship!"

Clutch just laughs and pulls out another. Then another.

"Ya got a 'fes'ation," she says.

"I found one inside, too," Doug mutters.

"Dey prolly chewed some of da harnessin' and piss on da lines," she says as she re-seals one panel.

"Honestly… that explains the smell I've never been able to trace. Ugh," Doug shirks his face in disgust.

She keeps working, moving quickly, efficiently—clearly in her element. Doug mostly watches, unsure what to do that won't get in the way.

"Just let me know if you need anything," he finally offers.

She doesn't respond, just keeps working until the last panel is sealed. Then she turns with a smirk, grabs the tether, and heads back toward her ship, dragging Doug along.

Once they're back in the airlock, Clutch cycles the doors and starts pulling off her gear.

"Less go look at dat scanner," she says, pulling her helmet free.

Doug nods and starts peeling out of the suit. His chest feels a little lighter than before. As they cross the threshold into Doug's ship, he doesn't float away as expected. The gravity is working again and that alone feels like a victory.

They head to the bridge, and Doug grins as he sees everything powered up.

"You fixed it," he says, practically laughing. "You actually fixed it."

"Ain't nutin' to it," she shrugs and slides into the pilot seat.

She leans close to the scanner display, flipping through logs with practiced fingers. Doug hovers behind her, waiting for her to reach the weird blips.

"There," he says, pointing. "Those. That's what I was talking about. They don't make sense, right?"

Clutch leans in, frowning slightly. Her eyes flick between lines of data. The pause lingers. Too long.

"What?" Doug asks.

Clutch doesn't answer right away. She looks at him, then back to the screen, and again, back to Doug, her expression unreadable.

"Well?" Doug presses. "Is it broken?"

"Nope," Clutch says finally, eyes returning to the display. "Scanner ain't broke."

"But that—what is that? That's not a normal signal," Doug presses, sure that there is a problem with his equipment. His luck would dictate it is broken.

"Don't make sense 'less ya know what it is," she says with a sly smile.

Doug crosses his arms. "And you know?"

"Douggie…"

"It's just Doug. You don't like ma'am, I don't like Douggie," Doug interrupts as though he has corrected many people before. One of the few things he feels confident in defending in his life.

Clutch grins. "Fair 'nough."

She leans back in her chair, arms crossed behind her head.

"As I was sayin', Doug, I don't fuck wif karma," Clutch says. "So, since ya 'scovered dees, I gotta invite ya on a 'venture. Treasure huntin' style."

"What are you talking about?" Doug asks, confused about what she just said.

"Well, ya can eidder give me dees readin's 'n go yer own way, or ya can come 'long fer da riches," Clutch replies. "I cain't choose for ya. Dat'd be bad karma."

"I've never had riches. I'm in. Whatever it is I am signing up for," Doug says with a smile, a nervous twinge filling his body.

Clutch leans forward and offers her hand. "Guess I'll be sharin' my aileen treasure wif ya."

Doug shakes her hand, gripping tighter than he expects. "Hope you're ready for a lot of dead weight."

"Nah," Clutch replies, her grin widening. "I like carryin' folk who don't know what dey wurf yet. Kinda like fixin' ships— messy at firs', but wurf it if ya do it right."

Doug doesn't know what to say to that. He just nods.

Did she just insult me, or does she think I am worth more than I know?
Worth what to who?

Doug starts to spiral in his thoughts.

They sit for a moment in silence, the hum of his ship's systems now a quiet miracle in the background. The scanner waits quietly, awaiting new instructions, new inputs, new signals. Somewhere out there, something strange had left a signal behind—something powerful enough to get them both moving. To cross paths.

Doug glances at Clutch. She's already typing something into his nav terminal.

"Got a heading?" he asks, unsure what else to say or ask.

"Got a hunch," she replies. "We follow dees sig'als."

Doug exhales slowly. "Okay then. Let's go find out what can rumble in space."

Clutch smiles, the glow of the console lighting the grime on her face like warpaint.

"Strap in, Doug," she says. "Karma's got plans fer us."

And just like that, the two ships, attached together, adjust course, silent engines whispering to life as two unlikely scavengers point themselves toward the unknown.

Chapter 3

"Explain it to me again," Doug says, squinting at the display as though it'll start making sense if he stares hard enough.

"I been seein' dees grav'ational 'splosions all ova space," Clutch replies, half-trying to clean up her accent and half-giving up. "I seen 'nough of 'em ta notice a pattern. A line. Like beacons 'cross da void."

Doug leans forward in his chair. "But which direction is the line facing? Forward or backward?"

Clutch shrugs, a motion somewhere between frustration and humility. "Ain't figur'd dat part yet. Don't know if I'm seein' 'em in da direction dey're goin'... or jus' seein' da echoes."

Doug crosses his arms. "And my scanner data—does it help with that?"

"Let's plug it in 'n fine out," she says, already moving to her workstation.

She taps a few buttons on the console. The ship's main holoprojector flares to life, casting a transparent 3D map of space between them. Floating data markers pulse slowly— each one representing a gravitational explosion.

"I'm gonna make each 'splosion big so we can track 'em easier," she says.

"I don't normally ask people to change how they talk, but… you are hard to understand sometimes," Doug says with a half-smile.

Clutch chuckles. "Ain't da firs' time I heard dat. I'ill try, but when ya don't got nobody ta talk wif fer months, speech gets… fuzzy."

"Well, you got me now. At least until I screw something up," Doug shamefully admits.

Clutch just nods and continues with the data and the projection.

Doug watches as glowing orbs flare to life in sequence, but the animation runs too quickly for him to make sense of the pattern.

"Can you slow down the display? It went way to fast," Doug asks.

"Yeah it did," Clutch said with a chuckle. "One sec."

The hologram blinks, resets, and begins again—slower this time. The gravitational pulses appear one by one across the display. Each one blinks into and out of existence like an explosion, but without visible light, the gravitation metrics displayed by each, a mess of unreadable data.

"There's a definite direction," Doug says, eyes scanning the projection. "See that? It moves. From that one… to this one… to—wait, what's that?"

He points to a rogue explosion that pops up well outside the apparent line.

"No idea," Clutch says, looking closer at her display. "But da line clearly went fum secta' 9312T to secta' 787Y2 up 'til dat outlier."

"From," Doug corrects Clutch

"Ya tryin' ta 'rect my speech now?" Clutch asks, unamused.

"You said you would try and that you don't have anyone to practice with," Doug replies with a smile.

"Ain't da time, chuckles," Clutch replies.

"Okay," Doug says, putting his hands up as though he was caught doing something he shouldn't be.

Clutch stares at him a moment longer than necessary. Doug can't tell if she's annoyed or amused, but she finally turns back to the display.

"Should we check out sector 787Y2?" Doug asks breaking the tension.

"Ain't got nutin' else ta go on. Let's go see what's makin' space burp," Clutch says. "In da meantime, ya study da weird'n."

"Weird'n?" Doug asks for clarification.

"Weird one," Clutch corrects herself with exaggerated effort.

Doug just smiles like he just pulled a fast one on Clutch. Forcing her to correct her speech. She sees his smile and scoffs before she heads off to the bridge.

The ship hums through quantum warp, a soft vibration rippling through its frame as they tear through space. Doug replays the display again and again, eyes tracing the line, lingering on the outlier. Something about it bothers him—a wrong note in a song he doesn't quite understand. Maybe it's just space paranoia. Maybe it's intuition.

"Comin' up on da secta'," Clutch announces as the stars slow and the ship slips back into sublight.

Doug peers out the viewport. They're surrounded by vast emptiness. Space in this region is deceptively still—no moons, stars, or planet, no visual cues to give a sense of scale. More so than normal.

"Whole lotta nothing," he mutters.

"A section like dis can mean anytin'," Clutch says. "One sec could hold a mil'on stars. Or jus' cold dead nuffin."

"Let's head for the epicenter of the explosion," Doug suggests. "If we've got a trail, that's where the next clue might be."

"Good idea," Clutch replies. Then, with a sarcastic grin and spinning in a circle, looks back at Doug.

Doug raises an eyebrow.

"We is already here," Clutch continues.

"Funny," Doug says with a sigh. "And, of course we are. So, did you find anything?"

Clutch checks the scanners. "Nuffin'. Not even a black'le."

Doug frowns. "A gravitational explosion with nothing left behind? No residual energy, no collapsed mass? That doesn't make sense." Doug is clearly thinking out loud, not expecting a response.

"Which is why it's weird," Clutch says regardless.

Doug leans forward, rubbing his chin. "What if we got it backward? What if we're supposed to go the other way down the line?"

BAM!

The ship lurches violently. Alarms blare. Both Doug and Clutch are thrown to the floor as the lights flicker.

"Fuck!" Clutch snaps, already scrambling to her feet.

BAM!

Another hit. The ship shudders again. Doug grabs the edge of the console and pulls himself up.

"What's going on?!"

"Prolly pirates," Clutch growls, sliding into her captain's chair.

She slams her fists onto a panel and activates the tactical systems. On the monitor, a ship appears—a clunked together, jagged thing firing small missiles. Large enough to stop a ship in its tracks, but not so big as to destroy a ship.

"Un ship," Clutch mutters. "Dey ain't bring backup."

Doug braces himself. "What can I do?"

"Sit down 'n shut up," Clutch barks. Her fingers dance across the controls. She jerks the ship sideways, just in time to dodge another missile.

Then, with a cold calm, she arms her single laser. Her trusty weapon with versatile options for defending her ship.

A lance of light tears through space.

It hits the pirate's ship square in the bridge. A red glow erupts through their viewport as the interior cooks instantly. The attacking ship stutters, its weapons falling silent—but Clutch's laser doesn't stop.

"Aren't they dead by now?" Doug asks, voice low, wondering why the laser is still firing.

"Sure," Clutch says. "But if I turn it off, some'un new migh' walk in n' star' shootin'. I ain't riskin' dat."

She keeps the beam locked while she angles her ship to dock and the viewport is no longer accessible by the laser.

Doug blinks. "Wait… you're boarding them?" His voice filled with a terrified fervor.

"Yup. Dey pick da wrong ship," Clutch says, confidence and anger filling her voice in return

"Doesn't seem smart giving them a door straight to us…" Doug says, attempting to keep Clutch from doing something stupid.

"Ain't no need ta worry," Clutch says, getting up and heading to the docked ship.

Doug hesitates, but curiosity gets the better of him. He follows her to the airlock.

Clutch is already geared up. Her weapon is strange—a metal tube that conceals whatever mechanics lie within. Its smooth surface is so shiny, he can see reflections from all directions. Her hand disappears inside it, grasping something Doug can't see.

The airlock opens.

A pirate stumbles through—ragged clothes, teeth like yellow quartz, beard matted and filthy. He sees Clutch and charges.

Clutch doesn't flinch. She swings the metal tube.

CRACK.

The man flips backward and crashes to the floor. She steps over him and hits him again—harder. In the head, ensuring he doesn't get up.

Doug flinches but follows.

Two more pirates appear as Clutch enters the pirate's ship. One grabs for the weapon, but the moment his hand touches it, electricity arcs out. He screams as volts dance across his body and then collapses in a twitching heap.

The other hesitates. Bad move.

Clutch swings. The end of the tube connects with his jaw. He drops, blood pouring down his chin.

Doug stares in awe. "What the hell is that thing?"

"Some'em I made fer close fightin'," Clutch says. "Nobody 'spects it. 'Cause it don't look like nuffin'."

She pulls a small handheld scanner from her belt and sweeps the room. After a beat, she tucks it away.

"All clear," Clutch says, then starts to wander further into the ship.

"That was…" Doug trails off.

"Impressive?" she says, grinning.

"Yeah. Definitely. I'm just glad you didn't use it on me," Doug says with a smile.

Clutch chuckles and starts prying open storage lockers and compartments with casual determination.

Doug follows her. "What are you looking for?"

"Anytin' useful. Fuul. Supp'ies. Tech."

"So… you're the pirate now?" Doug asks, half in jest and half serious.

Clutch pauses. "Guess so," she says with a half-laugh. "But dey started it. Dis is der karma."

Doug nods slowly. "Fair enough." He glances around and joins her. "Might as well see what karma left us."

Chapter 4

Clutch and Doug coast away from the wreckage, their ship humming quietly as it exits the battle site. Plenty salvaged from the pirates, but no clues uncovered. This location didn't yield any information helpful to their search for existence of aliens.

With no specific destination set, Doug settles into the galley's recessed chair, the soft blue glow of the holographic display casting harsh shadows across his tired face. His eyes flick between the floating data points—each one a recorded gravitational explosion. He zooms in, slows it down, speeds it up, watching the strange sequence over and over.

Then it hits him.

"Time!" Doug blurts out, nearly knocking over his drink as he jumps to his feet.

Clutch, sitting at a nearby panel with her boots on the table, raises an eyebrow but says nothing.

"We haven't taken time into account!" Doug exclaims, spinning the holo-display toward her. "Each of these explosions shows up based on when we recorded them. Not when they actually happened."

Clutch remains expressionless, chewing slowly on a protein stick.

"Look—when I was stranded and got those readings, I was here." Doug points to his old coordinates in the hologram. "And the explosions were here... and here. Not far apart from my perspective. But the real explosions could've occurred way earlier."

"So?" Clutch says flatly, mouth half full.

Doug leans in, animated now. "So the line of explosions we think we're following might be totally backward. It all depends on when and where the scans were taken. If we factor in distance and delay, the sequence could be reversed. Or diagonal. Or completely nonlinear!"

"K." Clutch says, still completely unfazed.

Doug deflates a little. "You're not impressed?"

She shrugs. "Ain't dat I ain't 'pressed. I jus' ain't da type ta git es'cited."

Doug grumbles, turning back to the display. "Can we add positional data—like where you were when you took each scan? Convert all of that to when the explosions actually happened without the delay of time?"

Clutch swivels in her seat and starts tapping at her console. "We can do dat. Ain't a hard ask."

Doug watches her fingers fly across the keys. "Maybe the order of the explosions is only wrong because we're seeing them out of sync—like thunder after lightning. I don't really know. I am not an astrophysicist. And math ain't my strong suit"

"Seem I'm rubbin' off on ya," Clutch says, flashing him a grin. "Ya said ain't 'gain."

Doug smacks his forehead. "So I did. Great. I'm becoming you."

"I ain't good at math needer," Clutch says. "But dat's what 'pewters are fer."

She runs the calculations. The display refreshes. Holographic icons adjust, but the pattern stays mostly the same. The timeline wobbles slightly—some pulses shift by hours or days—but nothing drastic.

"Can you get the computer to calculate actual explosion timestamps?" Doug asks. "Using signal strength, distance, wavefront timing… all that?"

Clutch is about to reply when a shrill alert pings on her wrist display.

She glances down. "Better not be pirates 'gain."

Doug stiffens. "Wait—what?"

"Got a ping. Some'un tripped da scanner." She stands quickly and heads for the bridge.

Doug follows, nerves rising like bile. He doesn't know if it's pirates, a system malfunction, or something worse.

Clutch drops into the pilot's chair. The scanner notification blinks red. She studies the readout.

"It ain't pirates," she says calmly.

Doug exhales, relieved. "Good. I'm not in the mood for more trauma today."

"But it ain't nutin' eidder," she adds, squinting at the screen. "Couple more grav'ational 'splosions… but dey ain't in no line."

Doug's mouth opens to respond, but—

WHAM!

The ship jolts. Not from outside fire—but from space itself. The entire hull groans like it's being wrenched sideways. Doug is thrown into the wall, pain flaring in his shoulder. Clutch slams into her console, knocking her head with a sickening crack.

"CLUTCH!" Doug shouts, witnessing her head, bleeding from the side.

He tries to move, but the crushing force pins him against the wall. It feels like the ship is being hurled through space by an invisible hand.

Then suddenly—WHAM! again.

They're flung in the opposite direction. Backward. As if the ship is being slingshotted from one point to another and then reeled back.

Until finally, the g-forces drop. Alarms blare. Doug falls to the ground in a heap, gasping for breath.

"Clutch?" he croaks, blinking through the dizziness.

He spots her crumpled figure near the console—unmoving. Blood darkens her temple.

Doug scrambles to his knees and crawls toward her, but stops short. He can't help her and find medical supplies at the same time. He curses under his breath and races toward the nearest storage lockers, rather than applying pressure to the wound.

Behind the first hatch: weapons.

"Uh… should I be concerned about this?" he mutters aloud, staring at an arsenal that would make a soldier blush.

He moves on. More guns. More tools. Some things he can't even name.

"No medkits? Really?" He asks the unconscious Clutch.

Doug grows frantic. He sprints deeper into the ship, opening cabinets, tearing through compartments. Eventually, he stumbles into Clutch's quarters—an organized chaos of gadgets, charts, and parts.

He heads to the drawers and starts rifling through them.

"Hey! Whatch'a doin'?" Clutch shouts.

Doug yelps and spins around.

Clutch stands in the doorway, one hand on her hip, the other on the door frame.

"Fucking shit, you scared me," Doug says through heavy breaths. "You were unconscious. Bleeding. I didn't expect you to just… walk in."

Clutch cocks her head. "An' I ain't 'spect ta find ya goin' true my s'uff."

Doug's face flushes red. He steps back from the cabinet like it's on fire. "I wasn't—look, I was trying to help. I saw the blood. I couldn't carry you and look at the same time. I was trying to find a med kit."

Clutch leans against the doorway, grinning slightly. "Mmm hmm. Sure. Jus' happened ta poke 'round my room in da process?"

"I panicked," Doug says, hands raised like he's surrendering again. "I thought you might be dying. Sorry I didn't have time to ask where the med kits are stored."

Clutch rolls her eyes and waves off the tension. "Ain't need 'em. I got nanos. Although, with ya on my ship, I prolly aught get one."

Doug freezes. "You what?"

Clutch confirms. "Little bots dat fix up ya body?"

Doug looks horrified. "You put nanos in your body?"

"Yeah. Ain't you?" Clutch asks.

Doug shakes his head firmly. "Fuck no. I'm not letting The Regimentary crawl around inside me with a kill switch and a tracking beacon. I don't care how handy they are."

Clutch lifts an eyebrow. "The Regy ain't got nutin' ta do wif mine. I built 'em myself."

"You what?" Doug asks, still concern and now also surprised.

"I buil' my own. Cus'om-coded 'em. Ain't kected ta nobody. Ain't ping nuffin' eidder. Ain't take orders."

Doug looks unconvinced. "You hope they don't."

"I know dey don't," Clutch replies, her voice sharpening just a bit. "Trus' me, I tore out all da parts dat even smellt like control."

Doug crosses his arms. "You know what The Regimentary does, right? Sure, they go into battles for all of humanity, and police what the local forces can't, but they created nanos. And their nanos can put a person to sleep, paralyze muscles, stop the heart. They act like they're here to help—but they're really just an enforcement tool."

Clutch nods. "Maybe dat true. I ain't seen it doh. Could jus' be conspurcy."

"I'm not willing to chance it. And if it is true, you're still okay with putting that tech in your body?" Doug asks one last time.

"I ain't. Dats why I made my own," Clutch presses.

Doug stares at her. She's either the most self-reliant person he's ever met—or completely insane.

"I'll pass," he says flatly.

"Suit yerself," she shrugs. "But if'n ya bleedin' out fer some reason, don't spec me to fix ya da ole way."

Doug scoffs. "You'd miss me too much if you let me die."

Clutch chuckles. "Yup. Ya my favorite cargo."

Doug finally exhales and lets the tension melt out of his shoulders.

"Ya done snoopin' true my socks now?" she asks.

He sheepishly closes the drawer. "Yeah. I'll go. Sorry."

As he walks past her, she grins. "If'n ya eva change yer mind 'bout da nanos, let me know."

Doug doesn't reply. He just groans and keeps walking, head low, ears burning.

Doug slinks back into the galley and takes a seat at the holographic display, still shaken—not just from the ship's sudden thrashing, but from the reality of Clutch's nanotech revelation.

She built her own nanobots. That's no small feat.

Chapter 5

Doug sits alone in the galley, hunched forward, looking at the holographic display, eyes tired, jaw tight. The image repeats in a loop—gravitational bursts forming, rippling across space. Different angles. Different timelines. Over and over.

He slows the display. Speeds it up. Rewinds. Fast-forwards.

Nothing helps.

His hypothesis about time—the idea that their data was out of sync—felt smart at the time. But adjusting for actual explosion delay only led to a different conclusion: the bursts weren't sequential at all. They were simultaneous. Spread across sectors billions of kilometers apart, but happening all at once.

Doug exhales sharply. "That makes no sense."

And yet… it does. In possibly the worst way.

What could cause multiple gravitational explosions to happen in different places at the same time?

His eyes drift to the mark on the hologram that aligns with where the ship had bucked forward and backward. One of the original gravitational readings. He rewinds the nav data, cross-checks the time of the ship's reaction. There's no physical object noted by sensors. No projectile. No mass. No anomaly.

But the motion clearly pushed the ship away from that location. Then yanked them back toward it.

"Come up wit anytin'?"

Clutch's voice cuts through the silence like a wrench on steel. She leans casually in the doorway, hair slightly damp, likely from washing off the earlier blood.

Doug doesn't even look up. "Not really. But I think that… whatever hit us—it was another gravitational burst. And we felt it firsthand. I mean, if we hadn't drifted off-course during that pirate fight, we might've been right on top of it when it went off."

Clutch scratches her head. "Ain't dat a gruesome taught."

"Yeah. Like being squished into a rock."

"Maybe we need be goin' a diff'rent 'rection," she suggests, tilting her head toward the display.

Doug sighs, running a hand through his hair. "But where? We've got one semi-linear trail, and then… that." He points at the rogue burst marker—the outlier that sits far from the rest.

"Ain't outliers der fer a reason?" Clutch asks, her tone like a teacher giving a student just enough rope to get the answer on their own.

Doug blinks. "We're already headed for it, aren't we?"

Clutch grins. "Yup."

Then she turns and strolls out of the galley like the conversation was already over.

Doug drops his face into his hands and groans. "Of course we are. Hours of staring at this, and she already had a plan." He lifts his head and squints toward the food shelves. "Maybe I'm just hungry. I can't think straight."

He digs through the galley's sparse pantry—mostly cans, ration pouches, and a disturbing number of unlabeled plastic cubes. He finally finds a box of stale Jublees—thin, dry crackers with the flavor of recycled air and even less nutritional value.

He opens the box and pops one into his mouth. It flakes instantly, crumbling like dust against his tongue. "Ugh." He grabs a bottle of water and takes a long drink to wash it down.

The dry food only magnifies a gnawing ache in his gut— not hunger, but loneliness. Being in space had always been isolating. But this… this was something else. Before Clutch, the most conversation he'd had in a cycle was yelling at malfunctioning equipment or grumbling at vending machines.

Nobody checked on him. Nobody called. The factory crew back at Elaron Salvage might've asked where he was, but only because it affected their quotas. If he vanished, someone else would just pick up his shift.

Doug pictures his ship—clamped by scrapper arms, disassembled on the conveyor belts he used to operate. It would be poetic, if it weren't so sad.

"Could've been watching my own ship get torn apart," he mutters, staring at the dry crumbs in his hand. "And no one would even blink."

He looks up at the doorway Clutch had disappeared through. This might be the most time he's spent with another person in… what, ten cycles?

Before he can spiral further—

BLEEP.

A soft alert sounds from the center of the room. A new ping.

Doug jerks upright, eyes darting to the display.

"Another burst!" he shouts, excitement rising like a fire in his chest.

Clutch returns just as he leans into the console. "Whatcha mean 'nother? We jus' 'rived at dis one."

She walks over to the display and stops cold. Her eyes narrow. Another marker has appeared—far from their current location. Another outlier.

"Damn," she mutters. "Ain't dis gonna be noyin'. If we gotta hop from one point ta da next 'cross da galaxy, we gon' need a betta' plan."

"I agree. But maybe we'll figure it out before we reach the next one." Doug hesitates. "Since we're here, did you see anything at this outlier? Any debris, radiation, weird tech?"

Clutch shakes her head. "Ain't nutin' here. Not even pirates."

Doug sighs, relief washing over him—then unexpectedly replaced by something else. A feeling he can't place. He looks at Clutch. Watches the way she casually leans on the edge of the display, the way her fingers fidget with a data drive from her belt.

He hasn't felt like this in years. Cared like this. Or… maybe he's just not used to someone being there.

"You okay?" Clutch asks, catching his stare.

Doug blinks. "Sorry, I was… what did you say?"

"We be need'n some supplies," she repeats. "Fore we start chasin' bursts all ova da stars. Nearest post should do. Ain't suppose ya got creds?"

Doug gives a weak smile. "No. I was heading to earn credits before my ship died. We could sell the ship if we need to. But that'd leave me stuck with you."

Clutch smirks. "Ain't get much fer dat ship out here. I'ill front da cost. We'ill sell it later."

"Deal," Doug says, no hesitation.

She walks off, heading toward the bridge to chart their course. Doug stays behind, watching her disappear through the doorway.

He already knows where she's taking them. There's only one place it could be in this part of the galaxy.

Warp Waystation.

Grungy. Remote. The kind of place people vanish from and don't get missed. A hub for smugglers, traders, and plenty of folks who make pirates look honest.

Doug sighs. "Great. A hotbed of criminals. Exactly what I was told to avoid at all costs."

He sits down and finishes the last of the Jublees, chasing the crumbs with another long drink of water. His eyes drift back to the new burst marker. Another anomaly. Another mystery.

"At least I won't be alone," he whispers.

She's tough. Smart. Dangerous in a way that comforts him more than it scares him. And as reckless as she might seem, she's got the kind of grit that makes survival possible out here.

"I just hope she doesn't leave me defenseless at Warp," he mutters. "Maybe she'll bust out the weapons cache I found. Maybe she'll trust me enough to carry one."

His eyes linger on the data display again, but his thoughts have already wandered far from gravitational bursts.

Chapter 6

"Couldn't we go to a different waystation?" Doug asks, watching nervously as the docking clamps engage with a dull clang as the ship lurches into place.

"Ain't got da fuul," Clutch says without even looking at him. "Sides, dis un got good Yeltive ribs."

Doug frowns. "Aren't those the cows that are grown in low gravity so they're more tender?"

"Yep. Dose da ones," Clutch replies, already unstrapping.

"Well, fine. But…" Doug hesitates, lowering his voice. "Hey… do you have any more of those unassuming weapons? I don't feel comfortable walking in there defenseless."

Clutch stops and looks at him over her shoulder. "Ya ain't da trus'in' type, is ya?"

"Not when I'm walking into the outer rim version of a mugger's market or a place you go to when you want to die," Doug mutters. "This place doesn't exactly have the reputation of a secure paradise."

"Dis place ain't bad," Clutch replies, stretching her arms. "Jus' gotta know where not ta go."

"And where's that?"

She smirks. "Jus' stay by me. Ya be fine."

Doug nods. He swallows dryly, but forces his feet to follow her. He doesn't trust the station, but he trusts Clutch—and she moves with that kind of self-assured swagger you only get from surviving a hundred bad ideas.

They step out of the ship and into the docking corridor, a narrow metal tunnel that opens into the main hall of Warp Waystation—a sprawling, grimy artery of commerce and chaos. Glowing strips flicker overhead. The air smells like oil, boiled meat, engine coolant, and old socks that have been recycled and used by too many people's feet.

Vendors line the walls on either side—some in permanent stalls lit with flickering holosigns, others just tables with crates and scavenged parts. People bustle through the concourse, shouting, haggling, laughing, and occasionally shoving one another out of the way. Doug feels overwhelmed immediately.

He takes a breath and immediately regrets it. Someone near him reeks like fermented regret.

Doug subtly sniffs his own armpit. "Damn it." He winces. He's one of the problems.

"Keep up," Clutch snaps, already ten paces ahead.

Doug hurries forward, eyes darting everywhere. The people here look rough—scarred faces, prosthetics, tattoos in languages he doesn't recognize. A guy with no nose and glowing blue eyes is selling "memory enhancers" from a box full of what looks like oiled up and chewed-on toothpicks.

Doug tries to stay focused, but then he spots something like salvation—a sign for showers. A worn-out placard over a doorway: Traveler's Bathhouse.

"Shit, I really need this," Doug mutters. "I haven't even seen a shower on Clutch's ship."

Without another thought, he peels away from their path and heads inside.

The door slides shut behind him with a hiss and a gentle click.

"Damn it," Doug mutters, slapping his forehead. "I should've told Clutch I was coming in here."

He turns to leave—only to be met by two massive figures now blocking the entrance. Towering, broad-shouldered, and built like vending machines.

"Leaving so soon?" the taller of the two asks with a grin that shows too many teeth.

"Just… have to tell my friend I came in here," Doug says, trying to sound casual. "She might get worried."

"Sorry, but no," the other says, stepping forward. "You can't leave until you've had your bath."

Doug's throat goes dry. "And… how much is a bath?" His voice cracks. "That was going to be my first question."

"Oh, you don't pay with credits," comes a third voice from behind him—soft, eerie, and entirely out of place.

Doug turns to see a smaller man in an oversized coat. He's got slick black hair, sunken eyes, and a smile that reminds Doug of old teeth floating in soup.

Oh fuck, Doug thinks. *She told me not to leave her side. I am such a fucking idiot.*

"Look," Doug says quickly, "I've only got a few credits. I do smell like a dying lizard, and yes, I need a shower, but—"

"The smellier the better," the third man says, almost sighing the words with glee.

Doug backs up slightly, scanning the three of them. "Okay. Time for introductions. Tall guy, not-as-tall guy, and—what, the shortest guy? That's all I've got so far."

The smaller man laughs. "Tall one's Hank. Other one's Teeter. And I'm Patrick. And you are?"

"Doug," he says quickly, cursing himself for not dragging out his response to buy time. Time for what? Anything that delays whatever is going to happen next.

They all smile.

Doug shifts on his feet. *Fucking fuck fuck fuck*, he thinks. *This is it. I'm going to die in a fake bathhouse, hidden behind a meat vendor with trench foot.*

Hank suddenly whips out a weapon from under his coat—a sleek dart gun—and fires.

SNAP.

Pain erupts in Doug's stomach. His eyes go wide as he looks down and sees a metallic dart sticking from his abdomen, like a steel mosquito lodged under his skin.

"What the fuck!" he yells, gripping the dart.

Patrick steps forward, smiling like someone who just won a bet, holstering his dart gun. "Doug… you've been marked. You're ours now. You'll get your shower—but after that, you're gonna start working for us."

Doug wants to fight, scream, run—but he does none of it. He's frozen.

Patrick gestures toward the back of the room, away from the entrance. "Come on. Let's get the fun started."

Hank and Teeter flank him, guiding him forward like handlers. They stop at an actual shower unit—stained, cracked, reeking of mildew and metallic sludge.

Patrick turns. "Strip. Shower. Change."

Doug blinks. "Wait, what? Here?"

The three men don't move. They just wait. Expecting.

Doug begins undressing—slowly, shamefully—backing into the stall while trying to keep his old clothes within arm's reach.

"Faster!" Teeter growls. "We ain't got all day."

Doug grits his teeth. 'All because my ship broke down. Because I'm broke. Because I'm alone.'

The water sputters on. It smells like chemicals and old feet. Like water recycled a few too many times.

Doug winces. "Is this even water?"

The men just chuckle. "We're waiting!" Patrick calls cheerfully.

Doug scrubs as fast as he can. The water doesn't make him feel cleaner—just colder. As he turns around to grab his clothes, they're gone.

"Seriously?" he mutters. He didn't even hear them take them and doesn't remember taking his eyes off of them.

In their place is a pile of new clothes—rough, synthetic, mismatched.

"Any towels?" he calls.

"Nope. Quit stalling," Patrick snaps.

Doug pulls the clothing over his wet body. The fabric clings, resisting every motion. The pants barely fit. The shirt smells like plastic.

Then Hank and Teeter grab him again—less politely this time—and drag him deeper into the building.

Here it comes, Doug thinks. *This is where I lose all dignity. Or this is where I die. Or wish I had. Or…*

They slam him into a metal chair across from Patrick, who lounges like a man completely in control. Getting slammed into the chair shakes Doug from his thoughts.

"Doug," Patrick says, his tone suddenly cold. "We own you. You'll do what we say. And if you don't—well—your insides'll be outsides real quick. And the only thing painting the walls will be blood and bowel."

Doug nods. Not because he agrees. But because he understands.

"Good," Patrick says, pulling a package from under the table and setting it down. "You'll take this to Reflextive Station. You'll meet someone named Stev. He'll give you another package. You'll keep doing this. Over and over. For the rest of your life."

Doug stares at the package. "How am I supposed to pay for fuel? For food?"

Patrick chuckles. "Find a weapon. Hijack something. Kill as you must to survive. Just don't forget—if you don't deliver, you don't exist anymore. Understand?"

Doug doesn't reply.

Patrick pushes the package across the table. Doug hesitantly takes the package. Teeter and Hank lift him up as he does, dragging him toward the exit.

"Oh," Patrick calls out, "and one more thing—we'll be listening. So if you tell your little friend about us… let's just say she'll be wearing your intestines like a scarf."

Then the door opens—and Doug is tossed into the station's main hallway.

The crowd bustles around him like nothing happened.

He stumbles forward, gripping the package.

His body trembles. His mind races.

He came in for a shower.

And now he's a prisoner—with no walls, no bars… just the threat of death and some device in his gut to remind him who owns him.

Chapter 7

Doug rushes through the corridors of Warp Waystation, his heart pounding like a war drum. Every turn feels like it might be the last before someone grabs him again. He hugs the package to his chest like a bomb, paranoid it might explode—or worse, someone might take it causing him to die from a completely different explosion.

Do I just take Clutch's ship? he wonders. *Just take off and go?*

The thought burns in his stomach.
No. I can't do that to her. She saved my life. Twice now. Leaving her behind... that isn't who he is.

He passes a cluster of docked ships and slows for a second, sizing them up. Most are small runners, one-man couriers. Easy to slip inside, maybe hijack during takeoff. Like Patrick said...

Doug shakes his head.
I'm not a thief. I don't have a weapon. Why the hell is being a pirate so hard?

He rounds another corner and sees Clutch's ship in the distance—relief hits him like a shot of clean oxygen—but with it, dread. How does he convince Clutch to take him to Reflextive Station without exposing the nightmare he's walking around with?

"Fuck," he mutters, slowing to a halt.

He lowers his head, gripping the package tightly. His stomach churns with shame, guilt, fear. 'What the hell am I supposed to do? I didn't sign up for this life. I just needed a ride… a break.'

He's about to cry.

Then a familiar voice calls out, almost too casually.

"Where ya been hidin'?"

Doug jumps, looking up to see Clutch standing a few meters away, arms crossed, her head tilted. Her eyes go immediately to the rectangular package tucked under his arm.

"I… um…" Doug stammers. "I saw a bathhouse. Realized I hadn't showered in a while and thought… yeah… big mistake." He tries to angle the package away from her view.

Clutch smirks. "Yup. Body odor ain't so bad 'pared ta what come outta doze places."

Her eyes scan him—clothes, posture, expression. "Got some new clodes, I see."

"Yeah… the new clothes came with the bath," Doug says with a nervous laugh. His voice cracks halfway through.

"Mmm hmm," Clutch hums, unconvinced but saying nothing. "Well, come 'long. We got what we need'd."

Doug falls into step beside her. He can barely think, his brain bouncing between panic and guilt.

"I feel like I was kind of useless here," he offers weakly. "Should've just stayed on the ship."

Clutch shrugs. "Maybe. But if ya hadn't gone, we'd never get ta see yer stylish new outfit."

Doug forces a smile. "Yeah. Hey—actually—I was thinking. Maybe… if it's not too far out of the way, we could stop by another station?"

"Oh yeah?" she asks, her tone casual but probing.

"Yeah. Like… Reflextive Station."

Clutch stops walking. "Reflextive ain't close. Ya got fuul money fer that kind'a detour?"

Doug hesitates. "I… have a friend there. He owes me. He can cover fuel. Yeah." His lie obvious. "I have a… package. A gift. For him. For his… birthday. Or something."

"What da fuck wrong wif ya, Doug?" Clutch cuts in, her tone sharp.

"I can't tell you," he says quickly, voice cracking again. "I just… I need to go to Reflextive Station. Please."

Clutch studies him. "Ya ain't good at lyin', are ya?"

Doug slowly shakes his head and instinctively places a hand over his stomach. "Please," he whispers.

Clutch holds his gaze for a beat longer… then gives a single nod.

"Let's get ta da ship den. Time's wastin' n' ya gotta git ta Reflextive."

Doug doesn't understand what just happened. Did she believe him? Did she not believe him? Either way, she doesn't press. She gestures to the crates nearby.

"Help me carry da supplies."

He silently picks up a crate, the package still clutched tightly under his arm. Every step back toward the ship feels heavier. He keeps looking over his shoulder, half-expecting to see Hank, Teeter, or Patrick watching from a shadowed corner, smiling with knives behind their backs.

They reach the ship without incident.

Doug sits silently as Clutch fires up the nav. The station recedes behind them. The ship slips into open space, stars stretching and warping as they enter low-quantum drift.

And then Doug realizes—this isn't the direction to Reflextive.

"This… this isn't anywhere near Reflextive Station!" Doug blurts, panic rising again.

"Listen, Doug," Clutch says without looking back. "I know what happ'nin'. We got 'bout twenty mins ta fix it. So sitch yer ass down, 'cause dis ain't gonna be fun fer needer of us."

She disappears for a moment, then returns carrying a large tool chest.

Doug jumps to his feet. "What do you think is happening? I don't have time! We don't have time! I can't—"

"Shut up n' lif yer shirt," Clutch snaps.

Doug freezes. "What?"

Clutch lifts her own shirt just enough to show a thin scar near her stomach—just left of center. A healed incision. A memory. A warning.

She lowers it and winks.

Doug stares… then slowly lifts his shirt.

Clutch opens the chest and starts pulling out tools—blades, clamps, surgical gel, and something that looks like a modified paint scraper with lights.

"This is going to hurt, isn't it?" Doug asks quietly.

"Ain't gonna be fun," she confirms.

Doug nods, mouth dry.

"Lean back," she says.

He obeys, lying on a low bench. Clutch places a square scanner across his abdomen and slides a sensor back and forth. A soft hum activates as a holographic projection of Doug's lower torso appears above them.

Organs. Muscles. Intestines. Movement.

And then—a tiny little object, lodged millimeters from his appendix.

"There ya are," Clutch mutters. "Stupid lil' bas'ard."

She grabs a knife.

"Wait, wait—what are you—"

SLICE.

"HOLY FUCK!" Doug screams, jerking.

"Stop movin'," Clutch says through clenched teeth.

"Stop cutting!"

Doug tries to breathe, but it's shallow and frantic. "Ow, ow, ow, fuck, please—"

"Almos' der," Clutch grunts.

Doug's world tilts. Pain rockets through his body. His vision pulses white. He grips the bench so hard his knuckles go numb.

Then—he blacks out.

A blurry voice calls through the fog.

"Welcome back."

Doug opens his eyes. The lights are dim. His body is slick with sweat, but... no pain?

"What... what just happened?" Doug asks.

"Ya pass out. I took da ting out. Ya free."

Doug blinks. "Wait—what?"

"I been in dat baf house once," Clutch says, sitting across from him, cleaning the blood off her tools. "Big 'stake. Same setup. Same dart. Took me foreva ta find it. Had ta cut it out myself."

Doug stares at her. "You... figured it out? Just from how I was acting?"

Clutch nods. "Didn't take much. Ya was shakin', talkin' weird, beggin' ta go where we ain't got no reason goin'."

Doug lays back again, breathing slow. "Thank you. I don't... I don't even know what to say."

"No need," Clutch says. "We got bigger things ta worry 'bout."

"Like what?"

Clutch pulls up a nearby screen. New scanner data flashes across it—more gravitational bursts. More anomalies.

"Got a few fresh readin's ta chase down."

Doug stares at the screen… then back at Clutch. Down to his stomach.

"Thanks Clutch, but what about the pain? You were digging into me pretty good," Doug asks, fully standing now.

"Ain't no need ta concern 'bout dat. We jus' gotta figa out our nex stop," Clutch replies.

Doug just looks at Clutch, unsure if he should feel relieved or even more paranoid.

Chapter 8

Doug leans over the console in the galley, eyes narrowed at the shifting holographic display. He rotates the map with a swipe, zooms in, adjusts timelines. Nothing adds up.

Two of the new gravitational burst readings are wrong. They don't follow the same trajectory. They don't fit the pattern.

They fracture it.

"This is so confusing!" Doug shouts. "We keep showing up at these places and it's either completely void of anything or we get tossed around like we're trapped inside a supersized heartbeat!"

Clutch enters behind him, wiping grease off her hands with a rag. "Ain't no ting," she says casually. "We jus' gotta wait fer 'nough readin's ta form da real picture."

Doug runs his hands through his hair. "I'm not a patient person, Clutch. I need to understand this. I want answers. I want to find something."

Clutch shrugs. "We ain't even know da q'estion yet. Jus' hopin' dese readin's mean sometin'."

Doug blinks. "Is your accent getting worse? I'm still finding it hard to understand you sometimes."

Clutch grins. "Prolly. I talk more 'round ya. Ain't used ta all dis company."

Doug shakes his head, chuckling despite himself—until the ship lurches violently.

BAM!

A sickening jolt hurls both of them across the room. Doug slams into a bulkhead. Clutch hits the floor hard and rolls to her feet faster than Doug can blink.

"That felt like—"

"Pirates," Clutch mutters, already sprinting for the bridge.

Doug follows, adrenaline rushing. The last time this happened, things got bad fast.

By the time they reach the bridge, Clutch is already flipping switches and pulling up sensor data. The holographic display blooms to life, showing three incoming ships—and one of them is pinging a connection request.

Clutch accepts without hesitation.

"Whatcha want?" she asks flatly.

Patrick's smirking face appears in the air. "We want that pretty boy of yours. He owes us a delivery."

Doug's stomach drops. He steps closer. "How did you find me?"

Patrick shrugs. "We've learned a few tricks over the cycles. Let's just say… well… we didn't just leave you with one parting gift."

Doug's breath catches.

"Tracker?" Clutch guesses.

"Obviously," Patrick says, then looks past Doug to study Clutch. "You know… you look familiar."

Clutch doesn't flinch. "I ain't no un 'portant."

Patrick tilts his head. "Nope. No, now I remember. That accent. The grimy ship. You cost us a lot of money a few cycles back. You vanished before we could collect."

Doug feels his heart pounding in his ears.

Patrick's voice hardens. "I think I'll kill you both, take your ship, and part it out for scrap."

Clutch folds her arms. "Ya ain't gonna do dat. Cuz ya'ill be dead firs'."

Doug steps up beside her, voice tight. "Yeah. I've seen what she can do. You should walk away while you still can."

Patrick laughs. "You two are hilarious. There are three of us. I haven't even started showing you what we can do."

Clutch and Doug glance at each other—an entire conversation passed silently between them in a single beat.

Clutch shrugs.

Then she opens fire.

The bridge pulses red as the first laser launches forward. It slams into Patrick's ship—only to scatter harmlessly across its surface.

Patrick grins. "What are you trying to do?"

Doug spins toward Clutch. "Uh… Clutch?"

Clutch remains calm. She targets the other two ships and unleashes two more shots.

"Hopin' dese two don't got LDs," she says.

"What's an LD?" Doug asks, ducking instinctively.

"Layza Disrupta's," she replies without missing a beat.

"You mean—disruptors?"

"Ain't da time, Doug."

The enemy ships move. Fast. The three ships begin flanking maneuvers, tightening the noose.

"Seriously," Patrick's voice chimes back in. "Just surrender. We've got the tech. You're boxed in."

Clutch keeps watching her display, tapping quickly.

Doug whispers, "We're in trouble, right?"

Clutch doesn't answer. Her eyes stay locked on the readings. Suddenly, one of the ships flickers—and goes dark.

"What the fuck?" Patrick's voice snaps back in, no longer amused. "Teeter, you've gone dark. What's happening?"

Silence fills the airways

Clutch grins. "Guess ya pal didn't get da message."

Before Patrick can react, her laser roars to life. The beam punches through the dark ship—Teeter's—and its cockpit begins to glow. The interior burns red-hot. Then—nothing. The ship explodes in a brilliant bloom of light, vaporizing in place.

Doug shields his eyes. "Holy shit!"

Patrick and Hank immediately return fire. Lasers streak past Clutch's hull, rocking the ship. Missile lock alerts blare in rapid succession.

"Clutch! They're—"

Before Doug can finish, Clutch slams a hand onto the warp switch.

The ship snaps into quantum space.

One second they're under fire. The next, they're alone.

Silence.

Empty stars stretch out around them.

Doug exhales the breath he didn't realize he was holding. "How... how did you do that?"

Clutch casually leans back in her chair. "While dey was braggin', I dropped an EMP pod on Teeter's ship. Knocked out da shields.."

Doug shakes his head in awe. "Why didn't you just use three of them at the same time?"

"Only had da un. Gotta build more now." She looks at her console like she's adding it to a to-do list.

Doug walks over and rests his hands on the edge of the console, still trying to steady his breathing. "They're going to come after us again, aren't they?"

"Prolly," Clutch says, unbothered.

"Then how did they track us this time? I thought you got the thing out."

Clutch doesn't answer immediately.

Instead, her eyes drift… to his stomach.

Doug follows her gaze.

"…Oh no," he mutters.

Chapter 9

Clutch crosses her arms and stares silently at Doug for a few seconds before finally speaking.

"Let me see dat package."

Doug tenses. "I think we should just... leave it outside and let it float away."

"Ain't no way," Clutch says flatly. "Dey tryin' ta kill us. Dey trackin' us. Might be da package." She eyes Doug. "Unless ya want me ta open ya up again 'n check der?"

Doug's eyebrows shoot up. "I'm good. Let's check the package."

'Of course. That's how they're tracking me.' Doug spins on his heel and bolts out of the galley. His boots clang on the floor grates as he rushes toward his room, heart racing. He heads straight to the drawer where he stashed the package and yanks it out, gripping it like a live grenade.

He turns to head back—and Clutch is already standing in the doorway.

"Taught I'd save ya some time," she says, cool as ever, holding a tool that looks purposely built to crack open secure containers.

Doug tosses the box to her with more relief than grace. "Here. Just... please make sure it can't follow us."

Clutch takes the package and heads to the galley. She sets the package down gently on the table and gets to work. Her hands are quick but steady. She's not just mechanically skilled—she's surgical. Doug watches the way she angles the tool, the way she braces the seams. Confident. Precise.

"Ya need ta relax more," Clutch says while prying at the edge. "Ain't no reason ta be stressin' so much."

"I don't know how to relax," Doug replies, pacing behind her. "I've always been high-strung. Anxious. Everything goes wrong and I spiral. And lately… life just feels like a constant emergency."

Clutch doesn't look up. "Ain't been workin' out dat way needer, huh?"

Doug pauses. "No. It hasn't. Freaking out about life hasn't helped make things better."

"Maybe tryin' a differen' way 'ill work fer ya."

Doug stops pacing and lets that sit for a moment. Is it really that simple? Just… decide to live differently?

"How do you do that?" he asks. "Change how you live, when the only way you've ever known is survival?"

Clutch shrugs. "Ain't no ting but takin' it un day at a time. Each ting, as it happens."

Doug nods slowly. He knows what she means—but he's never known how to do that.

Maybe that's what makes her different. She doesn't try to control everything. She just moves forward.

CLACK.

"There we go," Clutch says, finally popping the seal. "Lil' ting had a sec-pro on it."

"Sec-pro?" Doug echoes.

"Security protocol," Clutch enunciates, deliberately slow, like a teacher talking to a child.

Doug's face pales. "Wait. Was it rigged? Like... to explode?"

Clutch glances at him with an amused smirk. "Dere ya go 'gain. Freakin' out fer no reason. Problem's already solved."

Doug exhales through his nose, visibly trying to calm down. "Right. Okay. I'm fine. Totally fine. This is just... going to take some getting used to."

He leans over to look inside. "So? What's in the box?"

Clutch tilts her head. "Intrastin',"

Doug scowls. "That's not helpful. That's not even an answer."

He steps closer and finally sees it—a sleek, compact piece of black and silver tech resting in protective foam. It gleams with clean, high-grade alloy, built like it came off a government weapons lab shelf.

Doug squints. "What is that?"

Clutch grins. "It'sa implant imprint device. Mil'tary grade. CoreID 6—da newest model."

Doug's jaw drops. "No fucking way! That's a military grade imprint device? Don't you need one of those to inject secure credentials into implants? Shit! We may have stopped someone from breaking into every military database or weapons vault in the universe."

Clutch chuckles. "Stop wit'cha crazy taughts. Ain't nutin' more den sometin' dey was gonna use fer fancy robbin'. Get in, get weapons, sell 'em, make creds. Typical merc shit."

Doug raises an eyebrow. "Does it come with a speech enhancement implant?"

Clutch glares. "Now ya gettin' personal."

He smirks. She smirks back.

Doug exhales slowly, trying to think. "Should we... return it? Turn it in? Maybe even ask for a reward? I mean, maybe we don't need to keep chasing all these gravitational bursts..."

"Dey ain't take kindly ta tieves. Dey'd prolly shoot firs n' not ask nutin' later," Clutch replies. "Sides... I can use dis fer udder tings."

Doug frowns. "Fair. But if it's how they were tracking me, we need to be sure it's clean."

Clutch lifts her hand. In her fingers is a tiny chip no bigger than a grain of rice, blinking red.

"Already got it."

Doug blinks. "Where was it?"

"Bottom of da foam. Wrap' in false shielding." She walks to a nearby console and begins pulling up nav code. "I got a plan fer dis."

Clutch's fingers fly across the console. Doug watches as lines of numbers scroll by—coordinates, commands, and other things Doug doesn't understand.

She picks up the tracker, walks to the cargo bay, and rummages through a pile of junk. From under a dusty tarp, she yanks out an old, beat-up drone and drops it on a nearby crate.

Doug follows, wide-eyed. "That thing still works?"

Clutch shrugs. "Sure do."

She opens a side panel, slides the tracker inside, and taps on the tablet mounted under her sleeve. The display glows to life—now Doug sees it's more than just a tablet. It's connected directly to her ship's systems.

"You may wanna be sittin'," Clutch mutters.

Doug quickly drops into a seat just as the ship lurches forward, then shifts into another location with a single pop.

"Where are we?" Doug asks, eyes wide.

Clutch smiles. "Just makin' it easy fer 'em ta track us."

She carries the drone to a small gear transfer hatch—about waist-high, meant for jettisoning cargo or sending gear between ships. She places the drone inside the inner door, seals it, and opens the outer one.

The drone drifts silently into the void.

Then Clutch taps a command on her wrist.

With a sudden burst, the drone takes off in to the void—far from their current location.

Doug watches the screen update. "You sent it toward a star."

Clutch closes her sleeve with satisfaction. "See, when dey com'a lookin', dey 'ill get wrong coord'nates. Dey'll pop right into da middle of da star."

Doug stares at her.

Then he stares at the gear transfer hatch.

Then back at her.

"Remind me never to get on your bad side," Doug says with a smile. "But seriously. What did you say? Your accent is getting worse."

"I think I can fit you in this little gear transfer box," Clutch says perfectly, without the accent, a smile growing on her face.

"Yeah. That was great. I understood all of that," Doug says with a smile, looks at the gear transfer door, and gulps.

Chapter 10

Doug stares at the star map like it's mocking him. For the umpteenth time, he tilts and rotates the projected readings, attempting to force the gravitational bursts into a coherent shape.

Lines become planes. Planes bend into corners. Angles shift into what might be geometric form—if only they could tell what kind.

"It's starting to look three-dimensional," Doug mutters, more to himself than Clutch. "Like a… lattice? Or a web? I don't know what it means."

Clutch stands beside him, arms crossed, sipping from a cracked canister of bitter Kaf-X, a synthetic coffee replacement that few people enjoy. "Ain't no system near any of 'em. Jus' floatin' points in da middle'a nowhere."

Doug sighs. "Yeah. We keep showing up and finding… nothing. Not even wreckage. Just empty space. And still, we keep following it like it's a trail."

"Ain't no marker worth followin' if ya don't know where it lead," Clutch replies, turning the map to examine a different angle. "But this? Dis got shape."

Doug stares at the projection. The bursts aren't forming a line anymore—they're curving toward a center. Clutch has been adjusting their course every time the data shifts. Always toward some inevitable focal point.

"You think we're the only ones looking for it?" Doug asks, eyes still on the flickering points.

Clutch cocks her head. "Whatcha mean?"

"I mean... what if others have the same scanner readings? What if there's a whole fleet out there piecing this together too? What happens when everyone shows up at the center?"

"Don't matter," Clutch says. "Ain't 'bout who get der firs. It's wedder der's anytin' ta find."

Doug grimaces. "That's what bothers me. If something can cause these gravitational bursts—at this level of precision—it means there's something advanced waiting for us in the middle. Or... maybe it's a trap."

Clutch shrugs. "Ya worry too much."

Doug raises an eyebrow. "You keep saying that."

"Ain't worth doin' if ya can't enjoy it. Dis whole ting? It's an adventer."

Doug chuckles bitterly. "Yeah, well, I'm not exactly enjoying the 'adventure' part. I've never been good at the journey. I like to reach the destination and then decide if it was worth it."

Clutch chuckles and steps toward the nav console. "Speakin' of, we need fuul."

Doug instantly tenses. "I'm not getting off the ship this time. Just you. You get the fuel. I'm just a liability."

"Ain't no ting," she says with a smile. "Jus' stay close dis time. Good fer ya ta learn."

"If I have to, you bet I will be close by," Doug replies, forcing a smile.

Clutch taps her screen. "Look like Ulmbra's da closes' station."

Doug's eyes widen. "Wait. Ulmbra? Don't you mean Ulmbria?"

"Yup," Clutch replies casually.

Doug groans. "Nobody sane goes to Ulmbria. That place is a warzone dressed up as a fuel depot. Everyone there's either looking for trouble or creating it."

"Ain't got da fuul ta go nowheres else," Clutch replies, unfazed. "We'ill be in n' out."

Doug closes his eyes, presses his hand to his belly, and takes a deep breath. "That's what I'm afraid of."

Ulmbria Station

The outpost looms ahead like a rotting husk. Jagged hull panels jut out like scar tissue. Glowing weld seams pulse around sealed breaches. Half the station appears to be held together with desperation and exposed cabling.

The radio crackles.

"Docking port 12," a voice instructs with mechanical disinterest.

Clutch winces. "Ain't like dat number."

Doug raises an eyebrow. "What's wrong with 12?"

Clutch grimaces. "Ain't no easy exit der."

Doug's heart sinks. "Can't you ask for another port?"

"Ain't gonna get it. Sides... I got my ways a dealin'."

They dock, and Clutch is out of her seat, headed for the station's entrance.

Doug watches her grab a bag he hadn't seen before and a square device the size of a meal tray. She slings the bag over one shoulder like it's part of her body armor.

"Comin'?" she asks.

"Yeah. Definitely," Doug mutters sarcastically, sticking close. "And this time, I'm not leaving your side."

They exit the ship into a narrow docking corridor. Clutch stands at the junction between hallway and main concourse and affixes the square device just out of sight. It disappears into shadow.

"What's that for?" Doug whispers.

"Best not be askin' questions here. Neva know who lis'nin'."

They continue into the station. Doug's senses are assaulted instantly: the reek of recycled air thick with oil and sweat, the buzz of old lights half-flickering, and the unmistakable stench of violence simmering just beneath the surface.

Vendors line the corridor, some with tables full of crude tech, others with nothing but their stare and a sidearm. No one looks friendly. No one looks unarmed. This station makes Warp Waystation look like paradise.

Doug keeps his mouth shut.

The deeper they go, the worse it gets. Shuttered stalls barricaded with rebar. Weld scars like spiderwebs. Bullet holes you don't ask about. A bar with no name and a door reinforced like a vault. No lights. No welcome signs.

They finally reach the fuel vendor.

Clutch steps up to the counter and slaps a few payment chits down. "Fill it. Dock 12."

Doug raises an eyebrow. "Your accent," he whispers. "It's almost… gone."

Clutch flashes him a glance—just a look warning him to keep his mouth shut.

The vendor, a sharp-eyed man with a suspicious sneer, leans forward. "Your fuel line wasn't attached. You'll need to go secure it."

Clutch's face tightens. "That's not possible. I have an automated system."

"Not connected," the vender replies bluntly. The vendor then snatches the chits before she can reach for them. "I'll just hang onto these until it's fixed."

Clutch snaps. "Ain't happenin', ass. We ain't done bin'ness. Ya don't git paid."

The vendor's grin widens. "Oh, now I'm definitely keeping these, little iron ant."

Clutch stiffens.

Doug leans in. "What's an iron ant?"

The vendor smirks. "She knows. And she's not allowed to buy anything. Not allowed to be here. She shouldn't even be talking."

Clutch's hands clench, but she doesn't move.

The vendor turns to Doug. "Unless you're her handler."

Doug flinches. "Her what?"

"Her handler," the vendor repeats. "She's not allowed to purchase without one. You the one givin' her orders?"

Doug stares at Clutch—then at the slowly growing group of people surrounding them. Predators. Watching. Waiting.

"If it gets us the fuel we need," Doug says quickly, "then yeah—I'm her handler."

The vendor raises an eyebrow. "Then why are you giving this iron ant chits? Why is she calling the shots?"

Doug gulps. "Because I don't like doing the work. That's what I have her for."

A beat of silence.

Then the vendor snaps his fingers.

Chaos erupts.

Doug is yanked backward by two large men. Clutch pulled away by others, vanishing behind a wall of bodies.

He struggles, twisting, but the grip is unbreakable. "Hey! Let go!"

Clutch passes into view for just a moment—held back by a group of enforcers, yet she smirks.

Doug stares at her. 'Why is she smiling?'

Doug, not sure what is going on, gulps hard, afraid of another dart to his stomach, or worse. "I wish I had her confidence," Doug mutters under his breath.

The man holding him tightens his grip. "What was that?"

"Oh. Nothing. Just talking to myself," Doug says. "I'm pretty sure you're all going to regret this."

The man scowls. "Tough talk for a rat in a cage."

Doug doesn't respond. He's shoved into a metal chamber barely larger than a coffin—too small to stand, too short to lie down.

The door slams shut. Darkness swallows him.

Yet strangely… he doesn't panic.

He closes his eyes. Breathes in.

Clutch smiled.

That means she has a plan.

Doug, somehow, trusts her and chooses not to freak out for the first time in a long time.

Chapter 11

"Ya ain't wantin' ta be doin' dis," Clutch warns as they shove her into a dim chamber reeking of mildew, sweat, and something far worse. The guards slam the dented metal door behind her, their chuckles lingering in the air like grease.

The room isn't a cell. Not officially. But it might as well be. A brothel ready room. Torn sheets hang from a sagging cot. A rusted table wobbles in the corner. One wall is lined with a flickering glow that bathes the room in sickly pink. Her stomach tightens.

Footsteps echo back toward the doorframe. Someone's still there.

A lean figure steps through. Skin slick with grime. Facial hair patchy and wild. He reeks of unwashed flesh and weeks-old food. His yellowed eyes and even yellower teeth settle on Clutch with hunger.

"You don't need to do much," he says, locking the door behind him with a slow click. "Just lay there. Be quiet. They'll take turns. You're an iron ant, after all. You know the deal."

"Ain't happenin'," Clutch replies flatly, her voice cold steel.

He smirks, not slowing down. "You iron ants always try to fight. Never works. But I like that fire. Makes it more fun."

He unclasps the holster at his waist, dropping it lazily on the table as if to prove he doesn't need it. His fingers tug at the fasteners of his jacket, then slide over his shirt, pulling it up. Clutch doesn't move.

She turns around. She starts to lower the top of her shirt from her shoulders and casually looks back to her right.

Shoulders exposed. Hair hanging loose over the nape of her neck. Her posture relaxes just enough to bait him closer. The man gets closer, smile still wide. He starts to rub his hands together in front of him, slowly, up and down, like he is getting ready to feast.

Clutch looks forward and lowers her head, chin into her chest.

He licks his lips. Stretches his arms. Walks up behind her slowly, like approaching a wild animal he's already caught.

He places both hands on her shoulders.

Clutch cocks her head to the left.

A faint pulse of energy.

He stiffens.

Then crumples like a marionette with its strings cut, slamming to the floor with a dull, wet thud.

Clutch rolls her head counterclockwise three times, nods forward and then back. The device on her shoulder shimmers, then melts back into her skin as if it was never there.

"Works every time," she mutters, fastening her shirt again.

She steps over the unconscious man, grabs his gear from the table, and quickly inspects it. A multitool with decent options. A single-shot flare pistol, crude but useable. And a long, jagged combat knife with black tape wrapped around the hilt.

She takes everything.

Then her eyes turn to the door.

She pulls the multitool, flips open the screwdriver extension, and moves to a nearby access panel embedded in the wall. Two screws, stripped and stubborn. She jams the tool into the top one, grinding it loose with short, practiced motions. The bottom one fights harder.

Voices outside.

Louder now.

Once the panel comes off, she fully opens the tool and places two portions of the pliers at distinct locations. The lock pops, door ready to be opened.

Clutch puts the tool away and pulls out the knife and gun. With the knife hand, she opens the door slowly, not sure what awaits her. Nobody stands guard.

Maybe dat guy was da guard, Clutch thinks to herself.

She barely gets door open an inch before she sees the long line of men, waiting in a line, presumably to take turns.

Some banging fists against the metal.

"Hurry the hell up!"

"Is she broken already?!"

Clutch doesn't flinch. She closes the door and ensures it is locked again.

Gotta find a way out, Clutch thinks to herself.

She glides across the room, scanning for exits. No windows. No hatches. Just faded drapes clinging to one wall like a bad memory.

One of them stirs slightly.

'Airflow.'

Clutch crosses the room, pulls the curtain aside, and finds a wide vent grate. Big enough to crawl through. She flips the tool again and starts working on the screws.

Outside, the shouting grows.

Someone approaches the door with keys.

The first screw drops.

Beeps on the keypad. An error code. She disabled the device from accepting anything.

Then the second screw comes loose.

The door rattles. A key enters the lock.

Third screw.

The bolt turns.

Fourth.

The panel drops into her hands. She slips inside the vent, curtain snapping back into place just as the door bursts open.

She holds the grate in place, heart thumping.

"Don't drop it," Clutch says to herself, holding the grate tightly.

Men swarm into the room.

"Where is she?" one man shouts.

"What happened to Torely?" another one asks.

"Fuck Torely! I want my turn!" a third man shouts.

The room erupts into arguments. Clutch can't see them because of the curtain.

She takes the chance, with all of the noise, to let the grate slowly lean against the floor and the wall. Giving away her escape route, but not letting the grate fall to the floor. She moves through the passageway in the only direction available to her. Back toward the main hallway.

She slides through the narrow passageway as quickly as possible. The shouting hasn't changed. The men haven't noticed her escape.

She finds an exit, looks through, and sees the crowd gathered at the door. The shouting quiets down. The men start to look around.

"Fuck," Clutch says quietly. She looks further down the passageway to see if it keeps going. Perhaps to another room. Another hallway. But she doesn't see one. Nothing above or below. She either needs to exit here or go back to the room.

She thinks about it for too long.

The vent groans.

Someone else is in the shaft.

Footsteps. Hand slaps. Scraping.

Others approach the grate where she is hiding.

Cornered.

Clutch's eyes scan upward. A pipe runs just above her. COOLANT is etched across it.

She raises the knife and jabs. She hits it repeatedly until finally...

HISSSSSSSS.

A cloud of freezing gas erupts into the vent. Chemical coolant floods the shaft, biting at her skin and eyes. She grits her teeth, holds her breath, and counts.

One.

Two.

Three.

She contorts her body and spins, turned the other way, she slams a boot into the weakened vent exit.

The panel shatters.

She tumbles into the hallway, coughing, blinking through tears. Her skin frostbitten, but already healing.

The group of men gathered in the hallway stumble back, clutching at their faces from the fumes. One drops to the floor wheezing.

The fog of coolant rolls into the corridor like a tidal wave, blinding everyone who tries to look through it.

Clutch doesn't wait. She grabs the gun from her belt, kicks open the next door she sees, and stumbles inside.

She collapses against door, drawing in clean air, breathing heavily.

"Well... look what we have here," a smooth voice echoes from across the room.

She looks up.

A tall, semi-clean figure in a long coat, arms crossed. Smiling. Unarmed, but confident.

"Neat trick back there," he says. "I watched the whole thing. That coolant trick was real smart. You saved me the trouble of clearing that corridor."

Clutch narrows her eyes. "Ain't wantin' ta be doin' dis."

The man steps forward slowly. "Oh, but I do. See, iron ants don't just walk into my workshop. You're a rare prize."

He licks his lips. "Just cooperate. Undress yourself, and this will go a lot smoother."

Clutch lets her shoulders fall. Her posture slackens.

She steps forward. One... two steps.

She turns.

Lowers her shirt again.

His hand reaches out.

Clutch cocks her head.

His eyes go wide.

He collapses.

Clutch resets the device and buttons her shirt, just like before.

"Second un today," Clutch says with a smirk.

She scans the workshop. It's cluttered, dusty, but glorious.

Weapons. Tools. Gadgets. Generators. Armored plating. Boxes of components. Racks of modules. Ship parts.

Everything she needs.

Clutch steps into the room, hands twitching with anticipation.

Chapter 12

Clutch moves through the workshop like a predator through brush, each step sharp and purposeful, her eyes scanning shelves and benches with calculated focus. The stale smell of rust and scorched metal fills the air, mingling with the lingering tang of old engine grease. Lights flicker above, casting long, erratic shadows across the cluttered space. The room hums with dormant potential—tools, coils, plates, welding kits—all waiting for someone who knows what to do with them.

She knows.

Without hesitation, she snatches up half-melted hull plating, a dislodged plasma coil, fragments of landing gear, and a heavy iron rod stripped from the armature of a broken loader mech. In her hands, these scraps aren't junk—they're weapons. Makeshift devices. Purpose in physical form.

At the far end of the workshop, the heavy utility door shudders violently under the pressure of bodies on the other side. Banging. Screaming. Desperation laced with rage.

Clutch doesn't flinch. She barely spares it a glance.

Behind her, the cavernous main docking bay looms in silence, its large overhead lights cold and off, casting the rows of half-dismantled ships into shadow. Cranes hang frozen like skeletal arms.

"Why ain't dey go 'round?" she mutters, rolling her eyes. "Dumbasses pickin' da hardest door."

The banging intensifies. Dust rains down from the door frame. Time's up.

She stalks forward and plants one of her new devices to the left of the doorframe. The little sphere locks in place with a magnetic clink and lights up, blinking red. The second—longer, flat, and wickedly humming—is wedged into the central hinge. That one pulses low, almost like a heartbeat.

Then she turns her back on the problem and walks away.

By the time she rounds the corner, the first explosion rocks the workshop.

BOOM.

The door flies inward, slamming into the ground like a steel guillotine. Screams follow as the first wave of attackers spills inside, tripping over the twisted remains of their own breach.

BOOM.

A plume of green smoke erupts with a hiss, rolling over the wreckage like a creeping storm. The sharp, acrid scent of the gas cuts through the air—a cocktail of stomach-churning stench and something that makes the eyes burn and lungs seize. More screams. Coughing. Chaos.

Clutch doesn't slow.

She reaches the edge of the main docking bay and grabs the ladder welded into the wall, her boots clanking on each rung as she climbs to the catwalk above. The catwalk groans under her weight, but it holds. From this high perch, the skeletal remains of gutted ships stretch beneath her like silent behemoths.

She crosses the narrow platform to a heavy door marked with faded yellow paint—EVA ACCESS.

Inside, rows of space suits line the racks like standing corpses. Most are too bulky, too cracked, too suicidal to wear. But one—her size, matte-black, sealed tight— catches her eye. She pulls it from the rack and drops it onto a bench.

Fast hands. Fluid motion.

She checks the seals, wrist rings, the oxygen readout. The helmet clicks into place with a satisfying hiss. She slides into the suit and locks it down. She breathes once, deeply, and her voice echoes inside the helmet.

'Time ta leave.'

Clutch powers up the EVA suit's system, her breath hissing in her helmet as everything comes to life. HUD displays blink green—oxygen levels full, seal integrity stable, propulsion ready. She heads for the airlock, boots clanging softly on the grated floor.

Just as the inner door begins to cycle open, a voice cuts through the silence like a blade.

"Don't even think about it!"

Clutch halts mid-step, her body stiffening for a split second before she smoothly pivots, eyes narrowing. A man stands there, silhouetted by the dim corridor lights, aiming a pistol directly at her chest plate.

"'N ya are?" she asks, calm and unmoved.

The man approaches, light finally meeting his face. He's taller than most, with an athletic build shaped by vanity. His skin is clear, his features sharp, and there's a cleanliness to him that somehow persists despite the grime streaking his clothes and boots. In his eyes burns a quiet confidence—unshaken, unflinching—the kind that no chaos or threat could easily extinguish.

"Can't let you leave, iron ant," the man says, voice clipped, taut with tension. "We need your ship."

Clutch tilts her head. "Git ya own ship."

He doesn't flinch. "We don't have one. We're trapped on this roach nest with the rest of the scum. No way out."

Clutch's eyes flick past him, scanning for others. "Who's 'we'?"

"My crew," he replies, voice softening just slightly. "Locked up. Just like your friend, I'm guessing."

There's something honest in his tone—desperation, not deception. Clutch chews the inside of her cheek, considering. Her hand twitches near the panel to open the airlock. Options narrow quickly in places like this.

"Maybe if'n ya help me," she says, eyeing him, "I'z can help ya."

The man raises an eyebrow, still processing the heavy accent. "Has anyone ever told you you're hard to understand?"

Clutch grins behind her visor. "Yup."

"So… help you with what, exactly?" he asks, keeping his gun low but still at the ready.

"Help me git my compan'on," she says. "I help git ya crew. Git ya off dis heap. Even find ya a new ride. Dat way, we boff win."

He hesitates. Weighs it. The idea of escaping this floating gutter clearly appeals to him, but trust isn't cheap. Especially not here.

Finally, he lowers the pistol.

"Clutch," she says, nodding in a salutation of greeting.

"Pranz," the man replies, placing his gun in its holster.

Clutch nods. "Weird name. Now suit up. We goin' outside."

Without waiting for him to respond, she spins back toward the airlock. Pranz follows, grabbing a suit off the rack— clearly unfamiliar with the process. As the distant sound of voices and boots echo down the corridor behind them, Clutch hears the first banging against the sealed door.

The gas from her earlier traps must've worn off.

"May want'n be hurry'n," she mutters, sealing the inner hatch behind them as Pranz stumbles through, fumbling with the collar clamps on his helmet.

"I'm going as fast as I can. Normally I have someone help me with this crap," Pranz grumbles.

"Assistant?" Clutch raises a brow. "Ya sum richy?"

Before he can answer, a figure appears through the airlock's small window—another station goon, waving a gun, yelling silently through the thick metal barrier.

"Why dey always do dat?" Clutch asks, rhetorically, shaking her head. "Ain't like we can hear 'em."

She moves over and begins locking down Pranz's suit properly, adjusting seals and tightening joints with swift, practiced hands.

Pranz shrugs—partially to test the mobility, partially in embarrassment.

Clutch finishes, gives him a nod, and hits the outer hatch.

The door opens to the cold void of space. Beyond it, the hull of the station stretches in all directions, pocked and battered from decades of abuse.

She glances once at the man on the other side of the window—more of them gathering now, faces twisted with anger—and lifts a hand in a lazy wave before launching herself into the black.

The stars swallow her.

Pranz scrambles forward, grabbing onto a narrow, curved guide rail bolted to the hull. It snakes around the structure, leading to key access points, like a track for engineers to crawl their way around during external repairs.

The outer hatch seals shut behind him. The two of them now alone in the vacuum—suits humming, oxygen tanks ticking, hearts pounding.

"Where are we going?" Pranz calls over comms.

Ahead of him, already a hundred meters away and accelerating fast, Clutch's voice crackles in response. "Dis way."

He spins, scanning frantically until he spots her—a dark shape streaking toward a far-off ship docked at the side of the station, her small thrusters firing with short, efficient bursts.

"Wait for me!" Pranz yells.

"Use ya pulsion," Clutch advises. "It's fas'r."

"I don't know how!" he replies, dragging himself along the guide rail like a man climbing the world's worst jungle gym.

Clutch doesn't bother responding.

"I'ma gonna be in my ship," she says, already closing in. "Git der as q'ick as poss'ble."

She lands on the dorsal hull of her ship. Moving with practiced ease, she reaches a hidden top-hatch, punches in a code, and slips inside.

"Use dis same entrance," she calls back. "Or ya might be gret'n it."

"Okay," Pranz wheezes, still wrestling his way along the guide.

Clutch cycles the airlock with a hiss, stepping into the familiar confines of her ship. She peels off the EVA suit in quick, fluid motions, hanging it on a reinforced hook near the hatch. The cold outer shell clinks against metal as she walks away, unbothered, already shifting into a different mode—battle-ready.

She heads straight for the cargo bay, boots thudding softly against the floor, her body moving with practiced rhythm. Tucked behind a stack of old crates is a barely visible seam in the wall—one that would be invisible to anyone who didn't know exactly where to look. Clutch pops it open and pulls back a hidden panel.

Inside, a narrow, velvet-lined rack holds an arsenal of hand-forged weapons, tools, and armor pieces. Each item is strange and sleek, looking more like scavenged prototypes than commercially available gear. She pulls out a compact chest harness and secures it tightly over her shirt, the magnetic locks snapping into place. Custom holsters follow, one for her stun-bolt launcher, another for a close-range arc slicer. A knife, long and curved, goes behind her back. Everything fits with eerie precision, like armor she was born into.

Just as she tucks the last strap into place and reseals the compartment, a dull knock echoes from the far airlock door.

Clutch groans. "Guess he finally made it."

She jogs back down the corridor and pauses at the control panel. With a smirk and a small shake of her head, she cycles the inner door.

A whoosh of air precedes the hiss of pressure equalizing. Pranz stands inside, panting slightly, his helmet fogged and suit misaligned in at least three places.

Clutch crosses her arms as he pulls off the helmet, his hair sticking out in awkward directions.

"Ya ain't use'aly out in da black, are ya?" she says, amused. "Use'aly jus' sittin' planet side givin' orders. Or..." she squints at him, "ya a t'ust fund baby."

Pranz raises both brows, already defeated. "How'd you guess?"

"Ya either know how ta nav'gate da void," she says plainly, "or ya don't. And ya don't."

He exhales and shrugs, too tired to be defensive. Instead, he raises a hand in a mock salute and gestures toward the corridor. "Lead on, warrior queen."

Clutch smirks, turns on her heel, and takes off at a brisk pace. She knows her ship inside and out, turning corners and opening sealed doors like she's walking through muscle memory.

They arrive at the docking access Clutch and Doug originally used to enter the station. Before Clutch even opens the door, a heavy zapping sound rings out on the other side—followed by a series of thuds and groans.

Clutch opens the door without hesitation.

The hallway beyond is littered with twitching bodies—at least a dozen men, strewn about in various degrees of unconsciousness or discomfort. A fine mist of ozone lingers in the air from her arc trap that has been protecting the ship. One guy flops over, still convulsing, muttering something incoherent about his teeth.

Pranz recoils. "Who are they?"

Clutch steps over a limp leg like it's a broken pipe on the floor. "Pay'pl tryin' ta board my ship," she says casually. "Didn' have pa'mission."

Pranz swallows hard, halting just inside the threshold. "Am I going to be one of them if I step wrong?"

Clutch doesn't even glance back. "Ya safe."

He follows slowly, stepping over the crackling remains like a man picking his way through a minefield.

Once clear of the chaos, they jog into the bowels of the station. Clutch moves with purpose; Pranz trails close, glancing over his shoulder every few seconds.

As they round a corner into a narrow, dimly lit corridor, a voice pierces the air.

"There she is!" someone shouts.

Clutch's hand is already reaching for her next surprise.

The hallway erupts with sound—boots pounding, voices yelling, fists slamming against walls and each other in blind fervor. A few dozen angry bodies surge forward like a wave, eyes locked on Clutch with primal hate.

She doesn't flinch.

Instead, Clutch reaches into her vest and pulls out a flat, octagonal disk, roughly eight inches across. Her fingers twist expertly in opposite directions, unlocking the magnetic seal. A soft click sounds as the edges expand slightly, subtle mechanisms inside waking to life. Without hesitation, she flicks the disk underhand down the corridor.

It skitters across the floor and spins to a halt right in front of the mob.

Then, with a mechanical snap, tiny filaments shoot outward from the disk in every direction—nearly invisible threads of monomolecular wire, so thin they barely catch the dim light. The filaments anchor themselves to the surrounding walls, forming a tight web just as the first wave of men charges forward.

They don't see it.

Three men hit the wires at full speed. The moment of impact is silent—but grotesque. Limbs sever. Bodies bisect. One man's face slides cleanly apart as the rest of him stumbles forward in twitching confusion.

The mob halts, screams rising as those behind push forward unaware. More get tangled, shredded. One unfortunate soul ends up caught in the web—suspended by a dozen shallow cuts, blood running in rivulets down his arms and legs. He'd be screaming if not for the filament that's sunk into his throat, pinning his last breath in place. As his consciousness waivers, so does his strength to stand, his body weight finishes the job and slices through every piece of him as he falls to the ground.

The floor becomes slick with blood. But Clutch? She just crosses her arms.

"Ya'll need ta stop tryin' me," she says, voice calm, even bored. "Jus' let me have my frein' 'n ya'll stop dyin'."

Pranz steps forward slightly, trying not to gag at the sight. "And my friends too," he adds weakly. His voice cracks. He looks anywhere but at the carnage.

A figure pushes forward from the surviving mass—an average-looking man with sharp eyes and a crooked mouth. His demeanor says "leader," but his tone oozes disdain.

"Iron ant, iron ant, iron ant," he repeats mockingly. "You think you're tough? You can't kill us all. You belong on your back or in a mine. You know the rules. We can't just let you go."

He stops in the center of the hallway, just outside the web, staring straight at Clutch. "In fact—yeah. Let's do this properly. Bring me the iron ant's friend."

A moment passes. Clutch doesn't blink.

Then, through the bodies and the tension, Doug appears.

He's shoved forward roughly by two thugs. His face is bruised, one eye nearly swollen shut. He stumbles as he walks, clearly injured, but upright. Barely.

The crooked-mouthed man grabs Doug by the back of the neck like a ragdoll and raises a pistol to his temple. "Turn yourself over, iron ant," he says, "or your friend gets painted across this corridor, or shoved through your little trap."

Clutch's eyes narrow. Her fingers move to her side pocket, slowly, deliberately.

She pulls out a small silver remote. Her thumb hovers over the only button.

"Don't," the man barks. "No funny business."

Clutch meets his gaze, unblinking.

She presses the button.

The filaments retract in a flash, snapping back into the disk with a faint zzzip and clatter. The disk rolls slightly, then rests on the floor—innocent again. The path to her is open.

The mob doesn't hesitate. They surge forward again, rushing past the mangled bodies and into the now-cleared corridor.

But Clutch is already lifting the remote again.

Click.

A muffled pop echoes from the disk, followed by a loud hiss. A thick plume of pale green gas bursts into the air, instantly enveloping the front ranks of the crowd. They cough, stagger, and one by one, collapse. Eyes roll back. Legs crumple.

Panic sets in. Screams turn to moans as the gas spreads fast, tendrils curling toward the ceiling.

Doug tries to hold his breath—but he's already inhaled too much.

Pranz, wide-eyed, looks to Clutch for answers. Her lips are pressed into a thin line, and she's holding her breath, nostrils flaring, calm as ever.

Pranz understands too late. He stumbles, leans against the wall—and then falls forward like a dropped puppet.

The hallway is silent again, save for the hissing disk and the faint drip of blood from the earlier carnage. Clutch, still holding her breath, looks around at everyone laying peacefully on the ground, and smiles.

Chapter 13

Clutch sits cross-legged beside Doug, her shoulder pressed lightly to the cool wall of her ship. One hand scrolls through station logs on her tablet, the other casually flicks between space feeds—news, chatter, system anomalies. Her eyes stay mostly on the latest readings from deep space, those strange gravitational bursts that only she and Doug seem to be tracking. The puzzle is still unsolved, and that gnaws at her more than she'd ever admit.

Doug stirs beside her, groaning softly. His hand twitches at his side, then lazily drags up to his stomach before flopping back down again.

Clutch doesn't look up.

Instead, she keeps scanning for anything useful. Maybe a station registry entry she missed. A log of unauthorized cargo. Anything to make her life easier, her ship faster, her odds of staying free higher. They'd taken everything the station owed them—fuel, rations, med supplies. It was only fair, given how close they'd both come to being either enslaved or dissected. Clutch believes in karma. She also believes in collecting on those karmic debts.

Doug mumbles again, his voice sounding more like a dying modem than a person. Clutch smirks, just a little, still not glancing up.

"Want doze nanos now?" she mutters aloud, as if the question's rhetorical.

Doug's only reply is to groan, eyes fluttering—then promptly passes out again.

"I tink dat was a yes," Clutch says with a low chuckle, already uncapping a syringe. With a swift jab to his lower abdomen, she presses the plunger down. The nanos flood into his body—her own design, nothing like the ones the Regimentary used. No tracking, no control, just pure regenerative power. Doug will be back on his feet faster than ever.

Clutch stands and stretches. Her joints pop from the tension she hadn't noticed she was holding. She casts one final glance at Doug—splayed out, half-conscious, mumbling nonsense—and allows herself a crooked smile.

Then she's gone, headed toward the cargo bay with silent determination. She grabs a weathered satchel hanging from a hook and slings it over her shoulder. From there she moves back into Ulmbria Station. She pulls a handful of silver spheres—about three inches in diameter—and begins placing them as she walks, letting each one roll away quietly into the station's shadows. They disappear like smoke in a crowd, each created for a single purpose.

"Gotta go git Pranz 'n his crew 'fore da res' of da place wake up," she mutters.

Clutch finds Pranz exactly where she left him, still unconscious on the cold metal floor of the hallway. She kneels beside him, pulls out a slim injector, and jabs it into his neck.

A sudden jolt. His limbs spasm, and he gasps, wide-eyed and clutching his chest.

"Cawln down, Pranz," Clutch says, stepping back calmly, watching him like he's a live grenade. "Let's go git ya crew."

"What the—what was that?" he pants. "Warn me next time!"

"Ain't gonna happen," Clutch replies with a wink, already turning away and moving toward the detention block.

"Thank you for coming back," Pranz says, his voice steadier now, trailing behind her.

"Ain't want da bad karma," she replies without looking back.

"Bad karma?" he echoes.

"Bad karma of leavin' some'un," Clutch says. "Or goin' back on my word."

Pranz nods slowly. It wasn't exactly poetic, but it made sense. He quickens his pace to keep up as they wind through the grimy, half-lit corridors.

They reach the cell block. A row of reinforced doors, each one heavy with history. Rust, blood, and silence linger in the air.

Clutch gestures to the panel beside the first cell. "Ain't got da key?"

"Nope," Pranz replies. "You?"

Clutch smirks. "I got some'm dat'll work."

She places a matte cube against the control panel and syncs it with her tablet. A few quick commands, a flick of red to green, and the lock disengages with a deep mechanical click. The door slides open—and the smell hits them.

Pranz recoils immediately, hand over his mouth. Clutch only catches a glimpse before she turns away. A woman—slumped over the bed, blood congealed around her, her body half-folded in an unnatural position. Bodily fluids soiling her and the surrounding area.

"Who was dat?" Clutch asks quietly.

"Melissa. She was…" Pranz trails off, his voice cracking.

"Let's check da next un," Clutch says gently, leading him away.

Another lock. Another hiss of hydraulics. The next cell opens. Pranz rushes in.

"Jack!"

Inside lies a man missing half his body—an arm, a leg, his side ravaged by something more than neglect. Jack opens his eyes weakly.

"Kil…kill…me…"

"No—I can't…" Pranz's voice breaks.

"I'ill do it," Clutch says, stepping forward. "Quick 'n painless."

Jack gives a shallow nod.

"Watch our backs," she instructs Pranz, kneeling beside Jack and pulling a small cylinder from her belt. She presses it behind his neck, taps it three times, and stands. Jack's body goes still.

"That was quick," Pranz says, blinking away tears. "Thank you."

Clutch pats his back as they walk away.

Three more cells. Three more deaths.

"What dey want wif ya 'n ya crew?" Clutch asks, her voice low.

Pranz doesn't answer. His jaw clenches. Eyes glisten.

"Money?" Clutch asks again.

He nods once. That's all she needs to know.

A sudden ping vibrates against Clutch's wrist.

MOTION IN THE CORRIDOR.

"Hang tight," she says, already turning. "Dey shouldn't be wake yet."

She moves fast, feet light on the metal floor. She reaches the corridor, glances around the edge. The bodies are still sprawled across the floor—motionless.

Then—

"Boo!"

Clutch spins, one hand already grabbing a weapon.

"Woah! Calm down, crazy woman!" Doug exclaims, hands up.

"Ain't no raisin to sneek up on some'un in a place like dis," Clutch scolds, trying to get her pulse under control.

"Not my fault you only looked one direction," Doug says with a crooked grin. "Thanks, by the way."

"Fer what?" Clutch asks, still annoyed.

"For saving me. For healing me. I like these nanos. I've never felt this good."

"Can't jus' let ya die on me," she says. "Ain't good karma."

Doug chuckles. "You and karma. Always with the karma." He leans in and whispers, motioning toward Pranz. "Who's this guy?"

"Some richy out here in da black," she says. Then louder: "Hey, Pranz, whatcha doin' out heres anyway?"

Pranz wipes his face, tears drying. "Can we just get off of this station? I'll tell you anything you want once we're safe."

Clutch doesn't argue. She gives a sharp tilt of her head and starts walking back to her ship.

Doug and Pranz follow as the crowd, laying on the ground, starts to stir.

Chapter 14

The stars stretch endlessly ahead, Ulmbria Station now behind them. Clutch's ship cuts through the black like a silent predator, the chaos they left behind already fading into memory.

Clutch, Doug, and Pranz sit on the bridge. The hum of the engines and the occasional blip of navigational systems are the only sounds for a while—until Doug finally breaks the silence.

"So, Pranz... what brings you out here?" he asks, voice careful, still unsure where the emotional boundaries lie.

Pranz's gaze is locked on the viewport, his expression unreadable. He's still reeling—his crew, his purpose, the wreckage of both weighing on him. He opens his mouth, then closes it again.

Clutch raises a hand. "Hold dat taught."

She taps a button on her flight console. A silent tremor passes through the ship.

Outside, Ulmbria Station bursts apart in a brilliant blossom of orange and white light—like a dying star swallowed mid-scream. The explosion spreads, visible only for a few seconds, erasing the station from existence.

Doug's eyes go wide. "Um. Wasn't that... a little karmically sketchy? I mean... you just blew up a whole station full of people."

Clutch doesn't flinch. "Ain't my karma," she says, shrugging. "Dey called dat on demselves. Fuckt 'round. Found out."

Doug leans back in his seat. "Can't say I'm torn up about it."

"Me either," Pranz chimes in, his voice heavier. "In fact... I'll make sure you get the bounty on all the criminals who were there. Should be a substantial payout."

Clutch side-eyes him. "So, you's a hound?"

"I wanted to be," Pranz admits. "Figured if I couldn't find purpose any other way, maybe tracking down bad people would give me one."

He pauses, swallowing hard. "But I'm not some self-made hero. My father... he's the purpose. I'm just the mistake he pays for. The byproduct of a fling. He funds everything. Equipment. Travel. My 'career.'" He says the word like it's poison.

Doug raises an eyebrow. "So what went wrong?"

"I thought my resources would make it easy. In some ways, they did. I tracked marks, got close. But in the end, that's all it did—got my friends killed. Got me chained up in a hellhole, waiting to die."

"Dey figa ya out? Wanted yer money?" Clutch asks, her tone a shade darker.

Pranz blinks. "I—uh—what?"

"She's askin' if they figured out who you really were and tried to take your money," Doug translates.

Pranz shakes his head. "I don't think so. If they had, they would've contacted my father. Instead, they just assumed we were soft marks—rich and stupid. A quick score. Easy bodies to break."

He snorts. "Not exactly the brightest group of criminals."

Clutch nods once. "Ya, I notice."

Pranz's eyes narrow. "But what about you, Clutch? How are you out here? I mean, no offense, but I've never seen someone like you free. An iron a—I mean—"

"Slave?" Clutch says, cutting him off. Her voice is as cold as steel.

"Sorry," Pranz mutters, guilt flooding his face.

"Wait. What?" Doug leans forward, eyebrows drawn. "What are we talking about?"

"May I?" Pranz asks, glancing at Clutch. "Might be good for you to hear this too."

Clutch nods and raises a brow out of curiosity.

Pranz straightens in his seat and speaks slowly. "The Fornokey Corporation owns asteroid mining. All of it. Every legal claim in the belt. They made themselves untouchable. And what nobody wants to talk about is... they use slaves. Real ones. Born and raised in those mining stations. They're usually smaller in stature, yet strong, forcibly quiet, and expendable."

"That's just a rumor," Doug says, eyebrows raised. "That can't be real."

"Have you ever met an asteroid miner?" Pranz counters.

Doug hesitates. "Well... no."

"Exactly. Nobody has. Because they don't get out. The system's airtight. If someone thinks they're applying for a mining job, they get rejected, or become a slave themselves, especially if they don't have any family to complain of a missing person. The governments look the other way because they're paid to. As long as the resources flow, no one asks questions. It's all sanitized."

Doug looks at Clutch. "And you—?"

"Yeah," Clutch replies. "I's born on a rock. Raised ta dig. Wasn't sposed ta git out."

Doug's expression shifts from confusion to stunned sympathy. "Shit."

"Okay. But why are you referring to Clutch as an iron ant?" Doug asks, still confused. "That guy at the station used the same term."

"Cause dats what dey call slaves dat work on da stroids," Clutch replies. "Dergatory."

"Derogatory?" Doug asks, trying to understand Clutch.

Clutch nods. Doug nods in understanding.

Doug turns back to Pranz. "If it's so secret, how come you know so much about it? I mean, I have heard the term iron ants, didn't know much else about it. Thought it was some conspiracy bullshit and I never listen to that stuff."

"Ya ain't figa it out?" Clutch cuts in.

Doug blinks.

"Pranz's dad run Fornokey," she says. "Betcha Pranz's last name is Fornokey."

Pranz exhales slowly. "Close. Pranz is my mother's name. My father thought it would keep me hidden until he passed the company on to me. But I want nothing to do with it. I hate what he's done. I hate what the company is."

Doug rubs his face. "Damn, dude. Your dad sounds like an industrial-strength asshole. No offense."

"None taken. He's worse than you think," Pranz says. "If I took control of the company, I could maybe free them. People like Clutch. But I'd be dead before the ink dried. Shareholders don't care about morality."

The room falls silent. Even the ship seems to hold its breath.

Clutch breaks it. "I tink we might be able ta help e'chudder."

Doug looks at her. He nods, silent but firm, giving his consent.

Clutch taps a new control on the dashboard. A three-dimensional map projects into the air—an array of stars, each one pulsing slightly. Lines connect some. Others float like they're waiting to find their place.

Pranz leans forward, curious. "What's this?"

Chapter 15

"You've been chasing these signals all over the galaxy, don't know what they mean, and you're treasure hunting on top of that?" Pranz asks, brows raised as he tries to wrap his head around the mission. "You barely know each other, but you're flying together because Clutch believes in karma and didn't leave you for dead... and now you think my money and resources can help you?"

"Yup," Clutch replies plainly, not looking up from her seat.

Pranz blinks, stands confused. "How does this help me?"

"Whateva's causin' dese 'nomolies... it ain't nat'rall," Clutch says, her voice slower than usual. "Findin' it'll make us untouch'ble. Ain't nobody fuckin' wit da crew dat finds aileen shit."

"I seriously have no idea what you just said," Pranz replies. "Sorry."

Doug smiles and leans in to translate. "She means that whatever's causing these anomalies isn't natural. If we're the ones who discover it, we'll be the most powerful people in the galaxy—untouchable. Even if you topple your dad's empire. Overthrow slavery. Nobody will mess with the crew that finds the first sign of alien existence."

"Right. Okay." Pranz folds his arms.

"And yeah, Clutch, your speech is getting worse as we go. You okay?" Doug asks.

Clutch slumps a bit and waves a hand. "Prolly tired."

"You should get some rest," Doug says gently. "We'll check the newest readings while you nap. Maybe we'll even figure out what all this means before you wake up. Besides, the shape is starting to form. With new eyes, who knows what will happen next."

Clutch nods and wordlessly leaves the bridge, dragging her fingers along the edge of the console as she goes.

Once she's gone, Pranz turns to Doug. "You seriously barely know each other?"

"Just met a few days ago," Doug confirms, kicking his feet up on the edge of the console. "But it feels like we've been through a whole damn war together. She's saved my life... at least three times now."

"She must really believe in that karma stuff," Pranz mutters. "Risking her neck for someone she just met."

"I don't care why she does it. Just glad she does," Doug says with a smile. "Now. Let's figure this out before she wakes up. I want to surprise her with an answer."

The two men stare at the floating map of gravitational anomalies. It rotates slowly, a three-dimensional constellation of mystery. Doug taps a few keys, zooming in and out, cycling views.

"The shape's definitely not flat," Doug says, gesturing toward the model. "It's three-dimensional. But we're still missing enough points to tell what it is."

Pranz nods and points toward an open void between plotted anomalies. "We need at least one more over here. A sixth point. Maybe then we'll know if it's symmetrical... or something else entirely."

"Yeah, and even if it turns out to be a geometric shape, we still don't know what that means," Doug adds. "Is it a message? A gate? A trap? Just a weird part of space? Something science has never detected before?"

"Describe again what happens at those locations," Pranz says, sitting forward.

Doug exhales and scratches his jaw. "They're like... gravitational beacons. Each one seems to 'go off' in the same rhythm, like pulses. Because of the distances between them and us, we pick them up at different times. But it's the same pattern. And if you get too close to one, it's like you hit a wave—your ship gets shoved back and then pulled forward again. Feels like being caught in a tide. You don't see anything and usually end up with something broken that needs to be fixed. Ship part. Human part. Both."

Pranz frowns. "Sounds like a warning system."

"Or a test," Doug suggests.

"Or a breadcrumb trail," Pranz replies.

Doug raises his eyebrows, acknowledging the thought. "Clutch and I always assumed we were the only ones chasing them. But now... I don't know."

"You ran into pirates, right?" Pranz asks. "Wasn't that your first real trip out?"

Doug nods slowly. "Yeah. Clutch made short work of them. But maybe they weren't just random."

Pranz leans back, arms crossed. "You think maybe... we're not the only ones chasing these signals?"

"We thought about that," Doug says.

"And?" Pranz presses.

Doug shrugs. "That's as far as we got. Just... thought about it."

"Then it's time we stop thinking and start solving," Pranz says with haste in his voice.

"How do we do that? We haven't come up with a way to do it," Doug shares. "We've just been waiting for the signals to appear."

"Do you have any AI tools?" Pranz asks like it's not a big thing.

Doug flinches like he's been slapped. "No. AI was outlawed. Hard-banned. Nobody's supposed to have it."

"Yeah, well," Pranz says, pulling a sleek silver device from his coat. "Nobody's supposed to have slaves either."

Doug glares at the chip. "We're not outlaws."

"You're treasure hunters in unregulated space, following alien breadcrumbs," Pranz replies. "You blew up a station of people. And who knows what else. I'd say you've stepped outside the lines already."

"That's not the same as unleashing an AI system that could—"

Pranz cuts him off. "Listen. The government says AI is illegal. But they also know that it will be used against them by rogue groups at some point. So, they keep it around for themselves and use it all the time. So do corporations. My father's company runs black-box AI systems across all their networks. They scrub news feeds, fake mining logs, even generate propaganda videos showing how 'happy' the workers are."

Doug clenches his fists. "That's messed up. And I don't see how that helps us."

"It's reality. You think they'll let an AI sit in a junk pile when they can use it to control information?" Pranz asks. "So we're going to use my InfiniChip to figure this shit out before someone else does."

"Probably should wait to see what Clutch has to say about that. Don't want to mess up her ship without her knowing about it," Doug replies, hesitant to do anything with AI.

"We don't know how much time we have to spare. It's best to get a move on before someone else snags it out from under you," Pranz says with a devious smile.

Doug hesitates, then sighs. "Fine. Plug it in. But if your chip fries the system or wakes up some rogue protocol... I'm not stopping Clutch from doing whatever she wants to you."

Pranz grins. "Fair enough."

He plugs the InfiniChip into a console jack. The holographic map flickers, then reboots entirely. In its place, a pulsing cube materializes—its surface shimmering, spinning slowly, voice calm and mechanical.

"What can I help you with today?" it asks in a neutral tone.

"We have a collection of gravitational explosion coordinates," Pranz explains. "We need to understand what shape they form, what's at the center, who's behind them, and why."

The cube spins once, emits a soft chime, and responds instantly.

"The data suggests the anomalies are forming a hexagonal sphere. You currently possess five points on one plane and several forming a second. Projected symmetry indicates two complete hex planes intersecting. Additional predicted points are now displayed."

The map reforms in real time. New points light up in orange, interspersed with the existing green ones.

"That was... freakishly fast," Doug says, his voice caught somewhere between awe and fear.

"What's at the center of this thing?" Pranz asks.

"There are no known celestial objects within the projected core. However, there is a spherical void unaccounted for by any gravitational mapping or charted matter."

Doug furrows his brow. "That doesn't make sense. A perfect sphere of nothing that's not even charted?"

Pranz leans in. "What's the closest thing to the void?"

"There are several stars equally distant from that spot as though there is an empty sphere of space taking over the center point of the larger hexagonal sphere," the AI replies.

"Well, we probably don't want to find out what is there if nothing else seems to fit there," Pranz says. Doug nods in agreement.

"What do we do with this?" Doug asks.

Pranz shrugs and continues to stare at the newly formed chart.

"I guess we wait for Clutch and see what she has to say about this," Doug says, sitting back in his chair and looking at the map.

Chapter 16

"Who figur'd dis out?" Clutch's voice cuts through the bridge like a snap of static. She stands with arms crossed, one brow raised.

Doug and Pranz jolt awake in their seats, eyes wide, limbs scrambling to catch up to reality.

"Uh. Yeah. Don't be mad," Doug blurts out, rubbing his face and standing quickly.

"Mad 'bout what?" Clutch asks, taking a step forward, eyeing the navigation display. "Ya seem ta have solved da puzzle."

"Well… no. Not really," Doug admits, scratching the back of his neck.

"I have an InfiniChip," Pranz chimes in, a little too casually. "Doug didn't want you to be mad that I plugged it into your ship. But it helped us figure out the pattern, angles, and projected shapes."

Clutch's eyebrows rise, her eyes wide with surprise. She stares at them for a beat, then smirks. "I ain't mad. Always wan'ed AI." She looks at the pulsing display and adds, "Can I keep it?"

"Nope," Pranz chuckles. "This one only works with my presence, checking bio markers before interacting, but I promise I'll get you your own before we part ways."

"I'ill hole ya to dat," Clutch says with a grin that lingers longer than usual as she looks back at the display.

For a moment, the tension breaks. They share a laugh, light flickering across their faces from the rotating holographic map.

"Why ain't we head'd to da center?" Clutch asks suddenly, pointing to the void in the middle of the structure.

"Too dangerous," Pranz answers quickly. "That central area—it's like a pocket of missing space. Nothing reflects. It's like a void. No stars. No dust. If it's a black hole or worse, we'd blink out of existence before we even knew we were dead."

Clutch grunts. "Where we go den?"

"That's what we're still trying to figure out," Doug says. "The pulses all trigger at once indicating that this entire sphere activates in a single repeating burst, but the center still gives nothing. However, the AI thinks the midpoints of the pentagons located around the hexagonal sphere might be significant."

"Wurf a shot," Clutch shrugs, already tapping buttons on her cuff.

The ship hums and jolts forward, the quantum drives warping them through the veil of space. Moments later, they decelerate into the dark.

Out the viewport, nothing appears at first. Just blackness. Then a shimmer. The scanners flare to life with a ping. A large station a few hundred thousand kilometers behind them.

"Behind us," Clutch mutters. She swings the ship around, and there it is.

A mass so large it blots out the stars like a void come alive. A monolithic silhouette hangs in space—a presence larger than a mere object.

"Dis is more of sphere 'den even da AI came up wif," Clutch says, awe tightening her voice.

Doug and Pranz press forward in their seats.

"I'm not even going to ask what you just said," Pranz mutters. "Let's just go look at this thing."

Clutch rolls her eyes. "Da pent'gons bowed out. Dey ain't flat. Dey is like a bubble—jus' sayin'."

Doug nods but is already glued to the external cameras. "I'm with Pranz. Let's just see what the hell this is."

The ship approaches in a wide arc. The station remains dark, its shape only distinguishable by the stars it obscures. As they draw nearer, the black void reveals itself to be a perfect pentagon. Then, with careful strafing, they see the full geometry emerge—a pyramid, five-sided, pointing inward to the heart of the sphere.

Clutch activates the external lights. The pyramid's sides glow faintly under the soft sweep of artificial light. Sleek ridges trace from the center of each face toward the apex like the veins of something ancient and alien. The ship scans the surface in different wavelengths of light. The display shows the shape better than any visual can.

"Base is… twenty kilometers per side," Doug mutters. "That's not a station. That's an entire city in space, larger than anything we have created."

Clutch and Pranz look at Doug in awe, contemplating the sheer size of this thing.

They continue past the pyramid's tip. As the ship curves behind the structure, the illusion breaks. The pyramid is only the front.

Behind it lies something else. Massive thrusters at the end of a very long tube shaped hull. Large symmetrical structures. No rivets, no panels, no seams. It looks like the entire ship was formed from a single block of metal, extruded by a machine so precise it might as well be divine.

"This thing ain't human," Clutch whispers.

"No panel lines… That's impossible," Pranz says, his voice caught between wonder and disbelief.

"Any radio signals?" Doug asks.

Clutch checks her display. "Ain't pickin' up nuffin."

"Maybe a tight-band transmission? Line-of-sight?" Pranz offers.

"Migh' be," Clutch replies. "Or… we ain't meant ta hear it."

Doug and Pranz exchange a look.

"Not human," Pranz repeats. "You think we just found alien tech?"

"Maybe," Clutch replies.

"Shouldn't we tell someone?" Doug asks.

Pranz spins on him. "They will take it. They will kill us. They will bury it until they know everything about it and use its resources to their own advantage. If it is alien tech, they will reverse engineer everything and use it on their enemies."

Doug backs up a step. "Okay Pranz. Calm down. Just… exploring options. Besides, maybe we just tell everyone. Broadcast it wide."

"Worse idea. Everyone would come out here and it wouldn't take them long to figure out the structure of this thing. Everyone would swarm each of the pentagons, kill each other, and it would be a small war," Pranz shares.

"If'n dey don't kill us firs'," Clutch replies.

"Or… da ones who built dis," she adds, almost too quietly.

"Who?" Doug asks with concern.

"Who eva' built dis," Clutch replies. "Dey prolly advanced 'n shit."

"Wait, wait—are you saying they're still around?" Doug asks, tension rising.

Clutch shrugs. "I ain't know. Could be. Migh' be long gone."

Pranz clears his throat. "Here's what I suggest. We board this thing, gather intel, figure out its purpose—anything. Then we document our presence by filing a claim with the Salvage Claims Office. No one checks those. They don't send out a party. They just see if the claim already exists. It gives us legal grounds over this area of space. Then we make the announcement letting everyone know we found proof of aliens. Everyone will want to know more, they will want access. We can bring them proof and let them throw money and fame at us. Let the galaxy drool while we hold the keys."

"Ain't some'un gonna fig'a out da salvage coord'nates claim 'n da…"

"I'm going to stop you there. I have already lost you," Pranz interrupts. "But yes, someone could figure out our claim and put the pieces together. But only we and one other person at the claims office will know we even made the claim," Pranz interrupts.

"Ya said dey have AI?" Clutch asks, reminding Pranz of what he said.

"Okay. Yeah. They could have AI looking for such anomalies and could figure it out. Fuck. Well, fine. Let's just go get proof and start with the rich and famous part. Then we can put in the claim," Pranz replies.

"Let's go with the rich and famous part. Then I don't care who takes what. I'll be sitting pretty on Tralbor. That's where I want to go when I am rich," Doug chimes in.

Clutch looks at Doug without approval or disapproval, just a general stare, something else hiding behind her eyes. Doug sees it but before he can ask about it, Clutch chimes in.

"I'm all fa goin' 'n splorin' dis station," Clutch replies, then touches her display a few times. The ship heads for the ship portion of the station, looking for a place to dock.

Doug, Clutch, and Pranz remain silent, watching every inch of space disappear between them and this new alien structure.

"Tralbor is really nice. You'll like it there," Pranz says to Doug quietly.

Chapter 17

"Der isn't a stan'erd dock. Gonna have ta walk," Clutch mutters, securing the grapple with a loud clunk as the ship locks to the alien structure.

"Good thing I got some practice space-walking back at Ulmbria station," Pranz says with a nervous chuckle, clearly trying to cover his unease with bravado.

Doug doesn't respond. He stands frozen near the gear rack, his helmet tucked under one arm, his eyes fixed on the black void beyond the ship's viewport. A yawning unknown stretches before them, darker than the deepest night.

Bad people on a space station? He could handle that now.

But this?

Alien architecture. Possibly alien minds. A silent colossus floating in empty space.

Doug's thoughts spiral:

'What if something's still alive in there? Watching? Waiting?'

'Will they even recognize us as intelligent? Or friendly?'

'How do you convince an alien species not to dissect you before introductions are made?'

'Is this what fame looks like—dying as the opening chapter in someone else's documentary?'

"Doug!" Clutch's voice snaps through his thoughts, sharp and grounding.

He blinks. "Huh? What?" His voice cracks slightly.

"Git ya gear on," Clutch says, her tone crisp, no room for hesitation. "We goin' now."

Doug nods mechanically and turns to his suit. His hands tremble as he fumbles with the seals and fasteners. A glove slips from his grip. Then the wrist lock. His mind screams at him to move faster, but every motion feels like swimming through molasses. He's not just afraid—he's terrified of both what lies ahead and of being left behind.

"Deep breaths, Doug," Pranz says, watching him with concern. "We haven't seen anything threatening. Could be abandoned tech. Could be a drone ship. We don't know. No need to panic."

"Yup," Clutch affirms, checking her own gear and not looking up.

Doug finally gets the suit zipped and sealed. Clutch steps over, grabs his helmet, and helps him lock it in place with practiced hands. Once she confirms the seal, she gives him a firm thumbs up and turns toward the exit hatch.

They crowd into the narrow transition chamber, shoulders bumping as the inner door seals behind them. The hiss of atmosphere draining fills the small space. Lights flicker, and the outer door groans open to reveal the stars—and the station—looming just meters away.

They stand on the edge of everything unknown.

Each of them secures a tether from their belts to the external hook on Clutch's ship. No one speaks. The silence of space presses in, thick despite their comms. The alien structure looms large, impossible and dark, its hull smooth and devoid of any human hallmark. Only one feature—an irregular seam in the hull—suggests a possible entrance.

"That's our best bet," Clutch says, her accent temporarily gone.

Doug blinks. "That was... surprisingly clear. Did you do that just so we'd understand you?"

"Yup." Clutch's grin is audible in her voice. "Now look sharp."

They float forward, gripping whatever edges or seams they can find, scanning the surface for a control panel, an interface—anything resembling a way in.

The void is quiet.

Too quiet.

Clutch runs her gloved fingers along the seamless surface of the station, inspecting a section just slightly different in texture—if not in design—from the rest of the smooth alien alloy. Her hand pauses at a subtle indentation barely visible even under the ship's external lighting.

Without warning, a silent shift in the hull.

The material beneath her hand liquefies for a fraction of a second, then collapses inward like a snapping jaw.

Clutch vanishes, sucked into the alien structure.

The hull reseals with a soft motion as though she was never there.

"Clutch!" Doug yells, his voice cracking as he watches the tether go slack, now trailing into what appears to be solid wall. "Clutch?! Pranz! Clutch is gone!"

Pranz spins around, catching the panic in Doug's voice over comms. "What do you mean she's gone? Where did she go?!"

"I don't know! She touched something and the wall ate her!" Doug fumbles forward, floating closer to the point of her disappearance. He presses against the surface, feeling for any edge or mechanism. "Clutch, do you read me? Say something!"

Before he can get a response—or think about what to do next—the surface beneath his hands ripples.

The door opens again.

A sudden force yanks Doug inward with terrifying speed. There's no time to react, no resistance offered. The structure swallows him whole, and the wall closes just as seamlessly as before.

"Doug?" Pranz stares in disbelief. "No... no no no. How?! How do you get SUCKED INTO a ship from the vacuum of space?!"

Alone now, tethered outside the alien vessel, Pranz floats a meter away from the mysterious doorway. He stares at the surface, his breath quickening, palms beginning to sweat inside his suit.

He hesitates.

His thoughts darken.

He looks back at Clutch's ship.

'I could leave... take the ship... bring help later. Maybe stake the claim on my own. My father would. He wouldn't think twice. Hell, he'd already be halfway to a press conference...'

"No. I'm not him. I'm not my fucking father!"

Pranz sets his jaw, then reaches out and places his hand exactly where the others did.

The wall yields.

In a blink, the structure takes him.

He lands hard, tumbling to the floor in a low-gravity roll, skidding to a stop beside Doug, who's still reorienting himself. Above them, Clutch stands with her hands on her hips, helmet already removed, the confidence in her stance palpable.

"Ain't smart follow'n me in here," she says, her voice relaxed, almost amused.

Doug scrambles to his feet and gawks at her. "Why the hell is your helmet off?! Are you out of your mind?!"

"Atmo's good," Clutch replies calmly. "And I ain't picky when it comes ta air."

Doug looks to Pranz, who shrugs and—after a beat—releases the seal on his own helmet.

"Smells... weirdly clean," Pranz mutters. "Also, how did we just break the laws of physics and get sucked in from the vacuum of space? Seriously, that ain't sciencing right. And I swear your speech patterns are messing with me."

Clutch grins. "Ain't a bad ting." Then she gestures broadly to the walls. "I'ma goin' wif aileen tech as da answer."

"Real specific," Doug replies, finally taking off his helmet. He inhales, eyes narrowing. "Is this what clean smells like? I must have never actually been around clean before. Smells different."

"Not sure how to handle that information, Doug. Yes. This is what clean smells like," Pranz deadpans.

Doug shakes his head. "Whatever. We'll leave the science for later. Let's just figure out what this place is… and how the fuck we get out of it."

"Agreed," Pranz says, stretching his neck.

The trio turns in unison, finally taking in the room around them. It's seamless—no visible panels, no corners, no edges. Just a smooth, white oblique spheroid of a room that seems to hum softly, as though it's alive. The walls are matte, not reflective, but somehow still emit a soft ambient light, with no obvious source.

"No seams, no doors, no tech. This place is… unsettling," Doug says under his breath.

They each begin pacing the perimeter slowly, hands hovering close to the walls, searching for anything to break the monotony of the room's perfection.

Then, with a soft hiss, a section of the wall ripples and recedes. A doorway forms—just enough to let them through. Beyond it lies pure blackness.

"Ominous," Pranz mutters, the word falling from his lips like it was too obvious not to say.

Clutch steps forward without hesitation. As soon as her boot crosses the threshold, the hallway beyond reacts. Light blooms outward in both directions, not from bulbs or strips, but from the walls themselves—like the ship is deciding to see for them. The glow is soft but total, and somehow omnidirectional.

"Auta'maytion," Clutch says with fascination, a twinkle in her eye.

The corridor ahead is unlike any they've seen before. The walls curve upward from the floor, forming an unbroken nearly cylindrical passage. The surface is the same polished material as the previous room—unblemished and eerily smooth. The ceiling is higher than human standard, subtly emphasizing the alien scale of the place.

Doug peers down both directions, frowning. "So, uh… which way? Back to the ship sounds great to me."

Pranz points confidently toward the far end, where the pyramid structure—what they assumed was the tip of the larger station—would be. "That way. If this station has a brain or a purpose, I bet it's there."

Clutch doesn't respond. She just starts walking.

Doug groans under his breath, following reluctantly. As the three of them leave the white room, the entrance behind them shimmers and vanishes. The wall smooths over like water freezing in real time—leaving no trace a door had ever existed.

"Fuck!" Doug stumbles back, hands frantically patting the wall. "How the hell do we get back?! There's no door!"

He starts searching with his hands, pressing every inch of surface he can reach. Panic rises in his voice. "We're trapped. That's it. We're gonna die here."

Clutch checks the glowing interface on her arm, tapping at the readout. "Ya ain't back far 'nuff."

Doug pauses, then turns to her. "What?"

Clutch gestures casually. "Ya walked furder den ya taught. Go back lil' more."

He takes a few steps closer to where they first emerged— and just like before, the wall ripples open, revealing the room they came from.

Doug exhales heavily, visibly deflating with relief.

"I got a track'n sys'em runnin'," Clutch explains, pointing to her device. "Ain't losin' our way. Now, can we go splorin'?"

Without waiting, she turns and walks forward.

Pranz smirks and gives Doug a look. "See? We're not totally screwed."

Doug gives a dry laugh and falls in line, not wanting to be left behind again.

As they proceed, the lights follow them like a loyal pet— illuminating the hall up to a hundred meters ahead and letting the space behind them fall into darkness. The silence inside the station is total—no hum of life support, no clank of shifting metal. Just the soft hiss of their own breathing. An oddity they soon notice, despite the surface being smooth, there is virtually no echo.

Pranz begins to drift from the center, tracing the wall with his gloved fingers. His face is a mix of focused curiosity and something harder to place—like he's quietly calculating the value of everything he sees.

Then—shhhhk—a door ripples open where his hand touches.

Doug flinches. Clutch spins around.

"Whoa—what did you do?" Doug asks.

"Just touched the wall," Pranz replies, grinning. "Looks like we can open doors at will."

He walks inside without hesitation.

Clutch and Doug follow a second later, just in time to see him step back out, disappointed. "Nothing. Just another blank room. Like the hallway, but with less personality."

"Maybe da rooms is motion ac'vated too," Clutch says thoughtfully. She steps inside and starts waving her arms in slow arcs across the walls.

Suddenly, surfaces begin responding.

Sections of the wall extend outward—drawers, panels, flat platforms—all appearing and then disappearing in a mechanical dance that seems hyper-sensitive to her proximity. One panel opens fully, revealing what looks like a tall, narrow cabinet. It's empty.

Doug takes a turn, dragging his fingers along another section. A table slides silently from the wall, and a cylindrical stool rises from the floor beneath it. No seat back. No obvious shape. No guess as to who—or what—would use it.

"Anyone find a bathroom?" Pranz jokes, arms crossed as he watches.

Doug doesn't respond. He's staring at the pristine surface of the table. "This place... it feels too clean. Like no one's ever used it. Or it's cleaning itself constantly. Either way, it's unsettling."

"Let's keep splorin'," Clutch says, already halfway out the door.

The others follow, the room closing up behind them like it was never there at all.

Chapter 18

After walking for what felt like a never-ending stretch of seamless, glowing corridor, Doug finally slumps to a stop. His legs ache, his breath catches in his throat, and his shoulders sag beneath the weight of his suit.

The lights in the hallway flicker—not fully dimming, but stuttering like a nervous breath. A quick pulse, as if the corridor blinked without ever closing its eyes. Doug blinks in response, unsure whether it was the lights or just his own vision faltering. He glances at Clutch and Pranz, but neither of them react. No flinch. No pause. Maybe it's nothing. Or maybe it's just him. Believing he is just tired, he shakes it off.

"I haven't walked this far in… well, ever," he groans, leaning against the smooth curve of the wall and sliding down to sit. "I need a break before my legs stage a rebellion."

Pranz, who's been quietly pacing just ahead, turns and squints down the corridor. "It does seem endless. Maybe the beings who built this place had a more efficient way of moving around. Rails, floaters, teleportation—anything other than foot travel."

"Or maybe they move swiftly. Or don't have feet. Or…fuck. We don't know shit about this place," Doug says, frustration simmering just beneath the surface, but exhaustion dulling its edge.

Clutch taps at her cuff-mounted interface, her eyes scanning the display with quiet intensity. "We ain't even close ta da main ting," she mutters, glancing up only briefly before returning to her cuff.

Doug lets out a dramatic sigh and sinks lower, running a gloved hand over his face. "Of course we aren't."

Clutch frowns in concentration. She spends the next five minutes lost in her display, fingers dancing with surprising precision across the tiny surface. Her expression remains unreadable, until finally she gives a short, thoughtful nod.

Then, to everyone's surprise, she sits.

Not in a hurry. Not irritated. Just calm. Deliberate. She plops down beside Doug and rests her arms on her knees, her head tilting slightly as she watches the empty corridor ahead.

Pranz approaches with a puzzled expression. "What are we doing?" he asks. "This is the opposite of finding something we can take back with us."

Clutch jerks her chin toward the floor and raises an eyebrow. "Might wanna get comfy, richy. N' move out da way."

Pranz blinks. "Why?"

"Jus' trus' me," Clutch replies, leaning back against the wall.

Doug watches her curiously, then chuckles as he rests his head against the cool surface behind him. "This isn't what I expected when I met you."

Clutch grins, side-eyeing him. "Oh yeah? Wha'd ya spec?"

Doug hesitates. The obvious answers aren't what seem to be forming at Doug's mouth.

He opens his mouth, but nothing comes out at first. Then, after a beat too long—"Aliens?"

The word feels like a deflection. A weak attempt to pivot away from what he really wanted to say. And Clutch knows it.

She smirks. "Ain't what I was spec'n needer," she replies. "But we found it—ta'gedder."

Her voice is soft, less broken than usual. That single word—together—hits Doug with a surprising amount of weight.

Her smile holds there, patient and genuine. Doug feels the heat rise to his cheeks and quickly averts his gaze, pretending to study the flawless floor beneath them. He offers a shy smile of his own, lips pressed tight.

Pranz stands a few feet away, arms crossed, watching the whole thing unfold. He rolls his eyes and mutters under his breath with a small smile. "Unbelievable. I'm third-wheeling on an alien megastructure and those two don't even know it yet."

A low vibration hum begins to seep through the corridor walls, subtle at first, like the growl of something vast and mechanical awakening.

Doug bolts upright. "Is that them?" His voice trembles with sudden panic.

"Dem who?" Clutch asks casually, still sitting, not a hint of concern on her face.

"Aliens," Doug whispers. His eyes are wide and darting down the dim hallway, as if expecting something to crawl out of the shadows.

Clutch stands up and places a reassuring hand on Doug's shoulder. "Ya need ta ra'lax more," she says softly, giving him a look that lands somewhere between amusement and sympathy.

The low vibration fades—but before anyone can feel relief, a new sound replaces it: a deep rumble layered with a rising hum, like heavy machinery gliding across some invisible track. The corridor behind them slowly begins to light up, one section at a time, as if the hallway itself is being chased by an unseen force.

Doug instinctively backs up, sliding behind Clutch. A moment of cowardice, he knows it. "Coward," he tells himself, ashamed. His stomach churns with adrenaline, but he clenches his jaw and steps forward again, forcing his body to stop retreating. He breathes through the fear, planting his feet beside Clutch.

The sound gets louder. The glowing sections chase closer.

Then—three dark dots appear in the distance, growing larger with every second.

The sections of light surrounding the dots finally meet the sections of light surrounding Doug, Clutch, and Pranz.

Doug squints. So does Pranz. The silhouettes approach fast, too smooth and synchronized to be alive. Finally, they come to a precise stop just in front of them. Doug braces, half-expecting an alien to leap out and vaporize them on the spot.

Instead—

"Pop speeders?" Pranz exclaims, stunned and delighted. "Those haven't been manufactured in centuries. I'm impressed you have three operational units."

"Stole 'em," Clutch replies, almost proudly.

Pranz blinks. "From where? The mines?"

"Yup. Da slavers had 'em. Made it eas'er fa dem to git 'round," Clutch says. "Now dey gonna help us git 'round."

Doug circles the nearest one, eyes narrowing. "How do they work? There's no controls… no handlebars…"

Clutch strides up to the first speeder and swings her leg over it with practiced ease. The sleek black orb hovers silently, the low hum of power almost imperceptible. A minimal seat appears above the ball—no connection points, no stabilizers.

"Ya sit, lean for'ard. Dat's it."

She leans forward ever so slightly, and the pop speeder jolts into action, racing down the corridor with uncanny speed.

Pranz's grin widens. "Had one as a kid. They're pretty intuitive." He hops onto the second one and follows Clutch, gliding with smooth precision after her.

Doug stares at the last speeder like it's a bull he's about to mount. "No way this ends well," he tells himself.

Still, he straddles it and eases himself onto the seat. His nerves make him relax at the wrong moment, and the speeder lurches backward. Doug flails and tumbles off, slamming into the hard floor with a grunt.

Clutch and Pranz stop and look back.

Doug picks himself up, wincing, and tries again. This time he keeps his body rigid and leans forward just a bit too far. The speeder rockets forward, but Doug's balance is off—he tilts sideways and the orb compensates too sharply. He's flung off in a graceless arc, landing hard on his side.

"Should we turn on the training settings for Doug?" Pranz asks Clutch.

"Dey is 'bout da only ting dat ain't workin'. He jus' gonna have ta learn qick," Clutch replies.

"No better way than trial and error," Pranz replies.

"Yup," Clutch replies, a smile on her face.

"Small movements!" Pranz shouts from down the hall, trying not to laugh.

Doug groans and drags himself up, brushing off the pain and his wounded pride. His cheeks flush with embarrassment. One more try. He climbs back on, breathes deep, and leans just his head forward.

The speeder inches ahead.

Doug smiles.

A little more forward—and it moves faster. He shifts his hips, it veers. He leans into it, and the speeder surges. It's like riding a thought.

He whooshes past Clutch and Pranz, grinning ear to ear. "How do I stop!?" he yells, wind whipping past his helmet.

Clutch and Pranz smile and speed after him.

"Jus' stop leanin' for'ard!" Clutch calls out, laughing now.

Doug adjusts his posture, letting his body relax and center. The speeder slows, then coasts gently. His grin widens, filling his whole face. "This is awesome!"

Clutch and Pranz catch up, their expressions matching his—equal parts exhilaration and awe. In the glow of alien architecture, the three of them streak down the corridor on stolen slaver tech, laughter chasing their movements into the unknown.

A short time later, a massive wall begins to materialize in the distance, barely visible at first—its smooth surface catching stray light and shimmering like obsidian glass. The closer they get, the more immense it appears, dwarfing the already spacious corridor. The hallway, once just above their heads, now rises with each meter forward, tripling in height, as though preparing them to enter something far beyond their scale.

"I wonder," Clutch murmurs, the thought barely audible through the comms.

Doug slows down, uneasy, his eyes locked on the towering wall ahead. Pranz follows suit, cautious. But Clutch doesn't reduce speed. She leans forward slightly, guiding her speeder toward the very center of the wall, checking her cuff, adjusting course—directly at what seems to be solid black surface.

"Clutch! Stop!" Doug shouts, panic laced through every word. His heart pounds at the thought of her slamming into that monolithic wall.

But Clutch doesn't stop. The wall illuminates as she closes in, turning the wall from dark to light.

Just as her pop speeder is about to collide with the wall, a faint seam appears—an outline traced in silent light—and the surface parts with liquid grace. A doorway blooms open, seamless and silent, revealing a sliver of what lies beyond. Clutch glides through the opening effortlessly, and the wall seals shut behind her like it had never opened at all.

Pranz turns to Doug and smirks. "When in doubt, aim for the impossible."

Before Doug can respond, Pranz tilts forward and launches ahead. The pop speeder hums as he narrows in on the same center point. Doug hesitates for a beat, mouth slightly open, and then clenches his jaw.

"Screw it," he mutters, leaning in and accelerating.

Both of them reach the point together, the wall recognizing their approach. The gateway opens once again, elegant and quiet, swallowing them whole before sealing shut behind them without a sound—leaving only the fading memory of their passage behind in the darkened corridor.

Chapter 19

Doug takes a step forward. "What is it?" he asks, his voice barely above a whisper. Clutch and Pranz remain silent, eyes locked ahead, equally captivated.

"Is that... hmm," Pranz begins, trailing off, as if even trying to name it might be a mistake.

"Ain't nutin' I eva seen," Clutch mutters, dismounting her pop speeder with practiced ease.

Pranz and Doug follow suit, sliding off their speeders. The three of them fan out instinctively, eyes sweeping for anything—markings, controls, symbols—some clue as to what they are looking at, or how to interact with it.

Before them looms what can only be described as an alien power source, nested behind an immense crystalline wall. The surface of the wall shimmers and shifts as if it were liquid held upright by some unseen force. Ripples chase each other across its translucent plane, giving it the appearance of being alive.

Suspended within the crystalline veil floats a massive orb, nearly thirty meters in diameter. Its surface is a mesmerizing dance of shifting energy: blues and greens flow like solar tides, pulsing outward in hypnotic waves. Occasionally, streaks of violet lightning crackle across its skin, sharp and sudden like veins of static fury.

At the heart of the orb churns a molten nucleus of golden-white fire, chaotic and alive. It pulses with intensity, throwing long, distorted shadows across the chamber. The room is filled with an eerie hum, a blend of frequencies that form something almost musical—a haunting harmony that vibrates in the bones.

Thin conduits of dark, obsidian-like metal snake from the orb outward, embedding themselves into the station walls like roots from some colossal, energy-fed tree. They look dormant—silent, waiting.

The very air around them buzzes with energy, lifting the hairs on their arms and necks. The power is palpable, suffocating in its magnitude.

Doug opens his mouth to speak again, but the orb suddenly shudders. The rippling surface breaks into chaotic turbulence. The harmony fractures, replaced by a shrill, high-pitched whine that cuts through the chamber like a blade.

The orb convulses—a violent twist of form and light—before releasing a massive pulse of golden energy. A wave of raw force explodes outward, a blinding shockwave that flattens the crew to the ground.

The crystalline wall flexes like a living membrane. A thunderous BOOM echoes through the room, rattling bones and stealing the breath from their lungs.

Blinded, Clutch and Pranz cover their eyes, trying to shield themselves from the lingering brilliance. The shockwave fades, the whine giving way to stillness. The orb calms, its rhythm returning to the steady, hypnotic pulse from before, as though nothing had happened at all.

"What the fuck was that?" Pranz asks, breath ragged as he steadies himself.

Clutch doesn't answer right away. Her eyes adjust to the aftermath, scanning the chamber—then narrowing in on Doug's motionless body sprawled near the floor. She rushes to his side. "Doug. Git up," she says, voice firm but laced with concern.

No response.

Clutch kneels beside him, her boots scraping softly against the smooth floor. Blood. A slick crimson pool forming beneath Doug's head.

"Shit," Pranz mutters, finally turning and realizing what she's doing. "Is he—what happened?"

"Look like he hit his head in da blast. He'ill be fine," Clutch replies calmly, but doesn't take her eyes off Doug.

"Fine? His head's bleeding!" Pranz kneels, alarm spreading across his face unsure if he wants to use his hands to help stop the bleeding.

"He got nanos," Clutch says, already standing again and heading toward the shimmering energy wall.

"Nanos? Doug?" Pranz raises an eyebrow, both impressed and confused.

"I gave 'em to 'em. My own makin'. Betta den any Regy garbage," Clutch says, her voice cool and confident.

"Well damn," Pranz mutters. "You really are full of surprises. And yeah, my father insisted on Fornokey nanos instead of Regimentary ones. He probably knows something he shouldn't."

Behind them, Doug groans. "Ugh..."

He rolls slightly, then pushes himself upright. The pool of blood beneath him is gone—completely absorbed. The floor pristine again.

"Are you kidding me?" Pranz asks, eyes wide. "You've got blood recyclers embedded too?"

"Yup," Clutch replies without looking back.

"But those aren't even real yet. They're still theoretical. Years from deployment. Just sell that tech and you'll be rich!"

"Real 'nuff," Clutch says. "Dem people ain't deserve it. Dey 'ould jus' use it ta control udders," Clutch adds. "Plus, dey ain't gonna listen ta a iron ant."

"You could be rich," Pranz insists. "Get a patent. Work with a front. There are neutral brokers who can—"

"Ain't trust nobody needer," Clutch cuts in, hands on her hips as she turns and gives him a sideways glare, head tilted just enough to shut down the conversation.

Pranz raises his hands in surrender. "Alright. Message received."

Doug finally stands fully, shaking the disorientation from his eyes. "What happened?"

"We dunno," Clutch replies, finally pulling her gaze away from Pranz. "But if I'm right, it's gonna happ'n 'gain in 'bout an hour."

"Great," Doug mutters. "Maybe next time I won't bounce my skull off the floor."

Pranz chuckles. "Any chance those miracle nanos can fix your speech too, Clutch?"

"I love the way she talks," Doug says, brushing past them toward the energy wall, wincing slightly but holding himself upright.

"How hard did you hit your head?" Pranz teases.

Clutch is already mounting her pop speeder. "We should watch da next pulse from da black," she says. Her tone serious now, her eyes locked forward.

Doug nods and moves to his own speeder without protest.

Pranz lingers for just a moment. He scans the chamber, eyes darting over the walls, floor, conduit lines—hoping for anything tangible to take back. Evidence. A fragment. A trophy. But, like every other room, it's seamless. Alien perfection. Nothing detachable. Nothing meant to leave.

With a reluctant sigh, Pranz climbs aboard his speeder and follows the others. One last glance over his shoulder, then he speeds off, leaving the heart of the station behind.

Together, the trio race back toward the ship, the faint echo of the orb's hum still trembling in their bones.

Chapter 20

The three companions stare out from Clutch's ship at the alien structure, now ominously silent after its last pulse. A countdown ticks steadily on the dashboard—a timer predicting the next eruption of power from the station. No one speaks. The ship's AI system hovers in a state of standby, waiting for input to process.

Doug watches the timer drop to twenty seconds. He glances over at Clutch. There's something about the way she sits, focused and calm, that radiates a confidence he's always wanted for himself. Being near her makes him feel safer, even now. He lets himself hold onto that.

"Here we go," Pranz mutters, slicing through the silence.

The timer hits five seconds.

The room stands still. Everyone stops breathing. The anticipation is thick. Nobody knowing what to expect.

Four seconds.

The ship hovers just past the plane of the pyramid's base. A perfect position to see the pyramid and the rest of the ship.

Three.

Doug looks at Clutch again, holding on to her confidence rather than being fearful.

Two.

Doug turns yet again and stares at Clutch's face—the curve of her cheek, the stillness of her lips. The moment stretches. He shakes himself back into focus.

One.

'What was that thought?' Doug asks himself.

Zero.

A beam of light pierces through Doug's ship, slicing through the port side of Clutch's vessel before streaking toward one of the pyramid's corners. In an instant, the entire structure ignites. Each corner receives its own focused beam, energy channels activating simultaneously. The pyramid pulses with life, converging into a central, colossal blast aimed toward the middle of the hexagonal sphere. But the blast falters. It flickers and cuts out. Everything falls dark.

Inside Clutch's ship, alarms scream. Emergency systems kick into overdrive. Air escaping, power failing, stability gone.

"Fuck!" Clutch shouts, diving into the pilot's seat as emergency lights flash red. The ship groans, power surging and failing in uneven bursts.

Doug instinctively pulls himself into a seat, strapping in before artificial gravity collapses. He moves with the speed of someone who's survived a dying ship before.

Pranz, caught off-guard, floats upward as the ship lurches violently. The bridge seals itself off from the rest of the vessel as air begins venting through the breached port side. The ship lists, port thrusters failing.

Clutch fights with the controls. The displays flicker. The thrusters sputter.

Pranz slams into a wall with a painful thud, his body ragdolling. His head definitely hit the wall. One side of his chest caves unnaturally.

"Can you get back to the alien structure?" Doug asks, his eyes wide, unsure what to do to help.

"Tryin'!" Clutch shouts. "If Pranz float by ya, grab 'em!"

Doug unstraps, gripping his seatbelt as a tether. He launches toward Pranz but misjudges the next jolt. Both men spin helplessly into a bulkhead.

"Shit!" Doug grits out, seeing stars.

With the next lull in motion, Doug kicks off hard, launching toward Pranz. He manages to snag the unconscious man mid-float. Now, the floating object that has been smashing into everything has doubled in mass.

He times it. One second… two… the ship jerks again. Doug extends a leg, catching the wall just right, springing both of them toward a seat. He barely manages to jam Pranz into it, locking his arms around him like a human seatbelt before...

Another jolt. Doug's grip loosens but he's able to keep Pranz in the seat. He finally get's Pranz buckled in, just before the next jolt.

Doug looks to the second chair. Out of reach.

"Damn it," he hisses.

As the ship rocks again, he pushes off, floating halfway there—then the gravity slams back on. He hits the deck with a painful grunt, unable to move. "Too much gravity!" he croaks feeling the weight of six men laying on top of him.

"Ain't my faw't," Clutch fires back, hands flying across the controls.

Doug wheezes. The crushing weight lifts. He floats again, gasping, just as the ship jolts. He slams into the ceiling, then shoves himself down toward the empty chair and grabs hold.

"Finally!" Doug calls out.

"Fin'ly what?" Clutch asks without looking.

"I'm strapped in! And Pranz is secure!"

The ship convulses one final time, then powers down. Emergency lighting takes over, casting the cabin in a low red glow.

Clutch spins her chair around and grins at Doug. "Ain't want ta do dat 'gain."

Doug exhales a tired laugh, returning the smile. For a moment, they lock eyes. The moment lingers. Too long for Doug's comfort. He looks away, suddenly shy. Clutch catches his gaze one more time before both turn to check on Pranz.

His body is slack, blood staining his clothes.

Clutch and Doug unbuckle and drift toward him.

"Wouldn't he have nanos?" Doug asks, eyes scanning the damage. "I thought rich people all had nanos."

"He said he do," Clutch says, already floating to a nearby cabinet. " But all da same, I'ill get some a mine."

She floats over to a storage closet and pulls out a small box, retrieves a syringe, and injects it into Pranz's chest. Then, methodically, she reseals the kit and stashes it away.

"Now we wait," she says, hovering nearby.

Doug looks toward the view window, out into the darkness. "Where are we?"

Chapter 21

Doug and Clutch exit the ship, their boots eerily silent as they descend once again into the belly of the alien structure. This time, they steer their pop speeders toward the rear—where something different and unknown resides.

"You really think we'll find something to help your ship?" Doug asks, his voice tense as they accelerate down the glowing corridor. "It took a pretty nasty hit."

"Ain't know 'til we look," Clutch replies, steady as ever, her tone unreadable yet calm.

Doug glances at her from his seat, then back to the endless hallway ahead. "Do you think Pranz will wake up soon?" he asks, searching for conversation more than answers.

"Ain't know dat needer," Clutch replies, unfazed.

"You don't really like to guess, do you?" Doug asks, cracking a small smile, hoping to tease a grin out of her.

"Use'aly wrong when I do," Clutch says without a hint of irony. "So I stop guessin'."

Doug goes quiet for a moment, letting her words sink in. He turns them over in his mind, wondering if maybe his own life could've used a bit less guessing and a bit more moving forward with what was right in front of him.

As the two speed deeper into the structure, the hallway ahead begins to fracture—not just your typical fork or T-split. It breaks into five separate directions: one straight ahead, two veering slightly left and right, and two sharply branching into hard turns.

They pull their speeders to a stop, the hum of the devices fading into the ambient silence of the station. Each corridor looks the same: seamless, sterile, impossibly clean. No signs. No markings. No clues.

Clutch scans the junction, then points across Doug to one of the outer paths. "We should split up. Cova mo' ground fas'er," she says, motioning to the right for him and back over her shoulder for herself.

Doug lets out a short, almost-laugh. "You know what happens when I get separated from you, right?" he says, half-joking, half-serious. Inside his head is screaming, 'don't leave me alone!'

Clutch smirks just a little, not looking at him. "Ain't no'buddy here, dough. Ya be fine."

Doug gives her a long look, then nods—though not entirely convinced. Doing his best to feign confidence.

Clutch doesn't hesitate. She veers left and disappears into the leftmost corridor, the soft hum of her pop speeder fading quickly into the stillness.

Doug watches her go, swallowed by the sterile glow of the alien hallway. He's alone again.

He gulps and turns toward the far right corridor. "Alright," he mutters to himself, "just find the end, confirm it's a dead end, and get back to Clutch quickly. Easy."

He launches forward, pushing the speeder to its maximum speed. The wind brushes past his helmetless head, the artificial breeze doing little to ease the weight sitting on his chest. His mind churns.

'You're fine. She's probably already back. This is nothing. You've done worse.'

But the dread creeps in.

'What if this is the wrong path?'

'What if she needs you and you're not there? Or what if I need her? That's the more likely scenario.'

'Why am I such a failure?'

'No. I'm not thinking that way anymore. Remember?'

Doug briefly smiles and then right back to the dread.

'What if something's at the end of this hallway, waiting? An alien who's been watching us this whole time? A guard of some kind.'

He grips his legs tightly. "Get a grip, Doug. You've been through pirates, near death, alien power surges. This is just a hallway. Just a...weird-ass hallway."

The corridor finally veers left, guiding him deeper into the rear of the structure. After a few more minutes of high-speed travel, the hallway ends—abruptly. Just another blank wall.

Doug slows, climbs off the speeder, and approaches the smooth surface. Same alien material. Same impossible cleanliness. Same lack of visible seams or controls.

But he's learned a few things.

He presses a palm flat to the wall and moves along its surface, hoping for the motion sensors to trigger. A beat later, the wall ripples. A seam appears, splitting open into a chamber.

Doug steps inside, immediately noticing a difference.

The room's design is as minimal as before, but each section of the wall bears faintly outlined pentagonal shapes—five of them evenly spaced, slightly recessed like hidden compartments. He walks up to one of them, raising a hand in front of the shape.

Nothing.

"Not like the other rooms," he says aloud. "Maybe you need more than a wave."

Doug takes a breath, sweat already forming at his brow despite the stable temperature, and touches the wall directly.

The pentagon splits open—silently, cleanly—unfolding in five smooth directions like a blooming mechanical flower.

Inside is a compact holographic interface. A small, flickering image floats in the air, displaying shifting alien symbols and an unfamiliar schematic. The entire interface is ethereal, hovering, glowing—but without buttons, text, or any labels he could make sense of.

He glances around. No obvious way to control it. Still, curiosity gets the better of him. He reaches in and brushes the back half of the image with his fingers.

The diagram rotates.

"Shit," he whispers. "Did I just turn the whole ship?"

He frantically tries to reverse the motion, spinning the diagram back to its original position—at least, what he thinks was original. But the image just continues to rotate on different axes, responding to his gestures like it's reading his intent, not his precision.

As the panic fades, realization sets in.

"Oh," he exhales. "It's just… a model."

He experiments more, using both hands to tilt, rotate, and zoom. The diagram floats silently under his control. Then, as he pulls his hands away to rest, the entire projection suddenly expands—bursting out into the center of the room. A massive, fully-detailed hologram fills the space, bathing the walls in a soft, otherworldly glow.

"What the fuck…" Doug says, frozen in place, staring up at the intricate design.

The diagram is a multi-layered cutaway of something. A schematic of sorts. Very alien. Very unrecognizable. Tiny animated nodes pulse within the model, mimicking real-time activity. Embedded within the hologram are hundreds—maybe thousands—of alien symbols, changing dynamically as the diagram shifts. Some look like energy flows. Others resemble system readouts, possibly statuses or temperatures. None of it makes sense to him. None of it recognizable.

But it's beautiful. And alive.

He walks up to the floating image, mouth slightly open, caught somewhere between awe and a quiet, growing dread. This wasn't just a ship.

It was something more.

And whoever—or whatever—built it was far beyond anything humanity had ever touched.

Just as Doug extends his hand—drawn by instinct and curiosity but haunted by an unshakable dread—the door peels open.

He jumps, heart lurching into his throat, but manages to freeze in place. His head snaps toward the sound, breath caught somewhere between fear and reflex. Every muscle tightens. His eyes lock on the open doorway.

A figure steps in.

Doug's whole body slackens when he sees it's Pranz.

"You scared the fuck out of me!" Doug exhales, his voice half relief, half frustration as he finally breathes again.

Pranz raises an eyebrow, clearly amused. "Nice to see you too," he says, then scans the room. "Where's Clutch?"

"She split us up. Took another path. I have no idea where she ended up," Doug replies, glancing around the floating hologram to make sure Clutch isn't somehow behind it.

Pranz approaches the glowing projection, eyes wide. He circles it slowly, clearly mesmerized. "What the fuck is this thing?"

"I haven't figured that out yet," Doug says. "But I did manage to get it out of the wall and into the middle of the room."

"Well, don't go poking buttons or whatever passes for controls. For all we know, one of these glowy bits could activate a self-destruct," Pranz says, flashing a grin as he steps back. "Come on, let's go find Clutch. Maybe she's figured something out on her end."

He pauses and adds with a teasing smirk, "And if not, you can impress her with your mysterious find here."

Doug's face immediately flushes. He tries to hold Pranz's gaze but fails, eyes darting downward in embarrassment.

Pranz chuckles knowingly. "Relax. It's obvious that you like her," he says, turning toward the hallway.

Doug lingers a second, collecting himself, then follows. The hologram remains active behind him, still spinning and shifting slowly in midair like a sleeping beast with secrets yet untold. Unsure how to return it to the small recess, Doug simply walks around it.

Outside, Pranz is already straddling his pop speeder, idling lazily in the corridor.

Doug climbs onto his own. Pranz flashes him a sly smile.

"Lead the way, Cassanova."

Doug rolls his eyes, suppressing a grin, and leans forward. The speeder responds instantly, shooting down the corridor.

Pranz accelerates after him. "You're getting really good at these things!" he shouts.

Doug doesn't look back—but the smile growing on his face says plenty.

As they race down the corridor, Doug finally breaks the silence. "What made you go hard right at the junction?"

"I like turning right," Pranz replies simply. "Nothing scientific. Just felt like the best move."

Doug nods thoughtfully, accepting the randomness. He jets forward, passing the old junction and heading straight into the path Clutch had taken. The corridor mirrors the other wing—smooth, seamless, and hauntingly silent. Up ahead, parked in the middle of the corridor, is Clutch's pop speeder.

Doug slows to a stop and scans the wall. Before he can call out, the wall responds. A soft shimmer, then the doorway unfolds like a blossoming petal.

Pranz hops off his speeder and joins Doug at the threshold.

Without a word, they step into the room together.

Clutch stands quietly near one of the pentagon-shaped wall insets, her eyes scanning a faint, hovering projection flickering within.

"Hi Clutch!" Doug says, his voice upbeat as he and Pranz step into the room.

"Find anytin'?" Clutch asks, not turning yet, still studying the display in front of her.

"Yeah, I did. You?" Doug replies, a small smile tugging at the corner of his mouth.

"Jus' dis lil' holo," Clutch says with a shrug.

"Watch this," Doug says, excitement building as he steps up beside her. He places both hands inside the recessed pentagon slot and gently pulls outward.

The panel responds immediately.

The small projection flickers, then bursts to life—expanding into the room in a smooth arc of cascading light. The projection stretches across the entire chamber, the shapes and lines of alien schematics casting a soft glow across their faces.

Clutch glances around, then back to Doug with an impressed look. "Ya seen un'a dees ova der I'm guessin'?" she asks, pointing across the room.

"Yeah," Doug nods. "Found one on that side. Opened it up just like this—accidentally figured out how to pull the holo into the room."

He crosses the space and touches the pentagon he originally activated. It responds just like before, unfolding with an elegant pulse. The hologram in the center of the room dissolves, replaced instantly by the version Doug first discovered.

"Dis what ya saw?" Clutch asks, tilting her head, analyzing the new diagram.

"Yup. Same structure, but definitely different. Like... maybe the opposite of the one on your side? I don't know," Doug says, eyes flicking across the floating, alien shapes. "I didn't mess with anything else. I mean, I'd rather not blow up the station."

Doug throws a glance toward Pranz and winks.

Pranz chuckles. "Smart move. But seriously, what do you think this is, Clutch?"

Clutch folds her arms and stares at the display. "Ain't gah a clue."

"She doesn't like guessing," Doug adds with a grin.

Clutch meets his gaze and smirks, a rare warmth in her expression. For a long moment, they hold eye contact—an unspoken connection flashing between them. Doug's smile deepens, but he's the one to look away first.

"We should check the other three hallways," he says, breaking the moment. "These diagrams are incredible, but they won't help us patch up the ship. If we don't find parts soon, we're going to run out of options."

"Speakin' of," Pranz says, stepping forward, "What exactly happened to me and the ship?"

"You got hurt," Doug says. "Well, kind of..."

"Kinda?" Clutch laughs as she moves toward the hallway. "Ya ribs was pokin' outta ya chest like a bus'ed scaffold. I had ta hit ya wif some'a my cus'om nanos."

Pranz raises an eyebrow, instinctively running a hand along his ribs. "And now I feel completely fine. I mean— damn. That's some next-level tech. I guess I owe you a huge thank you."

Clutch glances over her shoulder, flashing a lopsided smile. "I ain't un ta fuck wif karma."

She turns back, heading toward the hallway door, her voice drifting behind her. "Come on. Let's see what da rest'a this place is hidin'."

Doug and Pranz exchange a glance, then follow.

Chapter 22

"Five identical rooms at the back of the ship," Pranz says as the three of them regroup at the central junction. "And I think we all agree—they're maintenance hubs. Most likely tied to propulsion."

"Seem dat way," Clutch replies, tapping her boot lightly against the floor, her eyes narrowed in thought.

Doug's nerves, long strained, finally crack. "We haven't found anything we can use. No parts. No escape route. We can't fix Clutch's ship. Are we just... going to die here?" His voice trembles with the weight of the question, dread dripping from every word.

Before anyone can answer, the station rumbles beneath their feet—a deep, unsettling vibration that pulses through the walls and into their bones.

Clutch steadies herself. "Dis station... eeder ain't been used yet... or it been left ta rot. Ain't sure which."

"New or abandoned, it doesn't matter," Pranz says, a rare edge sharpening his usually calm tone. "What matters is getting your ship operational enough to get us out of here. Then we come back—with tools, a new or repaired ship, and the means to prove this place exists. And that we found it first."

Doug's frustration boils over. "How? My ship's toast. Clutch's is barely alive. We're stuck on a station no one knows about, with no working comms and no food!"

"Ain't dead," Clutch says firmly, her voice even. "Jus' hurt bad."

Pranz turns to her. "How far could it get us?"

Clutch tilts her head, mentally calculating. "Depen's on how long she hold. Migh' not make it far. But far 'nough... maybe in un 'rection. Not much choice."

"We just need to be far enough to get out of local scan range," Pranz says. "If we can pull off even one decent jump, I can get us rescued."

Doug stares at him. "How?"

Pranz sighs, almost embarrassed. "Emergency beacon. Embedded. Deep. All the rich kids get them. My father's idea. I never wanted it, but it's there. And it supposably works. And, very likely, hurts like hell. Calls in extraction teams, no matter where you are."

"But you said it hurts?" Doug asks, squinting.

"It does. I think," Pranz mutters. "But I'll use it. If it means saving us and coming back prepared. If we can secure this place first, we'll be untouchable. Every government, every corporation—fuck, every outlaw—will pay to get a piece of it. My father included."

Doug lets out a shaky breath. "I just want to stop being stranded in space."

Clutch turns toward them, eyes dark but calm, a different look than either had seen from her before. "I want 'nough... ta end slav'ry."

Pranz nods with quiet respect. "Then I'll help you do it. Whatever it takes."

Doug watches them, feeling the weight of their convictions. They seem so clear. So driven. He wishes he could feel that way. Instead, he's just scared. But maybe... maybe he can fake the confidence until it's real. Maybe if he says the right thing, he'll start to believe it. And maybe Clutch will see him the way he's starting to see her.

I like her, he realizes, heart pounding a little faster. *I really fucking like her.*

"Doug?" Clutch asks, pulling him out of his spiral.

He blinks and looks up. "What?"

"Ya ready ta go back ta my ship? Try'n jump us outta here?" she asks, already seated on her pop speeder.

Doug swallows hard, then nods. "Yeah. And... I'll help you stop slavery. However I can."

His tone is a bit uncertain, but sincere.

Clutch doesn't say anything—just gives him a small nod. That single nod says more than words. Then she turns and speeds down the hallway, her form disappearing into the glow of the corridor lights.

"That a boy," Pranz says with a grin, giving Doug a wink before hopping on his own speeder and racing after her.

Doug stands there a beat longer, then gives himself a crooked smile. "Come on, Doug. Keep up," he says to himself.

He mounts his pop speeder and tears after them, not willing to lose sight—not of Clutch, and not of what he's beginning to believe he can become.

The three companions sit strapped into the bridge of Clutch's battered ship. Systems hum weakly to life as they prepare to detach from the alien structure—just enough to drift clear and make a jump. The goal: put distance between themselves and the station. Far enough that no one could trace where they came from.

"Slow and steady," Pranz says, gripping the armrests. His voice trembles slightly, knowing what's coming. "Even if we just push off and coast... we only need enough distance to jump clean."

"I ain't new at dis," Clutch replies, flashing a half-smile, her fingers already dancing across her console.

The ship unhooks from the structure with a quiet hum and a low shudder. No visible movement, at first. A faint plume of gas escapes the ship's nose—soft, controlled thrust, nothing aggressive. Nothing more available without causing problems. Clutch's hand hovers over the controls, her focus razor sharp. The ship begins a barely perceptible drift away from the station.

"Startin' jump check," she mutters, almost to herself.

Another tiny burst—this one—tilts the ship, slowly pushing the station out of sight. Clutch triple-checks the jump coordinates. The tension on the bridge grows thick, compressed by silence and the flickering light from the failing emergency panels.

"Hold tight," Clutch warns.

Doug clutches his restraints and slams his eyes shut. Sweat beads down his forehead as the fear coils inside him. This ship is in bad shape. Who really knows if the ship will survive.

A flicker of light—then the stars blur.

The jump completes.

No explosion. No alarms. No failure.

Just silence.

Doug opens one eye, then the other. His jaw loosens. They're alive.

"How far from the station?" Pranz asks, already straightening in his seat.

Doug takes a shuddering breath, his body finally releasing its tension.

"Furdist I could," Clutch replies. "Five tics."

"Five thousand light years?" Pranz's face lights up with relief. "Perfect. Nobody's going to track us from that far. Now... the hard part."

Clutch eyes him sideways. "Dis ain't da hard part?"

"First, you need to memorize the coordinates of that station and then delete all of the coordinates you have stored. I'll have the AI scrub the system for any trace of your findings," Pranz shares.

"Ain't happen'n," Clutch says defiantly.

"I don't think you understand what will happen when we set off the beacon. They will come in force. They will take your ship. They will examine it from top to bottom to see what part it played in my capture. It won't matter what I tell them.

They will make it impossible to hide anything," Pranz shares.

"I ain't likin' dis already" Clutch says, a growing anger appearing on her face.

"I'll do what I can to stop them, but I don't know that I will have any choice in the manner. I'll likely be unconscious," Pranz says with a nervous gulp.

"Why?" Doug asks, also nervous.

"Because of how you initiate the beacon. It's hidden deep," Pranz continues. "Inside the tibia. Eighteen centimeters below the paella. Whatever that is. You'll have to break the bone to activate it."

Clutch's brow furrows. "Why da tibia?"

"To keep it hidden. It's woven into a titanium matrix that looks like healed scar tissue under scans. It was designed to be undetectable." He pauses, breathing deeply. "But that also means it's going to hurt. A lot."

"How we s'posed ta break titium?" Clutch asks. "Dat ain't normal bone."

"There are micro fractures pre-engineered into the design, at exactly the right point. A single, precise break will do it. That's why I need to be unconscious after," Pranz says, the color draining slightly from his face. "I'd rather not be awake when you take a blunt instrument to my leg."

Clutch looks around the cabin. "Ain't got da meds for dat."

Pranz gulps. "Fine. Just... please, do it fast."

He positions himself on the table, lying down and bracing for impact. Strapped in to avoid floating away. Clutch moves to a nearby storage panel and pulls out what looks like an unremarkable metal bar—part of the ship's framework to the untrained eye, but anyone who knows her could tell it's a weapon. A trick she learned in the mines.

Doug hasn't said a word, just stares wide-eyed, his mind trying to process what's about to happen.

"Doug. Hold his leg," Clutch orders.

Doug stops staring and rushes to Pranz's foot. He grabs hold tightly, averting his gaze like a man trying not to watch a car crash.

Clutch anchors her feet so she doesn't drift from the hit and lifts the weapon high. Pranz closes his eyes and clenches his jaw.

She swings.

CRACK!

Pranz screams in agony. The bone doesn't break.

Doug flinches. "Shit!"

Pranz shakes his head slightly, biting his lip, tears welling.

Clutch swings again.

CRACK.

Another scream. Still no break. Doug starts to shudder.

Without pausing, Clutch brings the bar down a third time with full force.

SNAP.

The sickening sound of bone giving way fills the air, followed by Pranz's raw, primal howl.

And then—

THUD.

Clutch smacks him across the head with the weapon, knocking him out cold.

Silence.

Only the slow, drifting blood floating from Pranz's broken leg and unconscious body remains.

Doug slowly turns, his hands trembling as he meets Clutch's eyes. Hers are steady, unreadable. She releases the bar, letting it float away like it means nothing.

"I guess," Clutch says softly, returning to her seat, "we wait'n see if it work."

Doug swallows hard and straps himself in.

Waiting for rescue had never felt more uncertain.

Chapter 23

The ship drifts in silence. Cold. The last fumes of fuel spent in the jump. Lights pulse in low intervals, the only energy left committed to the emergency beacon. Either Pranz's embedded signal worked, or the ship's automated distress call will catch someone's attention.

"Am I dead?" Pranz mumbles from the floor, his voice low and dry, breaking the stillness.

Doug and Clutch jolt awake.

"Do ya feel dead?" Clutch mutters, rubbing the sleep from her eyes and sitting upright.

Pranz shifts slowly, testing his limbs. "Actually… no. No pain. Damn, your nanos are next level." He grabs at his leg, as if looking for signs of the trauma. "Seriously, Clutch. Just hand over your tech and you'll be rich."

"Ain't 'nough ta keep me from da mines," Clutch replies, already stretching. "Sides, we got aileen shit now."

Pranz nods, not pushing further. The weight of their situation settles again.

Doug drifts over, worry creasing his face. "How long is it supposed to take? For rescue?"

Pranz shrugs. "Depends. Where we are, where they are. If there's a subspace relay close by… all the usual variables."

"You've been out twenty-two hours," Doug says, glancing at the ship's timer, like the number itself might be useful.

Pranz blinks in surprise. "Wow. Okay. I figured someone would've found us by now. Where'd you drop us, Clutch?"

"Where I plot'd n' where we end'd migh' not be da same place," Clutch says, throwing a sideways look at Doug, who suddenly looks like he forgot how to breathe.

"Da 'puter still cal'caitin'," she adds with a shrug.

Doug exhales hard. "Fantastic."

"It's fine," Pranz says, waving a hand like that might calm anyone. "My father's reach is... massive. If the beacon fired correctly, someone's on the way."

Doug's stomach twists. "Yeah, and what exactly will your father do to Clutch when he gets here?"

The room goes still. Pranz looks from Doug to Clutch, guilt flashing in his eyes.

"She's a former slave, Pranz. A runaway. You think he'll just welcome her aboard for a drink?" Doug reminds Pranz.

"There's... a chance we can hide her identity," Pranz says slowly. "Disguise her. Change her clothes, change her speech patterns. Let them assume this ship is yours, Doug. I'll do the talking."

Clutch raises an eyebrow.

"You'll need to try to speak without the accent," Pranz adds gently. "It's... kind of the giveaway."

"I cun try," Clutch replies.

"Say that again?" Pranz says, urging Clutch to try it with a different dialect.

"I...can...try," Clutch says, deliberately over-enunciating the words, her tone rich with sarcasm.

Pranz blinks, impressed. "Good. That's... actually really good."

"And you'll probably need to shower. Maybe dye your hair," he continues, looking her over.

Clutch rolls her eyes and floats away, flipping him off without breaking stride.

Pranz just smiles and leans back into his chair. "What? That was a compliment."

Doug stays in his spot, arms crossed. "So... what should we expect when they get here? Are they going to thank us for keeping you alive? Or beat us senseless because we touched their golden boy?"

Pranz's smile fades. "I don't know. Depends on my father's mood."

Doug stares at him. "That doesn't exactly fill me with confidence."

"Doesn't fill me with confidence either," Pranz replies quietly.

An hour later, a sharp blare from the proximity alarm jolts Doug out of a zoned-out haze. He sits up fast, heart thudding, mind racing. Clutch floats in casually, checking her arm display as if the sound were a mere inconvenience.

"Look like dey's here," she says, still scanning the screen—until she notices the stunned silence in the room.

She glances up.

Two sets of eyes are locked on her—wide, unblinking, stunned.

"What?" she asks, confused by the way they're staring.

Doug is frozen, jaw slightly open, clearly caught off guard. Not by the alarm—by her. She's transformed. Her rough edges have been smoothed, hair dyed and neatly pulled back, and the dirt-streaked miner look has given way to clean lines and new clothing. She looks like someone else entirely. Someone...undeniably striking.

Pranz stares longer than he should, and his expression borders on inappropriate.

"Wow," he finally says. "You look...good. Like, really good. Honestly, if you don't speak, nobody would even think you're an iron ant—uh, I mean—shit, that was—"

"Ferget it," Clutch cuts in, her voice firm. "Let's make contact wif ya dad's people."

Pranz clears his throat and gestures to the console. "Doug, if you wouldn't mind."

Doug looks to Clutch, uncertain. She gives a small, affirming nod.

He activates the comm and leans in. "Hello? Uh...are you here to rescue us? We're stranded. We have your son."

Pranz winces. "Dude. That sounds like a hostage situation."

Doug's eyes go wide. "Right! I mean—we rescued him. He's safe. We just—we're the ones who need help now."

A beat of silence. Then a flat, mechanical voice responds:

"We require verbal confirmation from the subject. Failure to comply in ten seconds will result in full vessel obliteration."

Pranz calmly steps forward and presses the transmit button. "I'm here. All's well."

"Identifier," the voice snaps.

"Bricklayer Twelve."

A moment passes. "Copy. Standby for docking procedure."

Doug exhales hard, adrenaline fading—but Clutch's face tightens. Her arms fold across her chest.

"Ain't got a good feelin' bout dis," she mutters.

Doug and Pranz both turn to her.

"We'll be fine," Pranz says with forced confidence. "You saved my ass. That's got to count for something with my father."

Doug narrows his eyes. "What does that mean, exactly— 'count for something'?"

"Nothing. Just a saying," Pranz replies quickly. "Point is, we're getting rescued. Ship gets fixed, we head back to the alien station, make our claim, and boom—we're set for life."

"But ya already set fer life," Clutch says, voice quieter now. Her expression has shifted—fear creeping in beneath the calm.

Pranz hesitates. "It's just a phrase. Don't overthink it. I told you it's going to be okay. Just trust me."

Clutch stares at him a moment longer. Then, without a word, she turns and floats out.

Doug watches her go, then turns back to Pranz with narrowed eyes. "If you screw us…"

"I won't," Pranz says. "I swear. I hate that world. I'd burn it down if I could. Just…hang in there, alright?"

Doug doesn't answer. Just glares, jaw clenched.

A heavy metallic clank reverberates through the hull, yanking Doug and Pranz from their uneasy silence. The docking procedure has begun.

Clutch reenters the room without a word. Her arms fold tight across her chest as she drops into her usual seat. Her expression is unreadable—steeled. Watching. Waiting.

Then—three firm knocks echo from the airlock door. Sharp. Authoritative. The ship has been boarded. The docked ship initiates a power transfer to engage the grav panels. Everyone feels the firmness of the floor under their feet.

Clutch shifts her gaze to Pranz, her eyes scanning him like a lie detector. Looking for a crack, a tell. But his face is stone.

She says nothing. Just stands, walks to the ship's controls and opens the inner airlock door.

A wave of red and black surges in. Uniformed personnel march through like they own the place, weapons slung and visors down. Each one wears the sleek emblem of Fornokey Corp on their chest—precise, clinical, unmistakable.

They sweep the ship without pause or permission, fanning out to check corners, consoles, crawlspaces. The place isn't a rescue site to them—it's a threat.

Three operatives peel off and stride toward the bridge. One of them, clearly the leader, walks with a soldier's posture and a politician's stillness. He stops short in front of Pranz, Clutch, and Doug.

A subtle nod. The ship is secure.

"Clear to come aboard," the leader says.

Pranz's eyes narrow. "Theadore."

"Ted, sir," the man corrects, stiff and expressionless. "Please."

Pranz's lips twitch. "No thanks."

Ted doesn't flinch. No reaction, no blink. Just protocol.

A moment later, a new presence fills the doorway— grander, colder. A hulking guard steps aside to reveal a man in an obsidian-black suit with crimson accents. Tall, silver-templed, and unnervingly calm.

Gabe Fornokey. CEO. Master of a trillion-dollar empire. Father.

"Jason," Gabe says, flatly.

Doug instinctively glances at Pranz, eyebrows raised. Jason? That's his real name?

Pranz stares forward. "Gabe Fornokey."

"I'm your father," Gabe says, tone clipped. "You will address me with respect. There is only one person alive who gets to call me dad. You know that. I expect you to use it."

"Whatever," Pranz replies, voice cool and defiant.

Gabe's attention turns. "And you are?"

"Doug," Doug says, chin up, trying to stay composed.

Gabe gives a nod so shallow it could be mistaken for a muscle twitch. "Doug. Thank you for saving my son's life. Although, he looks perfectly fine for someone who supposedly has a broken leg."

"Wasn't me," Doug says, nodding toward Clutch. "Clutch saved him."

Gabe's head pivots. His gaze lands on Clutch.

His lip curls, his head tilts as his eyes scan her features. A realization hits.

"That's bullshit. Iron ants aren't smart enough for that. They don't do anything beyond orders. And she's not at her station." He gestures with a flick of his hand. "Lock her up. She is going to regret ever escaping from the mines."

Clutch doesn't flinch. Doesn't argue. She turns her eyes to Pranz—hurt and anger simmering beneath her composed face—and says everything with that look.

"Hey!" Doug explodes, stepping forward. "Where the fuck do you think you're taking her? She's not—she's not that. Look at her!"

"I am," Gabe says, eyeing her like a stain on his boot. He gestures toward the side of his own head, just about his ear. "She missed a spot."

Doug lunges. Two guards are on him in a flash, slamming him back into a chair and pinning him there.

"Dave, is it?" Gabe asks rhetorically and without actually looking at Doug.

"It's Doug," Doug growls through gritted teeth.

"Whatever." Gabe barely glances at him. "You saved my son, so I'll leave you your little ship. Jason, you're coming home. Full medical. Especially after exposure to an iron ant."

"No," Pranz snaps. "You're not leaving him here to die. At least give him fuel and some drones to repair the ship."

Gabe's expression sours. He glances around the bridge, then back to his son. Finally, he relents with a sigh.

"Fine. Fuel the ship. Leave a few repair drones. Then we're gone."

Ted nods, signaling his team. The soldiers peel off in practiced silence. Gabe vanishes through the door without looking back.

Only one guard remains behind, watching Pranz.

"I didn't think it would go down like this," Pranz says, barely above a whisper.

Doug stands in silence, arms crossed, eyes cutting straight through him.

Pranz hesitates. Then turns and walks out.

A few moments later, the last guard is gone.

The decoupling clamps release with a final clang, echoing through the empty ship.

And Doug is alone, floating again until the drones fix the ship's systems.

Chapter 24

Doug stands alone on the bridge of Clutch's ship. He's been pacing for hours, boots thudding softly against the metal floor, worn into a path of restless indecision.

His mind loops through the same torturous questions.

Do I take the ship and call it fate?

Just leave Clutch to whatever hell they threw her back into?

She escaped once. Maybe she'll escape again.

But then her voice echoes in his memory, sharp and certain:

I ain't one ta fuck wit karma.

Karma.

He's heard the word a thousand times. Thrown around in stories and bar banter. But now—now it stares him in the face like a judge.

"Clutch came and rescued me. Multiple times now," Doug mutters, pacing to the edge of the viewport and back. "I can't just sit here. I have to try and rescue her."

He glances toward the console. Fuel readings are clear—just what Fornokey left him. Enough for one jump. Maybe.

"But they only gave me one damn jump," he says aloud, voice rising with frustration. "One chance to get somewhere. Anywhere. But it has to be for more fuel or I'm stuck again."

He stares at the display, hoping an answer will flicker to life on the screen.

"But I don't have the credits," he growls, kicking the base of the pilot's chair.

"Fuck!"

He turns away from the console.

"Fuck!" he shouts again, louder, fists clenched.

His eyes dart around the empty bridge like it's holding out on him.

Pacing again. Back and forth. Too many options. None of them good.

I could go to a fuel depot and find work… wait tables, scrub cargo haulers, maybe earn enough to refuel.

I could go looking for Clutch in the belt, but if I pick the wrong system, I'm dead. They don't ask questions in the belt. They shoot.

I could return to the alien structure—but there's nothing there. No food. No power. No life.

I could go home…

Doug stops pacing, just for a second.

Home.

The word feels like a prison.

Sure, there's work. There's safety. But it'll take weeks—months—to get back out here. And Clutch… she'll be gone by then. Or worse.

He runs a hand through his hair, then grabs a handful of it and yanks like he could shake a solution loose from his skull.

"Fuck," he whispers.

His eyes drift to the pilot's chair—Clutch's chair.

Empty.

"I wish you were here," he says, barely above a whisper.

A tear slips down his cheek. He doesn't wipe it away.

A few moments later, the ship jolts with a sudden, unmistakable clang—the harsh metallic report of another vessel docking.

Doug freezes mid-step.

"Fuck!" he shouts, stumbling back from the console. "Pirates!? This is how I die. Great. Perfect!"

He bolts across the bridge, rifling through cabinets and compartments, flinging open drawers and panels.

He opens the cabinet where he initially found weapons—cleaned out by Fornokey guards.

"Come on, where does Clutch keep her insane death stick?" he mutters, yanking open a storage bin filled with nothing but sealed rations and fabric wraps. "Seriously!? Food wraps!?"

Doug spins, scanning the walls, the corners, the floor. Nothing.

In his blind panic, he doesn't hear the hiss of the airlock or the heavy clunk of boots landing inside. Not until a voice—calm, authoritative—slices through the silence behind him.

"Give us the map."

Doug spins and nearly collapses in fright. Standing in the doorway is a group of red-and-black clad soldiers—Fornokey operatives. Weapons holstered but eyes sharp.

"Fucking shit!" Doug gasps, stumbling back into the pilot's chair. "You scared the fuck out of me!"

"The map," the leader repeats. His tone isn't angry, but it's sharp enough to draw blood.

Doug forces himself to breathe. "How... how did you know I was still here?"

"We didn't," the man says flatly. "Pranz assumed you'd be lost. Said you'd probably stay put. We took a calculated risk. Now... the map."

Doug narrows his eyes, trying to play it cool. "Pranz, huh?"

The operative steps forward. "He told his father everything. About the station. About the alien tech. About the map. Last chance—hand it over."

"I have no idea what you're talking about," Doug says, forcing a shrug.

The man walks past him like he owns the ship, heading straight to Clutch's console. His gloved fingers start tapping across the interface, quick and purposeful.

"Hey, that's not your—"

"Silence," the man snaps, not even looking up. "Would be your best move right now."

Doug bites his tongue but his fists clench at his sides. The man keeps working—until he stops, frowning.

"Encrypted," he mutters to the others.

Doug can't help himself. A crooked little smile creeps onto his face.

The leader notices.

"So you do know what I'm talking about. What's the code?"

"I don't," Doug replies with a little more bite than intended. "But I'm loving that you can't get it. Whatever it is."

"The code," the man growls, taking a menacing step forward.

"This isn't even my ship," Doug shoots back. "I didn't encrypt anything. I couldn't if I tried."

A pause. The man tilts his head slightly.

"Oh? It's not your ship?" His tone shifts—more calculating now.

Doug stays silent. That might've been a mistake.

"Then you're a stowaway," the man declares coldly. "Take the ship. We'll get R&D to crack the system. As for him…"

He points straight at Doug.

"…lock him up."

Two guards grab Doug before he can react.

"Hey! Hey—what the fuck?! This is unnecessary! I didn't do anything! I'm not a stowaway—I am a guest here!" Doug shouts, heels dragging across the floor as he's hauled out.

They ignore him.

Outside, the rest of the team secures the ship with additional tethers and magnetic clamps, preparing it for towing.

Doug is marched across the short docking bridge and into the Fornokey vessel, the cold gray interior doing little to calm his frayed nerves. He's shoved into a holding cell. The walls hum with power. The door clanks shut with finality.

He barely catches a glimpse of Pranz standing at the far end of the corridor—watching, still, unreadable.

Doug wants to shout something—anything—but the door seals before he can.

His arms fall limp. He backs into the wall, slides down, and finally slumps to the floor.

"This luck…" he mutters bitterly, rubbing his face with both hands, "…this feels a lot more like mine."

"Hey," a voice whispers from the cell door.

Doug bolts upright, heart pounding. The lights are dim—night cycle. Most of the ship's crew is probably asleep.

His eyes adjust. Pranz stands in the corridor, silhouetted by the soft amber glow of emergency lighting.

Doug's jaw tightens. "What do you want, traitor?"

The last word cuts sharp and deliberate.

Pranz flinches, but doesn't back away. "I had to give them something. If I hadn't, they never would've come for you."

"Oh, so this was all for me?" Doug rises to his feet, voice dripping with disbelief. "You sold out the one person who saved your life just so your daddy would send a ship?"

"I knew you'd stay on Clutch's ship," Pranz insists, his voice low but urgent. "You had little fuel. No plan. I also knew Clutch wouldn't leave the map unsecured. I trusted her to protect it, and she did."

"You still handed over the existence of the alien structure," Doug snaps. "And Clutch? She's who knows where now. Back in some fucking mine or worse."

"I didn't know they'd take her," Pranz says, guilt threading into his tone. "Not like that. I thought I'd have more control over how this went. I swear, I never meant—"

"You don't get to swear to me!" Doug barks, stepping closer to the slit in the door. "You said you hated your father. That you'd rather see him burn. But here we are— I'm in a cage, and you're walking around like you're still wearing your fucking trust fund diaper."

Pranz doesn't respond right away. He swallows hard.

"I have a plan," he says finally. "I know where they're taking her."

Doug turns away, arms folded. "Sure. Another plan."

"If they can't break her encryption, they'll start asking her for the code. And they won't ask nicely," Pranz says quietly. "We don't have much time."

Doug doesn't move. Doesn't say a word.

"I am trying to help," Pranz says, a little softer now. "I'm not my father, Doug. I'm not built like him. But I can still make things right."

Doug lies back down and throws an arm over his eyes. "Talk is cheap. Come back when you've done something."

Pranz exhales through his nose, like he was hoping for more. Then a sudden metallic clink echoes from somewhere down the corridor—boots maybe, or a door latch disengaging.

He stiffens and backs away from the cell.

"You'll see," he says over his shoulder, disappearing into the dim light. "I'll prove it."

Chapter 25

Doug lies on the cell bench, staring at the ceiling. Time slips by like sludge. It feels like days have passed, but he knows better. A corp-owned cruiser like this can rip through star systems in hours. Still, isolation warps his sense of time and hope.

A faint whisper interrupts the stillness.

"Doug," someone hisses through the narrow cell window.

Doug sits up, heart kicking at his ribs. "What now, Pranz?" he says, his voice low but bitter.

"I can't explain here. Just... when they move you, don't fight. Go with it. I'll get you out," Pranz whispers, barely audible.

Doug springs up and rushes to the window. He catches just a glimpse of Pranz's back as he hurries away down the corridor.

"Figures," Doug mutters, eyes narrowing.

A second voice cuts in from the other side. "Looking for something?"

Doug turns sharply. A guard stands just beyond the door, laser prod in hand, wearing the deadpan look of someone used to giving orders without question.

"A reason," Doug says flatly, "for why I'm locked up when I haven't done anything wrong."

"You told us that ship wasn't yours. Whether you stole it or just sat shotgun, you're complicit," the guard replies as he begins unlocking the door. "Regardless, it isn't for me to decide. I'm handing you over to the Regy. They will decide if you are guilty and, when they do, what to do with that verdict."

The guard emphasized 'when they do' a little too much for Doug's liking.

Doug frowns. "This is about the encryption, isn't it?"

The guard shrugs as the door hisses open. "You know what they say—if you won't give them what they want, you're part of the problem."

"Wonderful," Doug mutters.

"Turn around. Wrists."

Doug hesitates but complies. The restraints click into place—cold metal biting into his skin like handcuffs made from disdain.

With firm hands on his shoulders, the guard escorts Doug off the ship and into the light-soaked chaos of Gervantion Station.

It's a city in the void.

The moment the bulkhead doors open, the sound hits him first: a constant hum of overlapping voices, the metallic clank of boots, intercoms blaring from every direction. The crowd outside is a roiling ocean of people—moving shoulder-to-shoulder in every direction. It's like stepping into old vids of pre-space Earth: New York sidewalks in spring.

Fornokey walks freely at the front of his own procession, red and black uniforms carving a corridor of respect for their employer. Doug, cuffed and silent, is barely noticed. Pedestrians brush against him. No one offers a glance.

Doug watches as Fornokey veers off toward the Fornokey wing, a gleaming extension grafted onto the side of the station like a palace sewn to a battleship. It doubles the size of the original facility. His name is etched across it's entrance in glowing platinum letters.

Doug can't help but mutter, "Why didn't we dock on that side? I'm sure he has his own…"

"Shut your mouth," the guard snaps, shoving him forward.

Doug stumbles but keeps walking. Ahead, a unit of military personnel rushes toward the Fornokey wing, moving with urgency, weapons drawn, heads on a swivel—clearly responding to something.

Doug's eyes follow them.

His heart skips.

Something is wrong.

Out of the corner of his eye—just before the guard shifts his weight—Doug spots someone trailing them at a distance. The figure wears a long coat with the hood pulled low, face shadowed, movements deliberate. There's something familiar about him, but Doug can't place it. Not yet.

The guard guides him through the sea of people and into the local holding facility: a single door and a pane of glass on an otherwise gray slab of bureaucracy tucked into the station's underbelly. A holding cage for the not-quite-yet-convicted.

A bored officer sits behind reinforced glass, feet up, chewing something obnoxiously loud. "Who'd you bring us today, Kyle?" he asks without looking up.

"Hey Terance. Been a while." Kyle gives a friendly nod. "This here's Doug. Won't give us a last name. Claims ignorance on everything. Caught him squatting on a ship we impounded—supposedly it is property of an iron ant. Which we both know is bullshit. She probably stole it."

"Oof..." Terance whistles low. "You don't see many of them make it out. As for this one, that's gotta be ten to twelve right there. Easy." He shrugs. "Per charge."

Doug stares at them in disbelief, as if they're discussing his sentencing over coffee. "I didn't do anything," he mutters, but it's barely heard.

Terance finally stands, unlocking the single door. "I'll finish the booking," he says. "Just bring me another box of those Welerver cigars next time, yeah? You know the ones— smell like burnt cinnamon but hit like a fever dream."

Kyle laughs. "You got it. Heading there in a few anyway."

The two exchange a casual nod, and Kyle turns to leave, the heavy door swinging shut behind him. Terance, taking hold of Doug and leading him through the door.

But it never closes.

A boot stops it short.

Terance blinks, startled, as the hooded figure steps inside, slow and deliberate, keeping the door propped open with his foot.

"How about you get those cigars now?" the man says, voice gravelly, eyes still obscured beneath the hood.

Doug was hoping it was Pranz, but he can't place the voice. It's unfamiliar to him.

Who is this guy? And why is he interested in me?

Terance crosses his arms, trying to mask the sudden edge in his voice. "I can wait. No rush."

"I'm sure you can," the man replies coolly. "But you don't have to." He produces a small, polished box and flips it open.

Inside are the coveted Welerver cigars—and nestled among them, like jewels in a case, are glowing green credit chips.

Doug's eyes go wide.

Thirty some chips. Green-tier. Ten thousand credits apiece. The kind of currency that doesn't just buy favors— it erases debts, makes friends and allies, changes the minds of the weak.

Terance slams the lid closed, while maintaining contact with the box, still in the hands of the hooded man. He leans in and scans the room, suddenly a lot more interested in discretion.

"What do you want?" he mutters.

"The prisoner," the hooded man says. "Unshackled. Now."

Terance hesitates, his fingers twitching around the box. "Technically, he's not booked yet. I could say he was never here. But I need the box first."

The hooded man pulls the case back slightly. "Not how this works. Remove the cuffs. Let him stand behind me. Then you get your prize."

Another beat. Terance glances over his shoulder, then sighs.

"Fine."

He steps forward and yanks the restraints off Doug's wrists. "Go," he mutters, shoving him past the stranger.

Doug stumbles behind the hooded man, wide-eyed.

The box is extended.

Terance snatches it like a starving man and immediately kicks the man's foot out of the doorway, slamming it shut behind them. A final, hollow clang echoes through the corridor.

The hooded man finally turns to Doug and nudges him forward. "This way."

Doug follows without hesitation, instinct overriding confusion. Whoever this guy is, he's the first person who hasn't treated him like trash all day.

And right now, that's enough.

"Who are you?" Doug asks. The hooded man says nothing, only quickens his pace.

They round a corner and duck into a small, dimly lit storage room. Metal shelves line the walls, filled with crates and parts covered in a fine layer of dust. The door shuts behind them with a quiet hiss.

The man turns his back to Doug and, without a word, pulls down his hood.

"Pranz?" Doug blurts, blinking in disbelief.

"Hang on," Pranz mutters, his voice gravelly and unrecognizable. He opens his mouth and slips out a set of false teeth with a wet click. "There. That's better."

His voice returns to normal—clear, familiar, and annoyingly smug.

"I had no idea it was you," Doug says, still stunned.

"That was kind of the point," Pranz replies with a crooked grin. He pivots toward the wall, placing his hand against what looks like an ordinary panel of reinforced steel.

A soft chime sounds, and the wall comes to life— illuminating beneath his palm as a scanner flickers to life. A thin beam glides across his hand, confirming his identity.

With a hiss and a subtle mechanical hum, the back wall slides open to reveal a cavernous chamber beyond.

Doug steps through and freezes, his mouth falling open. A secret stockpile stretches out in front of him—rows of gear, weapon crates, food rations, surveillance drones, and tools stacked with military precision. The lighting above bathes everything in an industrial white glow.

"What... is this?" Doug asks, eyes wide as he spins slowly to take it all in.

"I've been building it for years," Pranz says, a proud glint in his eye. "A contingency. My father thinks I've been wasting credits on art collections and gambling parties. In truth, I've been funneling resources into this."

Doug walks forward slowly, brushing a hand across a crate marked with black glyphs and a red security seal. "So what's the plan? Feels like you've been waiting for this moment."

Pranz's smile grows wider. "Now I just have to figure out how to pull it off... and when."

Doug frowns. "Pull what off? You're being vague again. Sounds like you have a plan you're not sharing."

"Just trust me," Pranz says, giving Doug a firm pat on the shoulder. "I'm going to make things right. For Clutch. For you. For a hell of a lot more people than you realize."

Doug's skepticism lingers, but something in Pranz's voice makes him pause.

This wasn't the boy who ran from his father's shadow.

This was someone stepping out of it.

Chapter 26

"Find her yet?" Doug asks—for what feels like the hundredth time.

Pranz exhales sharply, dragging a hand down his face. He sits hunched over the glowing console in the heart of his hidden bunker. "I can't work faster when you ask me every ten seconds," he mutters, irritation creeping into his voice.

"I thought you said your system was tied into your father's. Full access. All his dirty secrets," Doug presses, the edge in his voice sharpening.

"It is," Pranz snaps. "But it's not like they tag people with names in the black file logs. They treat her like cargo— unlabeled and disposable. I've got to backtrack the whole operation manually."

He slams a few keys, then curses under his breath. "Fuck! Another dead end."

Doug paces behind him. "Who took her off the ship when we docked?"

"Low-level security," Pranz says, eyes flicking across code. "Some grunt named Lonlyle."

"Has Lonlyle shown up anywhere since?" Doug asks quickly, his tone now urgent.

Pranz pauses. His fingers hover over the keyboard. Then he starts typing, slower this time. Focused. "Let me check… system logs, door pings, shift reports…" He trails off.

Doug leans in. "Well?"

"Huh," Pranz finally says, sitting back with a thoughtful frown.

Doug stiffens. "That doesn't sound like good news."

"Lonlyle hasn't checked in since the moment we arrived. No reports, no activity, nothing. It's like he vanished."

"Off-book transfer?" Doug asks.

Pranz nods grimly. "That would be my father's play. Disappear people, hide the trail, keep the risk contained."

"Or maybe Clutch turned the tables," Doug offers, grasping at hope. "Maybe she got away and she's hiding. Waiting for a chance to get back to her ship."

"Doubt it," Pranz says, shaking his head. "A ship left the station shortly after we docked. The timing, the other ship's location, the fact that we docked in the main station's docking array instead of the Fornokey docking bay—if I'm reading this right, Lonlyle got her off-station fast. Too fast for anyone to notice. Why draw attention to the existence of iron-ants if you can avoid it."

Doug frowns. "You checked the footage?"

"I pulled everything from docking to when you were removed," Pranz replies.

"And after that?"

Pranz freezes. Doug sees it—the exact moment the idea hits.

"They wouldn't use normal exits," Doug adds, catching on. "They'd go off-route. Maintenance paths. Forgotten corridors."

Pranz's fingers fly across the console, a blur of precision and speed. "Of course they would."

Doug steps closer, the glow of the screens washing his face in flickering light. Just as he leans in to get a better view—

BAM. Pranz slams both hands on the console and turns around, grinning ear to ear. "Found her!"

Doug spins toward the exit. "Then what are we waiting for? Let's go!"

"Wait, wait—no, I don't know where she is right now," Pranz says, raising both hands. "But I found footage. Clutch. Being escorted off the ship by Lonlyle. I've got a timestamp. A path."

Doug freezes mid-step. His body sags with disappointment.

"But now that I have the trail," Pranz continues, lowering his voice, "I can trace the rest. Piece by piece. We'll get her back."

Doug nods, though his expression stays locked between hope and fear. He turns away and clenches his jaw.

Pranz gently pats his shoulder, then spins back to his terminal. His fingers tapping the screen again, and the room settles into tense silence—two men in the dark, chasing a spark before it goes out.

"Doug! Wake up!" Pranz's voice cuts through the silence like a siren.

Doug jolts upright—then immediately tumbles off the edge of the cot he had found tucked away in the shadows of the lair. His body hits the floor with a dull thud, groggy limbs tangled in the thin blanket.

"What the hell?" Doug mutters, rubbing his shoulder as he staggers upright. He yawns as he stumbles over to Pranz, stretching his arms overhead. "You better be waking me up for something good."

"I found her," Pranz says, eyes locked on the screen, voice low and serious. "It's not going to be easy."

Doug's exhaustion evaporates. "Where?"

"Mine A8-H74FeB," Pranz replies. "Locals call it Crunch Rock."

Doug's face hardens. "Let's go get her. You've got pull— use your last name. Say she's your property, or a prisoner transfer. Lie. Whatever it takes."

"It's not that simple," Pranz says, turning to face him fully. "The mines don't answer to middle-tier managers. Only two people can override a placement at Crunch Rock—my father, or Ted."

Doug scowls. "That enforcer guy?"

"Yeah. You saw how loyal he is. If I show up sniffing around, they'll call him. Or my father. Either way, this whole thing collapses."

Doug folds his arms and starts pacing. "So, how do we get her out?"

"The whole mining system is locked down. They only allow one ship to come and go—standard resupply vessel. Inbound with guards and rations, outbound with ore."

"Of course," Doug mutters. "Efficient. Controlled. Impossible."

"There's more," Pranz adds. "The ship won't dock unless you've got the right imprints on your implant chips. If the system doesn't recognize you as part of the supply or security manifest, you'll be shot on site."

Doug slumps back against the wall, discouraged. "So it's a dead end." He pauses. Then his eyes flick upward—spark catching fire behind them.

Pranz narrows his gaze. "Wait. That look. What is it?"

"I might know how we can get the right imprints," Doug says, a slow grin spreading across his face.

Pranz raises an eyebrow. "That... helps. A lot. And with that, my friend—" he claps Doug on the shoulder "—I've got a plan."

Doug eyes him warily. "That smile tells me I'm not going to like it."

"Oh, you're going to hate it," Pranz says with a gleam in his eye.

Doug groans. "I already hate it."

"But first," Pranz says, turning toward a wall of gear and supply crates, "we need to get Clutch's ship off this station before someone cracks the encryption. It's too important to leave behind."

"Agreed," Doug says, already walking beside him. "We're not going anywhere without her ship."

Chapter 27

"That suit looks good on you," Pranz says, arms crossed as he leans against a locker, watching Doug study himself in the hovering holo-mirror.

Doug turns the holo-mirror slowly, watching his reflection spin in a seamless projection. He tugs awkwardly at the lapels of the sleek, deep-charcoal jacket. "Doesn't really fit me," he mutters.

"Fits perfectly, actually," Pranz says, tilting his head slightly, examining him from another angle.

"I mean it's not me," Doug clarifies, turning off the holo-mirror with a wave. "I've never worn anything like this. Feels like I'm impersonating someone I'm not."

"You are," Pranz replies with a grin. "That's the point."

Doug gives him a sideways look.

"Relax. You look like a natural," Pranz continues. "Just follow my lead. Look confident. Intimidate with silence. Works better than you'd think."

Doug exhales and starts fiddling with the cuffs. "All right. Just explain again—why do we need to look like we're about to close a trade deal with a planetary senator?"

Pranz turns off his own holo-display, the crisp lines of his navy-blue suit already making him look like he runs three corporations before breakfast. "Her ship's in R&D storage. That department is full of people who live in fear of executives. They see suits, they assume power. They scramble to get lost or fear having to explain themselves using small words. When people get nervous, they get sloppy. Sloppy means opportunity."

Doug shrugs. "Okay. Doesn't make a ton of sense, but I'll go with it."

"Here." Pranz opens a locker and pulls out a slim weapons case. "You'll need these."

Doug takes the two weapons inside—one a sleek laser pistol, the other a compact kinetic launcher with a dull black finish. He holds them awkwardly, like he's not sure if he's supposed to aim or polish them.

"Laser in your dominant hand," Pranz says, pointing. "Kinetic in the other. Just for show. You probably won't need it, but it completes the image."

Doug eyes the kinetic weapon. "Aren't these illegal?"

"In most places, yes. But Fornokey Corp has a special little arrangement. My father's exemptions go deep," Pranz says with a smirk. "It's how the rich keep power—they hold the rulebook and the eraser."

Doug stares down at the weapons in his hands. "Your family's influence really goes that far, huh?"

"Farther than you'd believe or even like to know."

Doug holsters the weapons and lets the silence linger. "So why risk all that? Why jeopardize everything you were born with to help me and Clutch?"

Pranz's smile falters. He looks away for a moment, almost embarrassed. "Because having everything doesn't mean shit when none of it means anything. I've spent years surrounded by things I didn't earn. Wealth I didn't choose. Status I never wanted. My father won't let me have a real role, says I'm not ready. So I play dress-up in hobbies—pilot training, engineering courses, hunting licenses. Anything to feel like I have purpose."

Doug raises an eyebrow. "And that brought you to bounty hunting?"

"Yeah," Pranz says, his voice softening. "I thought if I could catch criminals, make the galaxy safer... maybe I'd be worth something. Turns out I was just a tourist in someone else's war zone. Got people killed because I thought credits could replace training or instinct."

He falls quiet. Doug watches him, then says, "I guess the station's always nicer on the other end of the galaxy."

Pranz chuckles, a real one this time. "If we pull this off, maybe you'll find out."

Doug nods. The suit doesn't feel any more comfortable, but the moment carries weight now. The clothes don't matter—their mission does.

"Let's go secure Clutch's ship," Pranz says, turning toward the exit with renewed determination.

Doug follows, his stride just a little more confident.

"How do you even know about these passages?" Doug whispers as he follows Pranz through a narrow maintenance corridor. The walls hum faintly, and the air smells like ion grease and dust—forgotten spaces long out of reach for the average station dweller.

Pranz glances back, his voice low and calm. "I was a kid without supervision. When you're the trillionaire's son, people assume you're always safe. Turns out, when you show up to the right events—charity galas, photo ops—they stop tracking your in-between time. So I wandered. Explored. Found every duct, hatch, and panel they didn't think to lock."

Doug ducks under a beam, nearly catching his shoulder on a protruding pipe. "So this is just your childhood playground?"

Pranz smirks. "Basically. Also helps that I've got a master access key—gifted from dear old dad. He said it was for my protection. Probably just didn't want the hassle of finding me if I ever got locked out."

Doug's eyebrows raise. "Does that access extend off-station? Like… could we use it to bypass security at the mines?"

"Doubtful," Pranz replies with a shrug. "Most of my life's been spent here, in this shiny prison. The only time I left was for vacations. Alone, usually. He always had... meetings. 'Emergencies.' Better things to do than raise a son."

Doug looks away, masking the empathy tightening behind his eyes. He knows abandonment in his own way—but it never came with a platinum spoon.

They continue forward in silence, dropping into stealth when Pranz raises a hand to signal an approaching security checkpoint. They flatten against walls, move in shadow, wait out passing patrols. Doug's heart pounds harder the deeper they go, but Pranz remains calm, navigating like the station is an extension of himself.

After what feels like hours—maybe longer—and probably no time at all—they stop behind a slotted vent overlooking a wide chamber filled with soft blue lighting and humming tech.

"There's her ship," Pranz says in a whisper, pointing.

Doug presses his face against the grate. Clutch's ship sits near the center of the R&D bay, spotlit and surrounded by diagnostic stations and techs in white jumpsuits. "So what's the plan? Wait for a shift change? Everyone to go to sleep?"

Pranz chuckles, low and dry. "Nice idea, but no. They run in staggered rotations. This place never sleeps. We're going to have to take it by force."

Doug slowly turns to him. "That better be a joke, because I'm very much not in the mood to get myself killed."

Pranz flashes a grin. "Relax. I'm not talking blasters blazing. We just need to blend in long enough to get close. Their locker room's another thirty meters through these ducts. We grab some uniforms, join the shift, get close to the ship, and take the ship."

Doug sighs. "So, we trade one disguise for another? I thought these suits were supposed to be the magic keys."

"They were. But look at us." Pranz gestures at his once-sleek outfit. It's now scuffed, torn at the sleeve, stained from grime. "We've been crawling through the station's intestines. Corporate chic doesn't sell it anymore. My bad. I don't remember getting dirty from these areas."

Doug exhales sharply. "Great. So we change clothes, pretend to belong, and hope nobody notices two new faces popping up mid-shift?"

"Exactly," Pranz replies, already moving forward through the next segment of maintenance passageways. "Just trust me."

Doug groans. "I need to stop doing that," he mutters, and follows.

They reach the locker room and stand ready at a maintenance hatch. Pranz waves his hand over a concealed panel and it opens with a soft hiss. Doug pauses, raising an eyebrow.

'He really does have all of the access to this station?' Doug thinks. 'Imagine that kind of access to someone like me, who's always down on their luck. I would have everything, whenever I wanted and nobody would know it was me taking what I needed.'

"You coming?" Pranz asks over his shoulder, catching Doug mid-thought.

"Yeah, sorry—just... spaced out for a sec," Doug says, blinking rapidly and stepping inside.

Pranz tosses him a clean lab coat, a visor, and a fitted mask. "Suit up. Look official. Blend in."

Doug wrestles with the headgear for a moment before pulling it snug. The mask mutes the smell of sterilized metal and machine oil in the air. They each grab a tablet from a supply shelf and approach the bay door.

"Just walk a half step behind me. Eyes on the tablet. No sudden moves. If anyone asks anything, act annoyed that they're slowing your schedule," Pranz says as the door hisses open.

Doug gulps. "Cool, yeah. No pressure." He follows.

They step into the R&D bay floor—bright, buzzing, and orderly. Technicians in pristine uniforms move with purpose, gliding between consoles and workbenches. A few acknowledge Pranz and Doug with nods before returning to their tasks.

Doug bumps into the back of Pranz, misjudging his pace. "Shit—sorry," he mutters.

Pranz gives a subtle wave of his fingers behind his back. 'Relax.'

They make their way across the floor, passing a diagnostics station, then another. Pranz stops at a fueling interface near Clutch's ship. He doesn't linger—just taps a few inconspicuous commands into the tablet.

Doug glances over Pranz's shoulder. A faint hummm begins as fuel slowly starts flowing into the ship.

"Just a trickle," Pranz whispers. "Enough to move her. Not enough to raise flags."

They continue walking in deliberate arcs, circling from one end of the vessel to the other. Doug catches on, mimicking Pranz's body language—pauses, glances up at the ship's hull, back down to the tablet, then toward the floor like he's inspecting something.

"You're getting it," Pranz says quietly as they approach the cargo bay. "Almost convincing."

"Almost?" Doug whispers back, trying not to look terrified.

"Convincing people is an art. You're finger painting right now, but at least you're not eating the brush," Pranz says with a grin.

Doug rolls his eyes, then stiffens as they reach the ship's cargo bay door. Pranz slows down, scanning left, then right, eyes flicking between his tablet, the floor, the ceiling.

"What are you doing?" Doug hisses.

"Looking busy. Curious but not eager. Eagerness gets you noticed," Pranz murmurs.

Doug takes the cue and shuffles past him, feigning interest in a conduit panel. His heart pounds so hard he's sure someone will hear it.

Finally, they both step through the cargo bay threshold and vanish from the main floor's view.

"Okay," Pranz breathes, looking back to Doug with a smile hidden beneath his mask. "Now we move."

They break into a run, weaving through crates and spare equipment until they reach the bridge hatch. Pranz raises a hand to stop Doug, then pulls a compact weapon from beneath his coat.

"This part's going to be fast," he says in a low voice. "Could be messy. Be ready."

Doug swallows hard and nods, bracing himself.

The bridge door hisses open.

Every head in the room turns sharply. Silence slaps the air. Engineers freeze mid-task, their eyes locked on Pranz and Doug.

Pranz doesn't look up—his gaze stays glued to his tablet, mimicking the urgency of someone on a mission, not a trespasser.

A technician approaches, cautious but curious. "Can we help you? Are you lost?"

Pranz finally lifts his eyes. His voice is clipped, confident. "Nothing for you to worry about. Resume your work."

A guard steps forward from the shadows near the wall. "This is a restricted zone," he says, one hand already drifting toward his holster. "Everyone with clearance is already inside. Which means—you're not allowed here."

Shit.

Pranz doesn't hesitate. The weapon concealed beneath his tablet fires with a soft snap. The dart strikes the guard in the neck before he can finish his thought. He collapses instantly, twitching as he hits the floor.

A wave of panic spreads. Engineers jump. Someone gasps.

"Out," Pranz orders, leveling the weapon at them with a quiet but undeniable menace. "Now."

No one argues. The technicians shuffle past, casting wide-eyed glances at Pranz and Doug as they file out. A few mutter curses under their breath. Nobody tries to be a hero.

As the last one clears the threshold, Pranz slams the door shut and locks it.

He darts to the bridge console, hands flying across the interface. Doug watches, heart hammering.

"She encrypted the whole thing," Pranz says through clenched teeth. "I can't access the flight systems."

Doug rushes up beside him, jabbing at a few buttons. Nothing. The ship doesn't even acknowledge their presence.

"Shit!" Doug snaps.

The alarm system shrieks to life. Red lights strobe through the cabin. The R&D floor's internal klaxons join in—a chorus of panic. Their cover is blown.

"They called it in," Pranz mutters. "I should've shot them."

Doug tears off his mask, his head cover falling to the floor. His breath is shallow. "What do we do!?"

Pranz doesn't answer. He paces, taking off his mask and head covering too. Mutters. Glances out the side viewport.

Dozens of guards storm into the hangar, surrounding the ship with rifles raised and ready.

"Fuck," Pranz whispers.

Boots clatter against metal. They're boarding.

"Fuck!" again, louder this time.

Doug panics, spinning toward the main console—and then freezes. "Wait—look!"

The screen flickers. Then shifts.

The flight controls unlock.

"What the hell?" Doug breathes.

Pranz rushes over. "How?!"

"I—I don't know. Maybe it scanned me?" Doug guesses. "Or you?"

Pranz doesn't hesitate. He drops into the pilot's seat and begins hammering out commands. "Doesn't matter. We're taking off."

The ship groans as it lifts from its cradle. A red warning light flashes—airlock access requested. Pranz authorizes the opening.

Outside the ship, klaxons rise in pitch. Emergency lights blaze.

Guards and engineers not already evacuated scramble for the exits as decompression begins. The outer airlock creaks and then splits wide open.

A gust of suction rips through the hangar.

People vanish into the vacuum, their limbs flailing, screams lost in the silence of space. Doug flinches, watching a body slam into a distant bulkhead before being caught by a safety bot.

Inside the ship, more red lights flash—Cargo Bay Open.

"Shit," Pranz says. "The guards onboard—"

Doug looks at the screen. Their oxygen levels plummet.

'They're suffocating.'

Pranz slams the controls. The ship's bay doors seal, but it's too late. Whatever guards had boarded the ship are gone—either dead or dying in frozen silence.

The ship rockets out of the hangar, slipping through the airlock into open space. Alarms fade behind them. The vacuum claims the last few stragglers outside before rescue bots sweep them up.

Doug stares forward, stunned.

Without a word, Pranz initiates the jump.

The stars stretch and twist—and vanish.

One lightyear away, the ship blinks into empty space.

Silence.

Breathless, Doug finally exhales.

"That," Pranz says, slumping into the chair, "was not how I imagined that going."

Doug slowly turns his head toward him. "Yeah… me either."

They sit in stunned quiet, the hum of the ship filling the void where panic used to be.

And then—almost as if on cue—they both start laughing.

A little broken. A little wild.

But alive.

Chapter 28

"I can't believe that actually worked," Doug says, slumping into the seat beside Pranz, his breath finally steady again.

"Don't get too comfortable," Pranz replies, already tapping away at the command panel. "I guarantee there's a tracker on this ship. After what I had to tell them just to get us back on board, they're not letting this thing out of their sight."

Doug furrows his brow. "What exactly did you tell them? You gave up our big secret, didn't you?"

Pranz exhales sharply through his nose. "Nobody listens to me. I'm just the rich kid in the way. If I didn't say something that got their attention, they would've left you rotting on this ship, left for dead, with nowhere to go."

Doug leans back, arms crossed. "Wouldn't have been the first time I've been stranded."

Pranz pauses for a moment, glancing over. "I know. But I wasn't going to let it happen again."

Doug doesn't reply. He stares out the viewport, jaw tense.

"Anyway," Pranz continues, shifting the energy, "we don't have time for guilt or grudges. Get up here. I think the ship's tied to your face somehow. Might've been how we got out of there. Let's see if it gives us full control."

Doug sighs, then rises reluctantly. He drops into Clutch's seat.

The display flickers.

Multiple panels activate and shift. A soft chime echoes as a new notification blinks in the corner.

"What's that?" Pranz asks, pointing.

Doug follows his finger and taps the notification.

The screen changes—Clutch's face appears, and her voice fills the cockpit, rough and unmistakable.

"Doug. You'z da only guy I trus'. Dey prolly took me to da mount'n or da rock. Ya don't wanna fuck wit karma, so come git me. I only gave ya access to da ship fligh' stuff. Udder stuff 'ill stay crypt'd til I git out."

Doug's heart clenches. It's her. She recorded this for him.

"She left me a recording, but how does the ship know that I am here?" Doug asks.

"I can see ya 'n she tole me ta only let ya have access," the ship responds.

Pranz lets out a stunned laugh. "Okay, first off—she hacked my InfiniChip. Changed it into her own voice and system. I guess this is ClutchAI now. Secondly—no shit, she's hard to understand."

"She's not that bad," Doug says defensively. "You just have to listen like you're actually trying. And think a little."

Pranz smirks, but nods. "Okay, okay. I heard 'the Mountain' and 'Crunch Rock.' That gives us something and matches what we already know."

Suddenly, Clutch's voice returns, "Doug. In da 'vent dey trackin' ya, press dis."

A glowing icon pulses on the screen.

Doug raises an eyebrow. "That's... oddly convenient."

"Just press it," Pranz says, eyes flicking around.

Doug taps the icon.

Immediately, the console flares to life. Lines of code cascade across every screen. The ship begins running self-diagnostics, flipping through schematics, power scans, and system routes faster than either of them can keep up.

After nearly a minute, a list appears, labeled Anomalies Detected—each mapped with their location inside the ship.

"Doug, ya need ta check dees spots fer "nomalies," ClutchAI says, her voice now seamlessly blended with the system's interface.

Doug stares at the screen. "Clutch?" he asks cautiously. "Did you... upload your thoughts into the AI Pranz installed?"

"Yep."

Pranz stifles a laugh. "That... is so her."

Doug just grins, shaking his head in disbelief. "You heard the lady, Pranz. Let's go find us some 'nomalies."

The two begin their search, following the AI's prompts to the locations flagged by Clutch's voice—now hauntingly woven into the ship itself.

Doug heads to the galley first. The spot marked on the display leads him to a seldom-used cupboard tucked high and tight above the main food prep station—the kind of storage where outdated rations and long-forgotten utensils go to die.

He opens it, scans the shelves, and immediately closes it again.

"Ya need ta take everytin' out," ClutchAI says, her voice clear and sharp through the overhead speaker.

Doug freezes. The tone, the cadence—it's so distinctly her that he actually glances behind him, half expecting to find Clutch standing there, arms crossed, giving him that look.

He exhales and reopens the cupboard.

"Alright, alright…" he mutters.

Item by item, he begins pulling things out—old filters, a bent mess tin, emergency coffee pods with faded labels— until, tucked behind a loose panel in the back, he spots the small metal tracker. Blinking softly. Sleek. Corporate.

Doug scowls, plucks it from its hiding spot, and carefully carries it back to the bridge before heading for the next anomaly.

Meanwhile, Pranz makes his way toward the engine room.

He approaches the door, only to find it unresponsive. He tries the handle, pressing it, then shoving it harder with his weight. Nothing.

"I ain't want'n ya ta be in der. Doug only," ClutchAI cuts in—blunt and unwavering.

Pranz freezes, the rejection hitting harder than he expects. He leans against the door, folding his arms.

"Why don't you trust me?" he asks, voice low. "I'm not the same as them."

Silence.

"I get it, okay? I was born into all this," he continues, gesturing vaguely around him. "I didn't choose wealth. But I see the rot. The greed. And I don't want to be part of it. I'm trying to be different. So please... trust me. Let me help."

A pause. Then, cold and decisive:

"Ain't happ'nin now. Go check da cargo bay."

The door remains locked.

Pranz sighs and steps back, jaw clenched. He turns toward the cargo bay, frustration and resolve both swelling inside him.

Doug is just about to step off the bridge when ClutchAI's voice pipes in again—calm, precise, and eerie in its clarity.

"Go ta da engine room nex'."

Doug nods, more out of reflex than trust. Her voice—so familiar yet disembodied—makes him feel more like he's being watched than guided. He heads off, the sense of guilt coiling in his gut, yet a calmness of hearing Clutch's voice helps sooth the process.

As he rounds a corridor, he runs into Pranz coming from the opposite direction.

"Your girlfriend won't let me into the engine room," Pranz says casually, stopping in Doug's path. "She doesn't trust me."

"She's not my girlfriend," Doug says a little too quickly, a little too forcefully.

"Yeah, okay," Pranz says with a knowing grin. "But based on your reaction, you wish she was. I've seen the way you look at her."

Doug opens his mouth to respond, then closes it again and redirects.

"Anyway. I found the tracker in the galley. It's on the bridge now. Once we find the rest, we'll figure out what to do with them."

"Sounds good. I'm headed to the cargo bay," Pranz replies, already turning.

Doug makes his way to the engine room. The door hisses open automatically for him—unmistakably selective. He steps inside, immediately hit by a wave of heat and the deep, resonant hum of machinery. The smell is sharp— burnt coolant and recycled carbon—thick and metallic in the back of his throat.

He approaches the location highlighted by ClutchAI. It's tight—wedged behind a thick cluster of insulated pipes. He crouches, tries to wedge his arm between them, but a searing pain rips through his forearm as it grazes a hot pipe.

"Fuck!" Doug recoils, inspecting the red welt already blooming on his skin. "My arms aren't long enough."

He looks around frantically. A work apron hangs from a nearby hook. He yanks it down, wraps it around his arm like a makeshift barrier, and tries again—this time managing to reach the tracker but fumbling the grip. It slips from his fingers.

"Shit…" Doug mutters. Sweat rolls down his temples. "Clutch… you might need to let Pranz take this one. I'm just not tall enough."

He tries again. And again. His breath grows labored. The burn stings beneath the apron. After a fourth attempt, he sits down heavily on the floor, arms limp, chest heaving.

A moment later, Pranz steps through the doorway.

"Your girlfriend told me to come help," he says, a slight edge to his voice. "I have to admit, I'm not loving ClutchAI."

"I wouldn't piss her—or the AI version of her—off," Doug mutters. "She might just open the airlock next time we're sleeping."

Doug points to the pipe cluster. "It's tucked back there. Burns like hell. Here—use this." He hands Pranz the apron and steps aside.

Pranz wraps his arm, kneels, and in one clean motion pulls the tracker free.

"Must be nice to be tall," Doug says, rubbing his bruised forearm.

"It has its moments," Pranz replies with a wink.

They move on together, checking the rest of the AI-marked zones. Two more pings. The final two "anomalies" turn out to be stray tools—likely abandoned by engineers in a rush. The total count of real trackers: three.

Back on the bridge, they place the small devices on the console and weigh their next move.

"Let's just leave all three in one place and call it good," Doug suggests, but before he can finish—

"Nope," Pranz interrupts, already turning toward the nav console. "We need to leave two here, making it seem like we found them and tried to give them the slip, and then send one off on a fake jump. That one will make it look like we're headed somewhere important. Give them something to chase."

Doug tilts his head. "And where exactly are we supposed to be 'heading'?"

Pranz's grin returns—less playful this time, more calculating. "That, my friend, is the part where we get clever."

Chapter 29

"The drone with the last tracker is off—hurdling toward Covnovel Station," Pranz announces with a flourish, wiping invisible grime from his palms like the task had physically cost him something. "Now we get to go where we want."

He slides into the pilot's chair and initiates a jump, sending the ship lurching into a new slice of space.

Doug steadies himself, then furrows his brow. "What's even at Covnovel that would make them think we'd go there? It's just a regular hub—commerce, refuel, resupply. Nothing urgent."

"Oh, and the largest secret weapons depot in the sector," Pranz says casually, tapping at a few settings with a smirk. "Courtesy of my lovely, war-profiteering father and his cozy little contracts with the military."

Doug raises a brow. "Well… maybe we SHOULD go there."

"Tempting, I know," Pranz grins. "But I've got what we need for the next phase. Come on. I stashed something for you."

They exit the bridge and head through the dim, humming corridors toward a bunk room. Pranz leads Doug into the one he's been using and immediately kneels by a panel near the air vent. With a practiced twist, he removes it, revealing two rectangular containers tucked inside like contraband.

He pulls both out and tosses one to Doug, who catches it awkwardly.

"Hope I got your size right," Pranz says, popping open his own box.

Doug cocks his head and opens his container. Inside is a neatly folded guard's uniform—stern reds and blacks with a company crest on the shoulder. Underneath the fabric, a lineup of gear sits tucked into padded compartments: a baton, a laser prod, a tranq gun, a compact pulse pistol, and—just in case—a wicked-looking knife.

Doug lays each item out slowly on the bed like he's defusing a bomb. "This… is a lot of gear," he mutters. "A lot of gear I've never actually used."

Pranz sits on the edge of the bed, unbothered. "You'll manage. The baton's easy—swing, make contact. The pulse gun's straightforward too—pull trigger, hope for the best. Just don't miss."

Doug picks up the laser prod, inspecting its length and grip.

"That one's versatile," Pranz continues. "Great for crowd control or a surprise takedown. Fires at a distance or direct contact—stuns hard. Just don't fumble and zap yourself like I did once. Whole leg went numb for an hour—looked like a drunk puppet."

"It's the one I know the most. I have one that I kept on my ship. Definitely not as nice as this one," Doug says. "I think I'll only use this one if I have to."

"Suit yourself. Though, judging by how you handled yourself earlier, you'll be fine with any of them. You've got decent instincts… sometimes." Pranz flashes a crooked grin.

Doug sighs, flopping onto the bed. "Like I said, I've used the prod before. Everything else feels like dress-up."

"It's more about the confidence than the gear," Pranz says, standing and adjusting his clothes. "These guys see a uniform, a weapon belt, and a bored expression, they assume you belong."

"Bored I can do," Doug mutters.

"Good," Pranz says, motioning to the door. "Get some sleep. We dock in eight hours, and we'll need to be sharp."

"I thought there was only one transport ship in and out of the mines?" Doug asks, standing up to leave Pranz's bunk.

"There is," Pranz confirms. "We're hitching a ride in. Disguised as guards. It's already in motion."

Doug stares at him. "Okay. I'm not dead yet, I guess your plans are as good as any at this point."

Pranz flashes him a reassuring smirk as Doug steps out. "Sweet dreams, hero."

The door hisses shut, leaving Doug to wander alone to his bunk, with unfamiliar weapons—and the weight of the mission they're about to attempt.

Doug jolts awake, heart pounding, breath ragged. Cold sweat clings to his skin. The dream already slipping from memory, but the fear lingers like smoke.

The ship is in sleep mode—lights dimmed to the point of darkness, everything hushed. Even the gentle hum of the systems feels quieter, like the vessel itself is holding its breath.

Doug sits up, blinking away the haze. He grabs the bottle of water by his bedside and takes a long pull, trying to steady his breathing. Still restless, he rises and begins pacing the narrow room in tight, agitated circuits.

At the foot of the bed, the guard gear sits in neat, cold silence. A reminder of the mission. Of what they're about to risk.

Doug stops and stares at it.

"We're coming for you, Clutch," he whispers. "Just hang tough."

The silence breaks.

"She can't hear ya," Clutch's voice comes through the room's speaker, clear and unmistakably hers—except flat, hollow. AI.

Doug jumps, nearly dropping his water. "Fuck! Forgot you... right. You embedded yourself in the ship."

His breath spikes again, almost to the edge of hyperventilation. He leans against the wall, hand pressed to his chest.

"Didn't expect you to respond," he mutters.

"I know she can't hear me," he says a moment later, regaining control. "It's just something people do. We say things out loud. Hope the other person feels it... even if they're nowhere near us."

"Don't seem log'cal," ClutchAI replies in its digitized echo of her broken accent.

Doug half-laughs, exasperated. "You're the one who believes in karma. How's that any more logical?"

"Ain't me dat b'leaves," the AI responds. "Clutch do."

Doug lets out a long sigh and rubs his face with both hands. "Right. Okay. Talking to an AI ghost of Clutch. Perfectly normal."

He walks over, falls back onto the bed, and stares up at the ceiling—blank, expressionless metal panels staring right back.

"How long until we dock?" he asks.

"Tree hours," ClutchAI responds.

Doug closes his eyes for a beat, then opens them again. "I should try to sleep more."

He rolls onto his side, pulling the thin blanket over him. But his eyes stay open. The weight of everything pressing down: the mission, the risks, the unknown. And somewhere beneath it all—hope.

Hope that she's still alive. That she's still Clutch.

"Wake up, dude—we're here." Pranz's knuckles rap on Doug's door, a rhythmic knock that pulls Doug from a dreamless sleep.

Doug blinks hard, struggling to orient himself. The darkness of deep rest still clings to his thoughts. "Be right there," he mumbles, voice dry and thick with fatigue.

He sits up, exhales, and rubs his face. The gear lies ready—where he left it. The uniform. The weapons. The lie he's about to live. He fastens the last strap across his chest and steps out of the room, where Pranz is waiting with a smirk.

"Took you long enough," Pranz says, arms crossed, voice light with humor.

"I actually fell asleep," Doug admits with a stretch and yawn that doesn't quite chase the sleep from his limbs. "I mean, after I had a nightmare and a weird conversation with ClutchAI."

"Good. So, we've got to transfer to an unmarked ship," Pranz explains, his tone shifting more serious. "Clutch's ship is flagged. Probably marked as hostile or stolen—or both. It stays here, floating off-grid. We're boarding under forged identities. Leave anything and everything behind. Mining guards don't show up with any personal crap."

Doug stops mid-step.

"Leave everything behind," Pranz repeats. "Anything not assigned gets you flagged for contraband. Best-case, they confiscate it. Worst-case—become a miner yourself."

Doug's eyes go wide. He pats his pockets, even checking the lining of his boots, as if one rogue coin or wire might doom them both.

Pranz chuckles. "You're checking for lint? Come on, man."

But as he walks toward the docked corridor, Doug's eyes snap open like a man struck by lightning.

"Wait!" he shouts, already spinning on his heels. "Imprints!"

"What?" Pranz calls after him.

Doug doesn't slow. He races back through the ship, calling out as he runs. "Clutch! The imprint device! Where'd she put it?"

ClutchAI responds with that familiar vocal flicker. "Whatcha need dat fer?"

"To rescue Clutch," Doug says, urgency thick in his voice. "We'll need deep-system imprints—military level. That device will let us reprogram our IDs."

ClutchAI answers coolly. "It's in her room. Under da bed."

"Wait," Pranz says, catching up. "You two have a military-grade implant imprinter? Do you even understand what that is? That's... illegal in twelve sectors."

Doug shrugs as he opens her door. "Apparently it's the newest generation, too."

He steps inside and breathes her in—the trace of Clutch still lingering, even now. He hesitates just a second before dropping to the floor and peering beneath the bed.

"There," he says, spotting a brushed-metal case tucked behind some other boxes.

He pulls it out and places it on the bed. It clicks open with a hiss and unfolds to reveal a sleek interface, softly pulsing with power.

Pranz hovers, eyebrows raised. "You guys are full of surprises," he mutters with an appreciative whistle. "Even I don't have one of these."

Doug doesn't smile. His voice is steady, serious. "Clutch, can you configure this and give us the access we'll need?"

A beat of silence. Then ClutchAI responds, as casual as ever. "Ya."

Doug meets Pranz's gaze, holds up his wrist and says, "Let's become the guards they won't question."

Doug and Pranz, now armed with new identities and fresh imprint codes, step into the core of a small, circular structure floating quietly in the void—a mobile star station. It's called that not just for its size but for its design: five distinct docking arms radiating from a central hub like the points of a star. The architecture is efficient, stark, and intimidating in its simplicity.

They enter the hub, the air stale and humming faintly with station systems barely clinging to life. Metal storage bins and stripped-down supply racks line the interior walls, most of them strapped in tight due to the lack of gravity when the place is uninhabited.

Doug glances at the floor as he walks, expecting his boots to lose purchase. But they don't.

"I thought these little stations didn't have gravity," he mutters, eyes narrowing as he tests his step again.

"I got the deluxe model," Pranz says with a smirk, already ahead of him. "Can't do covert ops if your spleen's floating in your chest cavity."

Doug snorts lightly but says nothing, falling into step as Pranz motions him forward.

"This way. We need to move fast—don't want to miss our ride."

They stride across the central chamber toward one of the outstretched docking arms. There, tethered quietly like a loyal hound, waits a compact, two-seater transport vessel—sleek, black, and unmistakably Fornokey. The corporate insignia gleams across its hull, etched with silent authority into every panel, every surface. It's the kind of ship designed to whisper power without ever having to raise its voice.

Doug hesitates as they approach. "Won't they be able to track this thing? I mean… Fornokey logos aren't exactly subtle."

"Normally, yeah," Pranz says, sliding open the hatch. "But this one? Got it before they installed the tracker. My father talks too much when he drinks. I just made a habit of pretending not to listen."

He flashes a crooked grin and climbs aboard.

Doug follows, still uneasy, but sits beside Pranz. The cockpit is tight—built for utility, not comfort. As soon as the hatch seals, Pranz begins the launch sequence. Systems hum to life beneath their feet. He inputs coordinates with the ease of someone who's done it a hundred times.

The clamps release with a hiss. The station spins lazily away behind them.

Doug looks over. "Where exactly are we going?"

Pranz doesn't answer right away. He watches the starfield stretch and distort through the forward glass as they slip into the jump. The stars blur. The silence grows.

Then, finally, Pranz says, "Into the lion's den."

"How cliché," Doug mutters.

Chapter 30

Pranz docks the ship to Gelpsim Station, rising from his seat with a fluid, practiced motion. He straightens his uniform, checks the alignment of his gear, and absently pats the area over his implant, as if confirming it's still functioning.

"You just going to sit there?" Pranz asks as he strides past Doug.

"Is that an option?" Doug replies, genuinely hopeful.

Pranz smirks. "You're funny. Let's go."

Doug groans softly but gets up and falls in step. They exit the small corporate vessel and step into Gelpsim Station—a modest waypoint primarily funded and maintained by the Fornokey Corporation. It isn't flashy, but it has all the essentials: fuel, supplies, and just enough comfort to serve as a layover hub for corporate operatives. Occasionally, military transports pass through for brief rest stops, but today the station is quiet. A skeleton crew, a few vendors, and no military presence to complicate things.

Pranz walks with the poise of someone who belongs, commanding attention without trying. Doug follows a half-step behind, clutching a small, unmarked metal cube. As they near the central security checkpoint, they veer off to the side, slipping into a low-traffic junction just before coming into view of the guards.

"Are we close enough?" Doug whispers.

"We better be. Any closer and they'll see the cube and start asking questions," Pranz replies. He gestures subtly. "Tuck it into that junction slot down by the base of the wall."

Doug scans the area. "Which slot?"

"I'll point to it as we pass. It's close to the ground. Pretend you're adjusting your boot. Just drop the cube and move on."

Doug nods. "Let's hope ClutchAI got the coding right."

"Between Clutch and the InfiniChip? We're good," Pranz says confidently, then glances up at the ceiling and silently mouths, 'I hope.'

They move again. Pranz leads the way, maintaining the smooth, authoritative gait of someone on assignment. Doug trails behind at the right pace, ready for the cue. As Pranz rounds the edge of the wall and into partial view of the security checkpoint, he casually drops his hand in a precise gesture. Doug spots the narrow gap in the wall, crouches as he approaches, and mimics fiddling with his boot.

He slides the cube toward the slot, but it slips through his fingers and hits the metal floor with a sharp, echoing clang.

Doug freezes.

Wide-eyed, he reacts on instinct. He covers with a sudden, exaggerated coughing fit, doing his best to sound like a man suffering from mild space-lung rather than someone who just blew a covert op.

Standing up, he straightens his coat and adjusts his collar like it was all part of the act. When he looks up, he finds Pranz staring back at him, his expression a cocktail of disappointment and disbelief. A pair of nearby guards glance toward Doug, squinting in suspicion.

Doug coughs again, throws in a polite wave, and forces a smile.
Nothing to see here, just a guy doing illegal shit.

Finally satisfied that the commotion is over and attention has shifted, Pranz turns toward the checkpoint and walks forward. At the scanner, he lifts his arm—implant side up—and hovers it near the sensor pad. It beeps green. Smooth, seamless. He steps through without hesitation, giving Doug a subtle glance that says, your turn.

Doug exhales sharply. Moment of truth, he thinks. He steps up, mimics Pranz's movement, and hovers his arm over the scanner.

Beep.

Red.

Doug's stomach drops. The red glow paints his face in alarm. His eyes dart to Pranz for answers, help, anything. Pranz doesn't flinch—he simply lowers his hand to waist level and holds it there, palm facing down. A subtle signal: wait.

Doug freezes.

Two guards nearby immediately take notice. One steps forward. "You don't seem to have clearance," he says, giving Doug a once-over. "Where are you supposed to be?"

Doug clears his throat. "Just heading out to the rock. Gotta keep the iron ants in line," he says, forcing a casual tone that trembles beneath the surface.

The second guard squints at the scanner. "You're not getting out there without clearance."

"Maybe I pulled my arm away too fast," Doug replies, forcing a nervous chuckle. "Let's just try it again."

Pranz glances down at his cuff, fingers dancing over the display. Still holding the subtle 'stall' gesture, he gives Doug a sharp look that screams: keep talking.

"Have you two ever been out there?" Doug blurts. "To the rocks, I mean?"

The guards exchange glances. "Nope," says the first.

"Yeah," the second says, cracking his neck.

"Oh. Good," Doug nods quickly. "This is my first assignment. Thought I'd ask if there's anything they don't tell you in training. You know, stuff they leave out of the handbook."

Pranz rolls his fingers in the air behind the guards: stretch it out.

The second guard laughs. "You want off-the-record advice?"

"I mean, who doesn't?" Doug says, eyes wide with faux enthusiasm.

The first guard leans in slightly. "I also want to know."

The second guard chuckles. "Don't get smart with the higher-ups. Keep your head down, do what you're told.

You step out of line, you'll find yourself on the receiving end of a laser prod real fast. The rest you'll pick up easy enough."

Doug fakes a wince. "Sounds great. Good thing I've got a long history of blindly following orders."

That draws a genuine chuckle.

"And don't go sniffing around the female ants on your first shift," the guard adds with a smirk. "You won't get a chance until at least your second or third shift."

Doug forces a laugh, though his stomach turns. "Got it. No fun the first go. Second shift only."

Then Pranz nods—barely—but enough. Doug lifts his arm and waves it again over the scanner.

Beep.

Green.

Relief floods him, but he doesn't let it show. He offers a casual nod and walks through the checkpoint.

"Maybe I'll see you guys out there in a month," Doug says, glancing back.

"Not unless you're pulling double shifts," one guard jokes.

"I might. Could use the credits. And, well, you know… second shift," Doug says with a grin that he regrets the moment it leaves his mouth.

"Shut up," Pranz hisses under his breath. "You're going to say the wrong thing."

Doug nods silently and keeps walking beside Pranz. They stop at the staging room to grab helmets. Pranz secures his with a smooth, practiced motion. A face shield slides down, obscuring his features. Doug mimics him, locking his own helmet in place. Once hidden, they look like every other guard—just two more faceless enforcers in the system.

They enter the transport and settle into bench seats lining the interior. A few moments later, the rest of the guards begins to pile in. The doors hiss shut with finality.

Doug glances toward Pranz. Even through the tinted visor, Pranz can feel Doug's nerves radiating off him.

Pranz gives the smallest nod. A silent reassurance. No words exchanged. Not here—not when every inch of Fornokey airspace could be bugged and monitored.

With a sharp jolt, the transport detaches and accelerates toward their destination.

Minutes later, the ship eases into docking position. Through a small port window, guards begin craning their necks for a better view. The jagged, rust-colored asteroid looms ahead, with a twisted metallic spike protruding from its side like a spear—The Mountain. An iron-rich mine that lives up to its name.

Doug leans toward Pranz. "This isn't Crunch Rock," he says, anxiety bleeding into his voice.

"Yeah... I know," Pranz replies, brows furrowed behind his visor. "This was the only transport to take."

"Did we board the wrong one?" Doug asks, low and tense.

Before either of them can spiral further, a clipped voice crackles over the intercom.

"Guard group A will depart as soon as we attach. Everyone else will remain seated to avoid unnecessary delays."

Pranz lets out a long breath, relieved. "We're not group A. We stay put."

Doug nods, visibly easing. "Okay. Just... making sure."

They watch silently as the doors open. A team of guards disembark in unison, boots echoing against the steel. Another batch comes aboard. Then the doors seal again, and the ship lurches back into motion.

"Maybe it's a loop route," Doug mutters, his voice now contemplative.

"Could be. Let's wait it out," Pranz says, eyes locked on his cuff display.

The cycle repeats. The ship stops. More guards out. New guards in. Four more times.

Finally, the voice over the comm announces the next stop: Crunch Rock.

Pranz stands. "This is us."

Doug follows, adjusting his gear as they move toward the exit. The docking doors hiss open and the scent of scorched metal and stale air rushes in. They file out into the harsh, utilitarian corridors of the asteroid mine.

They hang back, letting the crowd pass. Pranz is glued to his cuff, rapidly swiping and entering commands with sharp precision.

A nearby guard spots them lingering. "Hey! You two—get moving!"

Pranz doesn't respond. He holds up one finger without looking up.

The guard sneers and marches toward them, baton in hand. "You don't get to fucking tell me what to—"

Before he can finish, Pranz executes a final command and raises his wrist. The cuff flashes a red seal. One most people don't see. One everyone knows.

The guard stops mid-stride, eyes widening. The baton lowers.

"My mistake," he says stiffly. "Carry on."

Pranz nods coolly and walks past without another word. Doug hustles after him.

Once they're around the corner and out of sight, Doug finally speaks. "Okay. What the fuck did you show him?"

Pranz smirks behind the visor. "Think of it like a corporate black card... for people who make problems disappear. Not many are given that level of clearance. Mostly high-ranking officers. Primarily, just assassins."

Doug stares. "Assassins? Seriously?"

"I can't let anyone here know who I really am. So, for all intents and purposes..." Pranz pauses dramatically. "I'm a Fornokey-sanctioned problem solver."

Doug blinks. "Do I get one of those?"

Pranz laughs. "No. But lucky for you—assassins are allowed to have assistants."

Chapter 31

"We've been searching for hours. Still no sign of her," Doug says, frustration thick in his voice as he rounds yet another corner.

"I know," Pranz mutters, his tone laced with equal annoyance. "It shouldn't be this hard."

"Can't you check some kind of registration system?" Doug asks, glancing toward Pranz's wrist display.

"There isn't one," Pranz says flatly. "Too much risk. If anyone hacked it, they'd have proof of what happens here. It's all word of mouth and shadow trails. You either know someone who knows, or you knock on every fucking door."

Doug rubs his face, groaning. "Can assistants ask guards any questions at least?"

"Not without drawing heat," Pranz replies. "We need to blend in."

Doug exhales sharply, the weight of it all pressing down. His thoughts churn—'Even if we find her... how the hell do we get out?'

"Hey..." Doug starts slowly, "when we find her... how do we leave?"

Pranz halts mid-step, his shoulders tightening. He doesn't turn around. For a long moment, the silence hangs between them, heavy and uncertain. Finally, he speaks— quietly, like he's trying to convince himself as much as Doug.

"Clutch escaped once. If anyone can pull it off again, it's her."

He pauses, then adds, with a hesitant edge, "And... I think my 'problem solver' clearance might let me extract assets without clearance."

Another pause.

"Maybe. Not totally sure."

Doug hangs his head and silently mouths, fuck over and over. He follows behind Pranz, each step heavier than the last.

They continue searching—bunkhouses, break rooms, supply corridors, even maintenance shafts. No sign of her.

"Are we allowed to talk to the, uh, 'employees'?" Doug asks. "Because this random wandering thing isn't working."

Pranz scans the area. "Let's try it. Carefully."

A hunched worker shuffles out of a nearby bathroom, eyes low.

"You!" Pranz barks.

The man flinches, instinctively lowering his head even more. "Yes'em?"

"We're looking for someone. Name's Clutch. Have you seen her?" Pranz asks.

"Ain't know no names," the man replies quickly. "Ain't 'llowed ta talk ta chudder."

"Carry on," Pranz says. He knows when a wall isn't moving.

But Doug isn't finished. "Hey!" he calls after the man, who pauses, reluctant.

Doug walks closer. "What happens to people who do talk?"

"Dey git boxed. Er beat. Er bof. If'n it a girl, dey git tabled," the man says, voice low, clearly scared.

"Tabled?" Doug repeats, trying to understand.

"Don't… don't wanna tink 'bout it," the man murmurs, eyes darting to the floor.

"Tied to a table. Raped by guards," Pranz says grimly. "Correct?"

The man nods, looking over his shoulder like he expects punishment just for being near them, or late to return to his shift.

"Where are you supposed to be right now?" Pranz asks, more softly.

"Prossess'n," he says.

"Let's get you there before you catch a beating," Pranz says, gesturing for him to lead the way.

They follow him through dim corridors. The noise builds— machinery, shouting, the clamor of industry. It gets louder with every step. By the time they reach the processing entrance, it's deafening.

A guard steps forward, inspecting the worker's cuff, ready to pounce—until he spots Doug and Pranz. Pranz flashes his cuff display without a word. The guard freezes, then nods and steps back.

Doug and Pranz retreat quickly, the cacophony swallowing the worker behind them.

"We have to find those tables," Doug says, urgency rising. "If Clutch mouthed off to someone…"

"She would've," Pranz says, voice dark. "I've heard what they do at the tables. They tie women down in restraints—different setups, different tortures. The guards come and go like it's a damn breakroom. When they're done… the woman is either dumped out an airlock or incinerated."

Doug clenches his fists. "Your father built this place."

"I know," Pranz says. "He's a monster. I've tried to tear it down, but I'm just a shadow under his name."

"You're also his son," Doug counters. "That's a weapon most people never get."

"Sometimes it feels more like a leash. Either way, I've never been this close to the corruption and lies. I've never seen the mines up close. And I've never been this close to dismantling it."

Before Doug can respond, a harsh voice cuts through the air.

"You two! Stop right there!"

They spin. A squad of guards approaches, weapons at the ready.

Doug grips the handle of his gun. Pranz instinctively readies his laser prod and raises his cuff, showing the signature seal.

The lead guard scoffs. "That trick won't work anymore. We know who you are, Jason Pranz. And your accomplice."

Pranz's jaw tightens. He glances at Doug and whispers. "Shit. They know. Get ready to run."

Doug freezes, heart pounding in his throat.

Too late. The guards close in fast.

Pranz fires first, hitting the lead guard square in the chest. The man drops. The rest scatter, taking cover.

Doug, wide-eyed, raises his weapon and fires, each shot echoing like a death knell.

"Run!" Pranz yells, sprinting up the corridor.

Doug turns and bolts after him, his breaths ragged, legs pumping.

"Where the fuck are we even going!?" Doug shouts between gulps of air. "There's no way out!"

Chapter 32

Doug and Pranz cling to the outer shell of the station, both gasping behind their cracked face shields, helmets fogging from the sheer panic of limited air. Hand signals are the only language now. They flash fingers, jab in directions, but no agreement forms.

Doug slaps his left wrist with his right hand—twice, sharp. A universal sign: time's running out.

The suits they managed to rip from the emergency racks on their mad sprint for the airlock had no oxygen canisters. Just the shells. No backup. No room to hesitate.

Pranz finally gestures decisively—follow me. No time for discussion. He turns and leaps off the station.

Doug watches as his friend soars across the void, soaring with perfect form over a black chasm between the docking wing and the asteroid's central mining unit—five hundred meters of dead space and very little gravity to pull you back.

Doug hesitates.

His boots grind against the edge of the platform. One mistake and you're not landing, you're exploring the universe at the slowest possible speed.

He pushes off.

The moment his feet leave the metal, he knows it's wrong. The angle's too high. The trajectory's off. The asteroid isn't coming closer—it's sliding away beneath him.

"Shit!" Doug curses, trying to course correct, arms flapping instinctively, uselessly.

Below, Pranz whips around and sees it. Doug drifting. Off-course. Hopelessly floating away.

Doug's vision tunnels. Stars blur. Panic rises.

And then a memory.

It crashes in like a punch to the chest.

Years ago.

Doug worked a maintenance gig for Rigspan Freight Systems, a mid-tier hauler outfit that specialized in cold-space delivery contracts—the kind that didn't bother with insurance or clean HR policies. He was barely twenty, working six-month contracts that paid shit but offered room, board, and a chance to keep moving, far from the station he grew up on.

His job? External module patch and recalibration. When an outside component failed—usually one of the thermal regulators or a container lock-joint—he got suited up, clipped in, and sent out to fix it.

Simple. Dangerous. Underpaid.

This time, it was an outer hull coupler that had been giving false readings. The ship's system flagged it as a possible disconnect hazard. Rather than turning the ship around or burning fuel to dock at a repair station, the company pinged Doug on his off shift and handed him a spool of thermal sealant and a wrench the size of his forearm.

"They said we were waiting for a station," Doug told them. "This isn't a fix that should be done on the fly."

"You've got a suit. We've got a time limit on this job," the shift captain said, waving him off. "You'll be fine. Tether's still good. Mostly."

Mostly.

The tether cable had frayed insulation, its outer layer peeling back like sunburnt skin. Someone had wrapped it in a strip of black tape and scrawled "DO NOT USE" on it in grease pen. The backup tether was missing—borrowed weeks ago for "reassignment."

Doug stared at the main tether, hesitating in the airlock.

He looked at the rescue drones, knowing the rumors. They were there for show. Internally scraped for parts.

He clipped in hoping he wouldn't need the drones.

Stepped out.

Cold silence enveloped him—pure vacuum and a billion stars. He inched along the rail, white-knuckling the coupler, checking readouts. The job took longer than it should have. Frozen grime had jammed the actuator, and he had to pry it loose with a chisel he'd stuck in his belt.

The moment he got it loose, he felt it.

A snap.

A gentle tug backward—soft, almost tender, like someone pulling at the back of his shirt.

Then—weightlessness.

His boots lost contact with the hull. His gloved fingers scrabbled at anything and nothing.

The tether had broken.

No snap. No alarm. Just… drifting.

The freighter's silver hull receded with agonizing slowness, growing smaller with each desperate breath.

"Shit. Shit. Shit."

He radioed in, but the crew was always slow to respond. Always slower when it came to the junior techs. There was a bitter joke that floated around between workers like him: "If you're not cargo, you're expendable."

Minutes passed. His oxygen readout ticked down.

He started to sweat. Inside the helmet. Inside the suit.

His breath warmed the air, fogging the edge of the glass. It felt like drowning in dry space.

Doug had no scream left. Only the gnawing sense that this was it. That he'd die where no one would hear him. That his bones would spin in orbit around some dead comet, lost and unmourned.

But then, a shudder in the void.

A capture drone, long-unused and supposedly busted, grabbed Doug by his hand.

He gripped the drone's arm with his other hand.

The drone sputtered back to the airlock, occasionally shifting off course, its propulsion system shady and likely nearing fuel depletion.

When he eventually came through the airlock, the shift captain just asked, "Get it fixed?"

No "you okay." No apology. No offer of reassignment. No humanity.

The tether was still coiled on the rack two weeks later—still labeled "DO NOT USE." No spare in sight.

Doug never forgot the silence. Or the sweat in his helmet. Or how much of his life had depended on a busted drone that shouldn't have worked at all.

He'd buried that memory.

Until now.

"No. Not again!" Doug shouts, wild-eyed. "Come on, move. Something, move!"

And something does.

Below, the boom arm of the mining drill retracts from its housing, shifting with jerky hydraulics. The rock-shredder at its tip spins as it repositions—rising. Chasing to get in front of him.

Doug sees it moving and starts to scream again.

"Yes! Yes—faster! Please don't miss me!"

The angle's wrong. Too far left. His path won't intersect—

Then it corrects.

The boom swings sideways, trying to get beneath him. A thin thread of salvation in the void.

But the shredder's still spinning.

"Oh fuck. Turn it off! Turn it off! I don't want to be space juice!"

The boom stretches, reaching its maximum extension just as Doug's body passes overhead.

He closes his eyes, bracing for impact. Then opens them. "Pay attention! You have to catch this thing!" He yells at himself.

His eyes start to droop on their own. "Stay awake!" he barks at himself, breath coming hard and fast. Oxygen nearly depleted. CO_2 levels rising past safe.

He slams into the boom with a sharp, jarring thud. Pain rings through his chest, but he's moving backward now. No anchor. No control.

He flails.

His eyes catch it—cable. A thick, carbon-reinforced tether snaking along the boom's edge.

He grabs.

His fingers slip.

"Grip, dammit! Hold on!"

He squeezes tighter, willing his hands not to betray him. He yanks himself downward, sliding along the boom toward the asteroid surface. His body shakes from oxygen deprivation. Vision blurs. Muscles tremble.

"I... can't... breathe..."

His grip loosens. Mind slipping. The world narrowing.

Then the ground rises.

A shadow moves.

Pranz—bounding across the rock. Reaching out.

Doug sees his friend's hand for half a second.

Then nothing.

His eyes close. His lungs fall still.

And the stars fade to black.

Doug hears voices before he feels his body. His mind stirs first, dragging him from a void of silence and weightlessness into something heavier, tighter.

His eyes won't open. His lids feel welded shut—like lead panels sealed with magnets. Every inch of his skin feels compressed, his limbs wrapped in invisible coils. He tries to move. Nothing.

Am I dead?

Where the fuck am I?

Why can't I move?

"There he is," a voice cuts through the static fog of his thoughts—calm, observant, male.

Doug tries to speak but can't. His mouth won't open. Something clamps his jaw in place.

"Don't try to move," the voice says, closer now. "You're in a pressure suit. Full containment. Your body nearly imploded out there."

Doug groans, frustrated. He forces a twitch in his fingers. It's barely a spasm.

"You're stubborn," the voice continues, with a note of amusement. "I can tell."

"You can let him out of that thing," another voice calls from farther off—familiar. Pranz. Confident. "He's got nanos. Next-gen. He'll be fine."

A pause.

"If he dies, it's on you," the first voice replies, moving closer. "We didn't have to pull him back, you know."

"I get it. Really, I do. But trust me. He can handle it."

Something begins to release around Doug—like a second skin slowly peeling away. Pressure eases in stages. He feels lighter. The vice grip on his face unclasps with a faint hiss, and light stabs through his swollen eyelids. He squints. Blinks. The world comes into focus through a searing glare.

The seal around his head peels back, revealing a red-lit room and two figures leaning over him.

His throat burns like sandpaper. His tongue feels like leather. But he forces out a word.

"Where...?"

"Easy," says the stranger. A man with red hair—rich auburn, like Clutch's, but his accent is clean. Refined. Controlled.

Doug blinks at him. "Who are you?"

"Rex," the man replies with a half-nod. Calm. Efficient. "Medical tech and general survivor, depending on the day."

Pranz moves closer. "That guy we questioned and kept from a beating, pulled you in. Rex patched you up. He's been surviving out here longer than anyone has a right to."

Doug's senses return in pieces. The smell of sterilized air. The hum of backup generators. The faint vibration beneath the floor. Some kind of med bay, built into a hidden bunker.

"Are we safe?" Doug asks.

"For now," Pranz says. "We've got a sliver of time before anyone comes looking. They know we are on this side of the asteroid and they saw our stunt."

Doug forces himself upright, shaking the stiffness from his limbs. "Clutch?"

Pranz's face darkens. "We haven't found her. Not in the mines. Not in the galley. Not even in the holding pens. No one's seen her."

"She's not in the mines," Rex adds. "And if the rumors are right, she's not been… tabled either."

Doug stares at him. "So where is she?"

Rex shrugs. "If she's still here, they're keeping her isolated. Somewhere new. Off-grid. Or worse—she's already been moved."

Doug stands. Paces. His heart pounds harder with each step. "What if she was never here?"

Pranz stiffens. "She is. She has to be. I paid well for the intel—the system, the video feeds, fuck."

"And you believed it?" Doug snaps. "You think these bastards care about honesty? You think they wouldn't feed you a lie just to get your money? To get you here, where they could trap us both? Maybe you got your intel from your father or his AI systems that look for things like you snooping around?"

Pranz's mouth opens—no defense comes out.

"You saw how hard they came at us. This whole thing was probably a setup. She has the encryption key. They can't unlock her ship. She's leverage," Doug continues, his mind clear, his focus sharp.

Doug slams a fist on the side of the table. "Why the fuck would they risk putting her out here on a death rock?!"

"I didn't think—"

"No. You didn't. And I didn't question it either. Fuck! I'm so fucking stupid!"

The silence that follows is thick. Rex stands in the corner, watching with measured caution.

Then Pranz takes a breath. His voice low. Steady. "I have an idea."

Doug glares. "Of course you do."

"It's not a good one," Pranz admits, cracking a small smile that doesn't quite reach his eyes. "But it'll reset our situation."

Doug folds his arms. "Reset. Meaning what, exactly? You get to keep playing spy? And I get dragged behind you as the expendable one? Right into a fucking cage?"

"You're not expendable," Pranz says.

Doug stares him down.

"Just... trust me, Doug. I won't screw this up again."

Chapter 33

"Hey, assholes!" Pranz yells as he strolls out from the hidden compartment, voice sharp and casual like he's greeting friends at a bar instead of armed prison guards.

The effect is immediate. Every guard within earshot turns, blinking in disbelief. A few of them straighten like they can't quite believe what they're hearing. A partially dressed guard—jacket off, weapons missing—sauntering straight into their territory like he owns the place.

Pranz doesn't flinch. He walks slowly, hands swinging loosely at his sides, breathing in the acrid recycled air like it's fresh spring breeze. If confidence had a form, it was this.

The guards hesitate, unsure if they're about to witness a meltdown, a joke, or an ambush. Two of them start walking forward cautiously.

Then the HUDs in their helmets flash. Red. Blinking.

Critical Alert: *Unauthorized Presence – Jason Fornokey*

Status: *Compromised Identity / Impersonating Guard – Detain Primary Immediately*

Additional companion also dressed as a guard, last seen with Primary

"Where is your companion?" one of the guards demands, his voice clipped and aggressive.

Pranz doesn't stop. Doesn't even slow. "She's back home. Probably worried sick about me," he replies with a smirk.

"The other guard, smartass. The one who was with you."

"Oh. Him?" Pranz shrugs dramatically. "Floated away. Gone to the big black nothing. Sad, really. I'll miss his quiet charm."

The guards fan out now, weapons lowered but hands itching toward them. They surround Pranz within a meter, tension thick in the air.

"You're to be taken into custody," one of them barks.

"Yeah, yeah. But I'm already turning myself in, right? Why complicate it with cuffs and drama?" Pranz winks. "Besides, I doubt daddy dearest would be thrilled if you zip-tied or cuffed his son like a street rat."

No one moves. The guards exchange a quick glance. Pranz can see the uncertainty flicker in their posture.

He smiles wider and points past them toward the corridor. "I'm assuming the VIP escort is that way?"

And without waiting, he casually strolls past them. The guards hesitate, then fall in behind him like confused bodyguards.

They pass through multiple checkpoints—processing bays, surveillance junctions, the claustrophobic back corridors that stink of coolant and sweat—until they reach the primary security terminal near the launch hangar. The staging area for guard transport and supply transfers.

Pranz walks straight to the waiting bench and plops himself down like he's waiting for a shuttle to brunch. He throws his arms over the backrests, one boot sliding up to rest on the opposite knee.

Half a dozen guards linger nearby, forming a nervous perimeter around him.

None of them speak.

Pranz leans back, scanning the ceiling lazily. "So, how long until that ride gets here? I'm famished."

Silence. The guards refusing to speak.

"Okay. Cool. Strong silent types," Pranz says with a grin. "I like that."

He leans his head back, closes his eyes like he hasn't a care in the world, and lets his voice drift like a lullaby.

"Wake me when my chariot arrives. I could use a nap."

And just like that, Jason Pranz, son of the galaxy's most powerful corporate tyrant, lays back in a prison mining facility surrounded by armed guards—and dares the universe to make the next move.

As Pranz is hauled away, Doug shuffles to the nearest airlock. The best suit the miners could patch together will keep him alive just long enough to traverse the asteroid. The helmet seals with a hiss, HUD flickering online with a low oxygen warning already flashing in red. He steadies his breath—slow and controlled. No room for panic now.

He cycles the lock and steps into the void.

The asteroid's surface greets him with the familiar crunch of regolith beneath his boots. Crunch Rock lives up to its name—jagged ridges and fractured ground stretching in all directions. Every step is a gamble, each foothold uncertain.

The stars spin silently above, cruelly indifferent to the life-and-death game being played out in their shadows.

Doug keeps low, ducking behind outcroppings of rock and old mining equipment left to decay in vacuum. His mind spins with one thought: *Get to the dock and wait, just like Pranz told me to do.*

Chunks of twisted metal, old conveyor lines, and mining towers mark his path like ghosts of industry. Occasionally, the HUD picks up movement far in the distance—workers, guards, even heavy machines. But out here, the silence is deafening.

Midway across, Doug stumbles. A rock gives out beneath him, and he crashes to his knees. He grunts in pain—a rock is impaled into his leg, piercing the suit.

Doug stifles a scream. Air he can't afford to use. His instinct is to pull the rock, but it's acting as a seal for the freshly made hole.

"C'mon," he mutters to himself through gritted teeth. "No dying out here. Not yet."

He presses on, sweat forming inside the helmet despite the cold. His thoughts drift to Clutch. The low gravity making it easy to move despite the pain of the rock in his knee.

Finally, the shadow of the dock looms ahead—no ship yet. But Pranz expects that to change at any minute.

I've got to get there before a ship arrives.

Doug ducks behind a set of docking fuel tanks, slipping between narrow gaps, avoiding windows, until he's nestled in the crook of a support girder. From here, he can see the ship's arrival.

He crouches in silence, watching. Waiting. Every breath now counts. Every second brings him closer to death.

Come on ship! Faster!

"Get up," a gravel-laced voice growls—just before Gabe Fornokey kicks Pranz's leg off his knee.

Pranz blinks slowly, stretching like he'd just awoken from a catnap under the sun, not surrounded by armed guards in a mining colony turned prison. "Wow. Feels like prep school all over again. You're really committed to the full nostalgic experience, huh?" He looks up with a smirk. "Didn't expect to see you here. And isn't it a little beneath your brand to arrive on a public transport?"

"Get. Up." Gabe's voice lowers to a lethal whisper. Each syllable tight as a wire. Rage simmering just below the surface.

Before Pranz can move, Ted steps forward and clamps a hand on the back of his neck, yanking him to his feet with practiced force.

"You all get back to your stations!" Gabe snaps, eyes flaring at the guards in the hangar. "I'm not paying you to just stand around."

One of the guards mutters, "Pretty sure that is exactly what he pays us to do." The other tries not to laugh.

"What did you two say?" Gabe hisses, narrowing his eyes at the pair.

"Nothing sir!" they blurt out in unison and immediately scatter like roaches.

Gabe marches behind Ted, who shoves Pranz into the corridor and up into the family cruiser—a gleaming, knife-shaped vessel docked with arrogant precision. No insignias needed. Everyone already knows who it belongs to.

Inside, Pranz steadies himself and brushes off his shirt. "Didn't know you let civilian ships dock here," he says, tossing the comment over his shoulder.

"You don't know anything," Gabe says coldly as the transfer door hisses shut and the ship undocks.

"Like using your fucking implant to get here," he adds.

"Whatever," Pranz replies, crossing his arm.

Gabe wheels around. "What the fuck are you doing at this station?"

Pranz raises his chin. "Funny, I was about to ask you the same thing."

"Don't test me, boy." Gabe steps in close, nose to nose. "Why. Are. You. Here?"

Pranz stares him down. "Fuck you."

The slap comes fast and brutal. Gabe's backhand snaps Pranz's face sideways.

He staggers slightly but doesn't fall. Blood touches the corner of his mouth. He meets his father's gaze—eyes wet, jaw clenched, silent.

"Why are you here?" Gabe asks again, looking at the back of his hand for any damage.

"Where is she?" Pranz finally asks, voice low and tight. "Clutch. Where is she?"

Gabe narrows his eyes. "Why do you care?"

"None of your business."

"You made it my business," Gabe barks. "You used your emergency beacon. You told me about a supposedly 'massive alien discovery,' and that the key to that information was on that stupid little ship. Which you stole! So, yes. It is my business. You dragged me into this."

"I told you the truth. I told you about the discovery. You're the one who responded by arresting the people who found it." Pranz glares. "We were going to file the salvage claim with the—"

"With the Salvage Claims Office?" Gabe cuts in with a sneer. "You mean the one I own? Every high-interest claim gets rerouted. We backdate a false prior claim and strip the rights. Standard procedure."

Pranz stares at him, stunned by how casual the admission is. "You're even more corrupt than I thought."

Another backhand. Pranz's face snaps sideways again.

"Where's the ship?" Gabe demands, voice lowering now. Icy.

"I don't know. You took it, remember?"

Gabe turns away, pacing. His tone shifts to something almost clinical. "We've perfected interrogation, you know.

Non-invasive, permanent damage minimized, memory extraction optimized. Cost-efficient, too. But still… unpleasant."

He stops pacing and faces his son. "I don't want to use it on you. But the information you have? It's worth more than your life. That's the calculus. Don't make me choose."

Pranz's hands tremble, but he keeps them at his sides. He finally replies with his own calm and disappointed voice, "Fuck you."

Gabe exhales. "I'd rather you be by my side, expanding this empire. You're my son. I'm building a legacy for you. It doesn't have to end with me interrogating you. Just tell me what you know."

Pranz doesn't flinch and speaks each word slowly and firmly. "Fuck. You."

A beat of silence. Gabe's jaw tightens.

"You know, we tried those same techniques on the iron ant. She didn't break. Any idea why?" Gabe asks casually, as if he's talking about a faulty appliance.

Something in Pranz shatters.

"Fuck. You!" he yells and spins away.

"Don't you fucking turn your back on me!" Gabe lunges, fist raised—

But he never lands the blow.

A searing zzzzap fills the room. Gabe jerks violently and collapses mid-stride, twitching.

Doug stands above him, holding a laser prod pressed into Gabe's ribs, his chest heaving.

"Dude!" Pranz shouts, keeping his voice low. "You weren't supposed to come out! No matter what!"

"Couldn't listen to that monster spew another word," Doug says, disgust curling his face.

"Give me that. Go! Hide before Ted comes back!"

Doug hands over the prod and scrambles back toward the hatch he'd crawled through earlier—one of Pranz's childhood hiding spots deep in the ship's structure. Disguised as a guard, Doug had snuck aboard in the chaos of the extraction, hiding until the time was right—or until everything went to hell.

Pranz stands over his father's stunned body, the prod humming in his hand.

"You're a shitty parent," Pranz says, and jabs Gabe again.

Zzzap.

"You're a fucking parasite." Another jab.

Zzzap.

"You're too scared of being small to realize no one gives a shit about your fucking empire!" Pranz lifts the prod above his head like a club.

But the strike never lands.

Ted tackles him mid-swing, driving Pranz to the floor. The prod skitters away.

"Don't be stupid," Ted growls, pinning Pranz's arms behind his back. In one fluid move, he secures them with restraints and drags him upright.

"Your father's going to kill you for that," Ted says grimly. "If you're lucky, he'll do it fast."

"Okay lapdog," Pranz mutters, breathless, taking an obvious jab at Ted.

Ted just shakes his head as he walks Pranz out of the room.

Chapter 34

"You've always wanted to be treated like a man. Like an equal. So why are you complaining now?" Gabe's voice slithers through the sterile room, calm, deliberate, poisonous.

Pranz thrashes in his restraints as they tighten around his arms and legs, locking him into the vertical interrogation table. Sleek, steel arms descend from the ceiling with gentle menace—calibrating, scanning, preparing.

"Let me go!" Pranz shouts, his voice raw with panic. "I don't know anything!"

"Everyone always says that," Gabe says, circling him like a predator.

"You know, you're being a really shitty father," Pranz snaps, venom behind every syllable.

"I'm building a legacy for you, Jason. For us. And you're throwing it away like it's some meaningless inheritance." Gabe's voice softens, a façade of parental concern undercut by the cold calculation in his eyes.

"Because your legacy is built on fucking slavery! Lies, blood, and manipulation!" Pranz shouts. His voice cracks—not from fear, but rage. "You exploit people. You ruin lives. You crush them. I don't want to be a part of that. I hate being your son."

Gabe pauses mid-step. For a moment, there's silence in the room—just the quiet hum of machines and the tightening of automated clamps around Pranz's body.

"You'll see it differently one day," Gabe says with eerie calm. "When you're older. Wiser. When you're not so... naive."

"No. I won't," Pranz spits. "You're not doing this for me. You never were. This is all about you. Your image. Your hunger to matter in the universe."

Gabe turns to one of the techs. "Is the neural map sync ready?"

The technician nods once. "Yes, sir. We'll begin the procedure on your command."

Gabe steps closer to his son—face to face now. "Then let's see what you really know. Maybe something useful is buried under all that self-righteous nonsense. And Jason..." He leans in just enough for only Pranz to hear, "...I swear to every stockholder in this empire, if you've wasted my time again, it won't be this machine that breaks you."

Pranz lifts his head slowly. His hair matted. His jaw clenched.

"Fuck. You," he whispers—eyes blazing, unbroken.

Gabe stares into those eyes for a long, measured beat. Then turns away, expression unreadable.

"Start the procedure," Gabe orders, nodding to one of the techs.

Pranz, strapped to the sleek interrogation table, breathes hard through gritted teeth. "I'm not going... to tell... you... anythi—"

"He's under," a technician confirms. The monitors flash into stable sync, waves calming as Pranz's body slackens.

Gabe steps forward, his voice calm but cold. "Jason Pranz, where is Doug?"

Pranz's head droops. His breathing, slow and steady.

"Unknown."

Gabe's lip twitches. "Where did you last see him?"

"In an area."

Gabe's eyes narrow. "What kind of area?"

"An area where someone can hide."

"Be more specific."

"On a ship."

"Which ship?" Gabe snaps, voice rising.

"Multiple ships."

"That doesn't make sense," Gabe growls, turning to the techs. "What is this? Why isn't the procedure working?"

"He's showing the same signs we saw with the iron ant," one tech says nervously. "He's under... but there's interference. Disassociation. Like there's another layer blocking direct access."

"Jason," Gabe says, his tone shifting—probing, wary. "What did she do to you?"

"She?"

"The iron ant."

"You found me with many iron ants."

Gabe's patience cracks. "The on you call Clutch. The one you tried to protect. The one with the encryption! What did she do to you?"

"She did what you never could," Pranz murmurs, eyes still closed. "She gave a fuck."

His eyes snap open—and he winks.

"You little shit," Gabe snarls, lunging forward. "Tell me!"

He grabs Pranz by the collar, dragging him forward against the restraints.

"Fuck you," Pranz whispers, calm now, the fight building in his body.

"This is going nowhere," Gabe huffs. "Release the restraints."

The techs hesitate. Gabe glares.

"Now."

They begin the release process. One by one, the clamps release. Pranz remains still—until the last one comes free.

In a blink, he lunges. He grabs Gabe by the neck from behind and pivots, slamming him against the interrogation table. Gabe gasps, his hands clawing at Pranz's arms.

"Didn't take you for someone with strength, you spineless asshole!" Pranz roars, tightening his grip.

"You've... never seen... what I can do," Gabe chokes out.

Gabe thrashes violently, smashing Pranz into the wall. Pain ripples down Pranz's spine, but he doesn't loosen his hold. Not this time.

The techs back away, frozen—caught between fear and fascination.

"It's your turn for interrogation, daddy," Pranz snarls, dragging Gabe toward the table.

"Not gonna... happen," Gabe gasps, pushing the both of them into a control screen.

"You'll talk just like you wanted me to," Pranz growls, slamming Gabe into the table again. "This is justice."

Gabe fights, bucking wildly, slamming Pranz into the edge of the console. Pranz sees stars, but holds on. Gabe's resistance falters. His strength fades.

With one final grunt, Gabe collapses into unconsciousness, and they both crash to the floor.

The techs move forward, but Pranz grabs a sidearm from Gabe's coat—one he knows his father always carries. He levels it at the techs.

"His turn. Strap him in. Now."

The techs freeze.

"Now!" Pranz barks.

Hands shaking, they lift Gabe onto the table and secure the restraints. The same ones Pranz just escaped.

"Put him under," Pranz orders. "Make him talk."

They begin the sequence.

"He's ready," the lead tech says, nervously stepping back.

Pranz approaches. Calm. Focused. Triumphant.

"Gabe Fornokey," he begins. "Who am I?"

"Jason Pranz," Gabe replies flatly. "My first born."

Pranz tilts his head. "Only son, right?"

"No. There are others."

Pranz's jaw tightens. "How many?"

"Unknown. Every few months I receive confirmation of another."

Pranz's lip curls in disgust. "How many women have you—actually, forget it. I don't want to know."

He glances at the wide-eyed techs, rolls his eyes, and says, "Learn something new every day."

The techs look at each other, letting smiles form, their nervousness turning to curiosity.

"Where is Clutch?" he asks, the real question.

"In restricted R&D."

"Where in R&D?"

"Holding cell."

"There are holding cells in R&D?" Pranz asks, eyes narrowing.

"Yes."

"How do I access them?"

"There's a hidden panel, left of the entrance. Before you enter the main chamber."

"Who is in charge there?"

"Walter Ter."

Pranz nods slowly. "What are you trying to get from her?"

"Her resistance to interrogation. Her encryption key. The location of the alien tech. And how she escaped the first time."

Pranz exhales. "Well, father... none of that is your concern anymore."

He turns to the techs, his expression shifting from vengeful to almost playful.

"How long can you keep him under?" he asks. "And... any questions you want to ask?"

The techs exchange looks—smirks beginning to bloom.

Chapter 35

"Doug," Pranz whispers, crouching near the hidden compartment, eyes still adjusting to the dim light. "You alive in there?"

"About time," Doug mutters with a groggy sigh, followed by a yawn that sounds like it came from his soul. "Was starting to think you forgot me."

"We have to move. Now," Pranz says, backing away to give Doug room. "My father's otherwise engaged—and by that, I mean strapped down and drugged up. It won't last forever."

Doug crawls out, blinking hard as he stretches. Pranz hands him a fresh uniform—sleek, black with subtle metallic trims. High-ranking corporate issue.

Doug squints at it. "This better not mean I'm the new regional manager."

"No more asteroid grunt disguises. It's time to upgrade," Pranz says, already turning away to change himself.

Too tired to joke, Doug just starts pulling the clothes on. "What took so long?" he mumbles, between yawns.

"My dad decided to play the good ol' mind-shatter game," Pranz replies, strapping on his boots. "Interrogation rig. Full sequence. Didn't work. Not on me. Same with Clutch. The nanos... the ones she modified... I think they disrupt the standard mind-mapping techniques. Seriously, she is sitting on a gold mine."

Doug pauses, hands frozen mid-zip. "Shit. That's… that's really messed up."

"You're telling me," Pranz says, shaking his head. "He thought he could break me like he breaks everyone else."

"You okay?"

"I'll process it later. For now, we move." He stands, fully geared. "Ready?"

"Since I have no idea what we're walking into, not even a little," Doug says, offering a tired, crooked grin. "But lead on, Mr. man who always has a plan."

They step off the ship and into the corridor, the station lights bathing them in sterile blue. Doug winces at the brightness.

"I'm shocked you still have access after all that," Doug says.

"I was giving it some thought. How my father found me. He said that I used my imprint. I remember that your imprint didn't register quickly, and we had to stall. It makes no sense that mine would have registered so much faster than yours. I'm guessing my normal imprint let me through and that sent a flag to Fornokey letting them know where I was," Pranz shares. "And now the military grade super imprint I have is allowing me all of the access I need."

"Seems logical," Doug says, nodding his head along to Pranz's theory.

Pranz smirks. "And as a backup, let's just say the facilities department isn't exactly loyal to my father. I've been bribing them with fine liquor, crash seat upgrades, and exclusive access to best clubs. In return, they gave me a box of full-access temp chips—untraceable unless someone catches you in the act."

"Wow. That's... terrifyingly useful."

"Right? Surveillance can still catch us using one, but by the time they respond, we'll be long gone. I rotate through the chips constantly—always keep extras. I just have to keep my imprint away from the scanner when I use one."

Doug yawns again, long and hard.

"Seriously, man," Pranz says, giving him a look. "You gotta wake up. You're the only guy I know who could sleep through a revolution."

Doug adjusts the new uniform and pats down his pockets. "Give me ten minutes and a cup of Kaf-X sludge, and I'll be ready to storm hell with you."

Pranz smiles faintly. "Good. Because we might be doing exactly that."

He taps his cuff, seemingly checking the route.

"Let's go," he says, looking up with a content look on his face.

They move briskly through the sterile halls of the station toward R&D. The deeper they go, the thicker the tension in the air. Uniformed guards become more frequent—posted at corners, along corridors, outside labs—arms folded, gazes cold. Most don't react beyond a flicker of eye contact, but Doug can feel the weight of their stares trailing behind them like smoke.

Pranz walks with the practiced confidence of someone who's used to being invisible in plain sight.

When they reach the R&D main entrance, Pranz swipes one of his temporary, all-access chips and the door slides open with a clean hiss. They step through—and instead of continuing forward, Pranz veers sharply left.

Doug stops mid-stride, confusion tightening his brows. "What—"

Pranz just winks and gestures for silence. He stands by a seemingly blank wall, hidden by support beams, running his fingers over the paneling like he's looking for a loose tile in a puzzle box. He waves a chip in lazy arcs, presses seams, tugs gently on edges, until, finally, a faint click echoes behind the wall, and a narrow seam splits open.

The hidden door slides away, revealing a corridor wrapped in deep shadows and sealed silence.

Pranz smirks, steps inside, and jerks his thumb for Doug to follow. "VIP tour."

Doug enters, still frowning. The door seals behind them, shutting out the lights and sounds of the main hallway.

"How the fuck do you know about this place?" Doug asks, keeping his voice low.

"I told you. My father is tied up right now."

Doug squints. "Wait—literally?"

"Yeah. Interrogated him myself." Pranz grins like he's talking about winning a board game. "That's how I found her."

Doug whistles. "Remind me not to piss you off."

They continue through the hidden corridor. Long, narrow, and lined with thick security doors on the right. Each door has a recessed panel glowing faintly—displays of status readouts and containment logs.

One door flashes a pulsing BIOHAZARD warning. Another reads SUBJECT: DECEASED in stark red text. Several are blank. A few display cryptic strings of data and numeric tags.

They stop at one door labeled:

SUBJECT 37B – EXTREMELY DANGEROUS

Pranz tilts his head. "Clutch?"

Doug raises a brow. "You think she got that kind of reputation already?"

Pranz shrugs and steps up to the control panel. He taps through the interface, flipping through logs and surveillance views. A live video feed reveals a man inside—bald, muscular, his face scarred with precision, like someone practiced surgery with a knife. His eyes don't blink. At the bottom of the screen:

Options: Terminate | Sedate | Paralyze | Observe

"Not Clutch," Pranz mutters. "Let's keep moving before he decides to blink at us and the building catches fire."

They pass more doors, glancing at each display screen. More empty rooms. More sedated subjects, and worse, rooms occupied by things not fully human anymore.

A voice slices through the hallway.

"Can I help you?"

"And you are?" Pranz asks without turning, looking at the next display panel.

"There are only three of us cleared for this sector," the man replies slowly. "And I don't recognize either of you."

"You must be Walter Ter," Pranz says without looking up.

Walter's eyes narrow. "I am. And who the hell are you?"

"That's above your paygrade."

"There's no such—"

"Is Gabe Fornokey above your paygrade?"

Walter hesitates. "Of course."

"Then it's very much a thing," Pranz says casually, swiping through the display. He finds the right cell and snaps his fingers in satisfaction.

Walter stiffens. "You can't be here for that subject. No one's supposed to know she's here."

"And yet," Pranz replies smoothly, finally look up to meet Walter's eyes, "I do. Why don't you tell me what you've been doing to her, Walter?"

Walter falters. "I only answer to one man. You're not him."

Doug steps forward and draws his weapon. Cool, practiced, unshaking. He levels it at Walter's chest.

"Don't do anything stupid," Doug says, voice low and cold. "Unless you want to bunk with subject 37B."

Walter's face drains of color. His tablet clatters to the floor. Slowly, he raises both hands.

"Open it," Doug says to Pranz, and then makes a demand. "Walter, get over here."

Pranz opens the door, Walter steps closer.

"Clutch, you okay?" Doug shouts the second the heavy door hisses open, keeping his eyes on Walter.

"Took ya long 'nough," Clutch replies as she steps into the light, her voice rough but steady, her hair back to its normal color, her posture rigid with exhaustion and defiance.

"Walter—inside," Doug orders, gesturing to the now-empty cell. "Jacket off."

Walter hesitates for only a second before shrugging off his coat. It drops to the floor with a soft thud, and he walks into the cell, face pale. Pranz swings the door shut and slaps the lock.

Doug hands the coat to Clutch. "Put this on. We're not clear yet."

Clutch slides it over her shoulders, wincing as it brushes against fresh bruises. "Ya diff'rent, Doug."

"Different how?" Doug asks, his voice cracking into a smile despite himself. Her eyes land on his, and something unspoken passes between them.

"Ya more conf'dent er sometin'," she mutters, gaze lingering a second longer before shifting away.

"Let's flirt with each other later," Pranz says as he walks by with a smile. "We have to escape before we can't."

Doug chuckles, embarrassed, and looks down, suddenly fascinated with the floor tiles.

They retrace their path through the shadowy corridor toward the hidden door—but Clutch mutters, "Dis place ain't right. Yer dad's a mons'er."

"Tell me something I don't know," Pranz says bitterly. "Tried to interrogate me earlier. Those nanos you made? Think they blocked it. They couldn't pull a thing from my head."

"And he calls his own kid names," Doug adds. "I zapped him with a prod on his own ship." He says it with a bit too much pride.

Clutch raises an eyebrow, a grin twitching at the corner of her mouth. "Ya been busy."

"We looked everywhere for you," Doug says, suddenly serious. "Crunch Rock. I almost died."

The name hits Clutch like a slap. Her shoulders stiffen.

"You have family there?" Pranz asks gently.

Clutch lowers her eyes. "Dey all my fam'ly. We gotta go back. Gotta free 'em."

Nobody replies as they continue down the hall in silence.

They stop in front of the hidden door. A digital display on the wall flickers to life, showing the corridor outside. Guards. At least six of them. Armed. Waiting. All looking in different directions.

"Fuck," Pranz mutters. "He's awake. He knows we're here."

"Is there another way out?" Doug asks, scanning the walls for seams or panels.

"Shoot our way out?" Pranz offers half-heartedly.

"Dat ain't gonna work," Clutch says, spinning on her heels and heading back the way they came.

They follow her through the long corridor again, past locked doors and flickering hazard signs. The silence grows heavier with each step, broken only by the occasional hum of machines behind walls.

"Whatcha dad do wit all dis?" Clutch asks, voice quieter than usual.

"I don't know," Pranz says, his eyes flicking to each door. "The more I uncover, the less I understand. But whatever it is—he'll do anything to keep it going. Anything. I'd bet he's got half the Senate locked up back here just for fun."

"If I get another shot with that prod," Doug growls, "I'll turn it up to lethal and let it ride."

Pranz gives Doug a look as they keep moving. One that can't be placed. Partially impressed, horrified, grateful, and sad all at the same time.

Eventually, they reach the end of the hall. A dead end. Just a blank wall.

"Shit," Doug mutters.

Without hesitation, Clutch turns and walks back to her old cell. The door hisses open.

"Can't get out?" Walter asks with a smirk, already halfway sitting up on the bench.

Clutch doesn't respond. "Where's da back door?"

Walter shrugs. "Why should I tell you?"

"Because if you don't," Pranz says, "we'll open the door to 37B down the hall and tell him you're the reason he was locked up."

Walter's expression goes slack. "That won't end well for any of us."

"Then just tell us where the other exit is," Doug says.

Walter lays back and stares at the ceiling. "If you do open that door... just make sure mine is locked."

Pranz steps forward. "So you're choosing to be a problem?"

"Pretty much," Walter says flatly.

Clutch doesn't waste a second. She grabs Pranz's pistol and fires at the door hinges. The blast echoes, and the door groans as it buckles. She hauls it aside and leans it against the wall like discarded furniture.

"Now ya gonna be da firs' he fine," she says with satisfaction, turning toward the hallway.

Walter bolts upright. "What are you—don't open that door!"

Pranz intercepts him and delivers a brutal punch to the gut. Walter collapses against the floor, choking for breath.

The trio marches back to the door marked EXTREMELY DANGEROUS. Clutch brings up the interface and scans quickly for surveillance feeds. The screen blinks and shows a live feed of the restrained subject—male, eyes like daggers, muscles twitching even under the tension of high-grade restraints. Gagged. Restrained at every limb. Still dangerous.

"He lookin' bored," Clutch says, examining the controls.

"Don't," Walter rasps from the hallway, still crawling on the ground.

Doug glances back. "You had your chance, Walter."

Clutch's finger hovers over the release. Her eyes flick toward the others.

"Ready?" she asks, a glint of mischief—or madness—in her eye.

Pranz gulps. Doug nods once.

Clutch presses the button. The door hisses open.

Clutch steps into the room first, her boots echoing softly against the reinforced floor. The man on the wall towers over her, nearly seven feet tall even while restrained. His arms are thicker than her torso, muscles bulging against the bindings like they're barely holding.

She doesn't hesitate. She meets his gaze—cold, calculating, and burning with a buried rage—and removes his gag with a slow, deliberate motion.

"Why's ya in here?" she asks, eyes narrowing as she studies him.

He doesn't answer. Just licks his cracked lips, savoring the freedom from the gag.

Clutch tilts her head. "If'n we letch ya down… ya help us 'scape?"

Still no reply—only a flash of emotion behind those hard eyes. Confusion, then anger. His gaze drops from Clutch to the ground, then slowly rises again. Not at her. Not at Doug.

To Walter.

Doug, watching from the doorway, takes a cautious step forward. "She's asking if you'll help us escape."

The man's eyes lock on Doug momentarily—nothing there but contempt—then shift back to Walter. Fury blooms, wild and hungry. He begins to thrash in his restraints, the full force of his strength causing the reinforced bands to groan.

"You wanna kill him?" Clutch asks, a small grin tugging at her lips.

"Yes," the man growls. His voice is so deep it seems to vibrate in the air—a low, guttural thunder that doesn't belong in a human throat.

"There's more where he came from," Doug adds, eyes darting to the display outside the door. "Guards. Fully armed."

The man doesn't care. He only has eyes for Walter.

Walter squirms in Pranz's grip. "You don't know what he is! You don't know what he'll do! If you let him go—"

"We're counting on it," Pranz replies, shoving Walter another step forward, closer to the beast.

"We need answers, Walter. A way out. Or he gets to play," Doug says coldly.

"You don't understand," Walter pleads. "We're studying him. He's not stable. He's not controllable!"

"Neither is your mouth. Let's fix that," Pranz says, glancing at Clutch. "Cut him loose."

Walter continues to protest, words becoming background noise as there is no stopping this trio now.

Doug backs away toward the door, holding it open. Clutch steps toward the man to remove the restraints. She starts with the leg restraints. Then the chest and head. The man never taking his eyes off Walter.

"Don't do it!" Walter screams one last time.

The left arm restraint removed. The final one she hesitates on—the right arm.

"Wan' me ta git yer udder arm 'fore ya kill 'em?" Clutch asks, more amused than concerned.

The man answers by wrenching free on his own. With a guttural roar, he tears through the final restraint, the sound of snapping metal like a thunderclap. Clutch darts backward and meets Doug by the door, clear of the blast zone.

Pranz doesn't waste the moment—he shoves Walter straight into the monster's waiting hands and retreats just as fast.

What follows is pure violence.

The man lifts Walter by the shoulders like a doll. Walter screams, but it's cut short by the sickening snap of bones. Shoulders, then ribs. One by one. Each pop louder than the last as the man squeezes Walter's body with surprising ease.

Then he hurls Walter into the air.

Before Walter hits the ground, the man catches him midair—grabbing both arms—and pulls. One arm detaches completely with a wet rip. Walter's limp body swings in a horrific arc, flung like a ragdoll through the air, blood misting in every direction.

Doug flinches. Pranz winces. Clutch just watches.

The man steps forward, drags Walter's nearly lifeless body close again, and grabs his head—one hand at the base of the skull, the other on his upper spine. He pulls. There's a crack, a snap, and then the head comes free. It all happens with terrifying grace.

With a final motion, he slams Walter's head into the wall. It explodes like an overripe tomato—flesh, bone, and brain matter splattering across the smooth white surface.

He turns, blood dripping from his massive hands.

Clutch stands waiting at the door, unshaken. "Ya good. Wanna git more of 'em?"

The man says nothing, just steps forward, past the threshold, and follows Clutch as she guides him to the exit.

Pranz and Doug remain frozen.

The man doesn't even glance at them.

Clutch leads him to the exit panel. She taps the display and peers outside. A cluster of guards, now more than a dozen. Laser prods in hand. Bored expressions. No sign they know what's coming.

"Dey's out der," Clutch says calmly, stepping aside. "Ready?"

A pause. Then, "Yes," the voice says behind her—closer now, colder, more terrifying than ever.

She opens the door.

The man walks out like death appearing from the ether.

Guards look up in confusion. They weren't expecting resistance. Weren't expecting a monster. They raise their weapons—but too late.

The man barrels into the nearest one and launches him across the hall like a bag of bones. He grabs another by the leg and swings him into a third, shattering limbs like twigs. Feet smash down on skulls. Fists crush chests. Screams echo, then die.

Laser prods crackle and jab—but they're useless. The man doesn't flinch. Doesn't stop. He tears through the guards like they're made of paper and rage fuels his every step.

Clutch calmly closes the door behind him.

She watches the display screen.

Doug and Pranz approach, the sounds of carnage muted behind the sealed door. On the screen, another guard's body flies across the frame. Another gets stomped into red paste until finally the screen goes dark with a deep reddish hue that obscures the feed.

"Ya'll ready?" Clutch asks, a smirk creeping across her lips. "Dey's gonna be busy fer a while."

Doug and Pranz exchange a glance. Then they look at Clutch.

And they all smile.

Chapter 36

The three companions move through the winding halls of the station, undisturbed. Panic travels in the opposite direction—Fornokey guards, station security, and thrill-starved mercs all rush past in loud, chaotic waves, pulled toward the distant screams and splatters of the monster they released. Every step of their escape is bought in blood, and they don't waste it.

Their stolen engineering uniforms—complete with full-face helmets and reflective visors—make them ghosts. Anonymous. Unseen. Perfect.

"We need a ship," Doug says, his voice low. "One they can't track."

"That's the problem," Pranz replies, navigating confidently through the corridors. "If it belongs to Fornokey, it's tagged. Every. Single. One."

Another squad barrels past, shouting half-formed orders and warnings into their comms.

"Let's go to Fun Town," Pranz says suddenly, pivoting at an intersecting hallway. "After a quick stop at my hideout."

"Fun Town sounds fun," Doug says.

Pranz and Clutch both stop.

Their visors turn toward him.

Doug senses the stare even through the opaque helmets. "...Oh. It's that kind of place." He realizes that there is nothing fun about Fun Town. "Stupid name for it then."

Clutch and Pranz turn and start walking again, content that Doug knows what he is walking into.

"At least we'll be ready," Doug says, nodding toward Pranz. "Wait 'til you see his hideout."

"I ain't un ta be 'pressed by much," Clutch says, her tone skeptical.

"Yeah, well... you'll see. It's—"

"Ritchy?" Clutch cuts him off, clearly looking toward Pranz.

Pranz grins behind his visor. "Yes, I use my father's fortune to fund my own little enterprises. And one day, it'll be his undoing. That's the poetry of it."

They continue in silence, tension rising with each step. The echoes of distant combat gradually fade behind them. The deeper they go, the fewer people there are. By the time they reach Pranz's hideout, it's as if the rest of the station doesn't exist.

As before, a panel slides open with a soft mechanical whisper. Inside: everything a rich kid with unlimited access might keep for future use. Racks of worthless things all the way to weapons nobody has ever seen or have been banned.

Clutch is through the door first. She doesn't speak. Doesn't gawk.

She removes her helmet, shrugs off the uniform, and gets to work like she owns the place.

Doug watches, expecting a moment of awe. Instead, Clutch begins dismantling and reassembling items on a workbench like a machine. Her fingers blur with purpose, already creating custom weapons, modded devices, and hybrid tools from parts Doug doesn't even recognize.

Pranz, already stripping down to swap uniforms, glances at Doug. "Doug!" he calls, voice too loud. "Stop staring at your girlfriend and get changed!"

Doug turns bright red and ducks behind a shelving unit stacked with grenades and fuel cells.

Clutch watches the moment play out in her periphery. She doesn't speak until Pranz gets closer, her eyebrow arches slightly. "Why ya keep sayin' dat?" she asks, not looking up.

"Because he likes you," Pranz says, grinning as he tightens a bandolier across his chest. "Like, likes you. But he doesn't have the stones to say anything. So I'm giving him a little… boost."

Clutch glances over toward the shelf. Doug is fumbling with his shirt, clearly trying to disappear behind a food rack. She stares for a moment, something unreadable in her eyes, and then turns back to her inventions.

They spend the next half hour preparing. Armor layered. Weapons charged. Tools tested. Every pocket filled with intent.

Pranz tightens the last strap on his vest and nods. "Time for Fun Town."

Clutch tosses them each a small object—a matte black ring with a subtle shimmer.

"Here, put dees on," Clutch says, handing rings to Pranz and Doug.

"Proposing to Doug already?" Pranz jests.

Doug smacks Pranz with the back of his hand.

"Dees is signals. Like a count ta three. Ya'ill feel it 'n know when ta act," Clutch replies.

"Bummer dude, I thought she was ready to settle down with you," Pranz says to Doug, a smile forming on his face like he is the funniest guy around while Doug's face just turns red again.

A moment of silence passes as they all look at the rings, now securely on their fingers, then they all laugh—quietly, but it's real. For a moment, despite everything, they're just people. On the edge of rebellion, of survival, of something bigger than themselves, bigger than humanity itself.

Without another word, they slip from the hidden compartment and ease into the main corridor of the station. It's quieter now—eerily so. No alarms. No screams. Only the distant hum of systems returning to idle and the metallic scent of scorched electronics lingering in the air.

They approach the sealed Fornokey section—thick slabs of reinforced alloy, now locked tight with glowing red panels on either side. No one in. No one out.

Doug glances at the doors, then at the emptiness around them. "Hopefully that... thing has been dealt with. Or at least it's not still breaking necks."

Pranz doesn't look away. "He could burn this entire station to the ground and grind the Fornokey logo into ash, and I'd sleep better at night."

They continue past the area, headed for Fun Town, when a voice slaps them like a gunshot.

"What the fuck, Jason!?"

Gabe stands ten meters away, disheveled but breathing hard, Ted looming at his side like a wolf sniffing blood.

Pranz doesn't flinch. "You can't stop us. Not anymore. You've got bigger problems now—like surviving whatever that thing is."

Gabe glares. "I should put you down myself."

Clutch steps forward without hesitation, raising a strange, freshly built weapon in her hand, its needle-like ends crackling faintly. "Ya try 'n ya git put down."

Ted shifts slightly from behind Gabe, preparing for engagement, eyeing Clutch's device attempting to assess its level of danger.

Gabe's expression twists. "So this is who you side with now? A degenerate coward," he sneers, nodding toward Doug, "and a filthy iron ant?"

"No," Pranz says, his voice low but steady. "I side with people who give a shit. Who help. Who care. You wouldn't recognize that if it punched you in the face." A quiet thump pulses against Pranz's finger—the signal Clutch gave them. He doesn't react outwardly, but inside, something sharp awakens.

"I've given you everything!" Gabe snaps, taking a step forward. "And this is how you repay me? You ungrateful little fuck!"

Another thump from the device. Pranz clenches his jaw.

"You want to know what they get that I don't?" Pranz says, breathing heavy, voice cracking as another pulse hits his finger. "Love. Respect. Empathy. A father who didn't treat them like a fucking investment!"

Doug's jaw tightens. Clutch narrows her eyes. Gabe, for once, is at a loss.

The pulse on Pranz's finger quickens—like a countdown.

The moment shatters.

Clutch moves first. She sweeps her arm up and fires. Her custom-built weapon hisses as ten shimmering probes shoot outward, attaching to Ted's limbs, chest, and skull. He stiffens instantly, then collapses like a puppet whose strings were violently cut. His body convulses on the floor, eyes rolled back.

Doug jerks forward, pulling out the laser prod, ready to act.

But Pranz beats him to it.

Years of fury explode as Pranz lunges at his father. His fist slams into Gabe's jaw with a bone-jarring crack. Gabe reels, then snarls—but Pranz doesn't stop. Another punch to the gut. One to the side of the head. He grabs Gabe's jacket and drives his knee into his father's ribs.

"You never—cared—about—me!" he yells between each hit, each word a hammer.

Gabe stumbles, dazed, and crashes to the ground. His breath comes in short, shallow bursts, but he laughs through bloodied teeth.

Pranz stands over him, panting. His hands tremble. His foot twitches, half a second from kicking—but something holds him back.

Doug puts a hand on Pranz's arm. "He's not worth it. Let's go."

Clutch is already on the move, her eyes scanning every corridor ahead.

Pranz doesn't look down again. He doesn't need to. Gabe is smiling.

That same smug smirk.

"You'll be nothing without me," Gabe croaks.

Pranz hesitates, a mix of emotions coursing through him.

Then turns and bolts, racing after Clutch and Doug.

They disappear into the maze of the station—headed for the place with the worst misuse of a name imaginable.

Fun Town.

Chapter 37

"My father's not going to let us win," Pranz mutters as they walk, his voice laced with simmering bitterness. "He flat-out admitted he owns the Salvage Claims Office. Says they fix claims when something's valuable enough—just stamp them denied and take what they want."

"Den we go ta da news," Clutch says flatly, like it's the most obvious solution in the world.

Pranz chuckles, but there's no humor in it. "You think that'll work? He has friends in every outlet. Probably owns half the networks outright, or at least their executives. The man controls information like it's a ship's control system. Fuck. He has to just to keep the mines functioning."

Doug walks a few paces behind, eyebrows tight with thought. "What if we just bring the alien artifact back? I mean, put it out in the open. Drop it on someone's doorstep with the cameras already rolling. Kind of hard to fake a claim or bury a story when it's broadcasting live across half the system."

Pranz glances over his shoulder, interest flickering in his eyes. "It'd have to be timed perfectly. We'd need the right media crew. No execs involved. No middlemen. And we'd have to hope the military doesn't just nuke the thing..." Pranz interrupts himself. "We don't even know if it can move. Or how to move it. No. We need to bring a live feed to it."

"Ya need a rogue 'porter ta come den," Clutch says.

Pranz's demeanor changes instantly.

Doug smirks. "Judging by that smile, Pranz, I'm guessing you know the type of reporter we need."

Pranz's grin grows, crooked and guilty. "I do… but she's probably the last person who wants to see me again."

Clutch arches an eyebrow. "Ya fuc't 'er 'n lef' 'er?"

The group walks in silence for a beat. Pranz actually winces.

"Not quite. We were a thing. Real thing. I loved her. Helped her dig up a story that would've made her career." His voice softens. "But my father made it vanish. Burned every file, scrubbed every trace. She thought I helped him. She thought I chose him."

Shame ripples across Pranz's face like a shadow. Clutch's gaze softens for a moment. She pats him on the shoulder.

"Den she prolly real mot'vated ta help now. She may jus' not know it yet."

"I don't want her revenge pointed at me," Pranz mutters.

"Guys?" Doug says sharply, his voice cutting through the moment.

They look up. A half-circle of scavengers has formed around them—leathered armor, mismatched weapons, eyes twitching with opportunistic hunger.

"Looks like Fun Town's welcoming committee," Pranz mutters, his hands drifting toward the weapons on his hips.

Doug's breathing quickens.

"What do we do?" he whispers.

Pranz leans in and mutters loud enough for the group to hear, "Doug. Take them. Do your thing. Fuck 'em up."

Doug's eyes widen. "Wait, what?" He says softly over his shoulder as Pranz pushes him forward.

"You got this," Pranz says with a grin. "These aren't soldiers. They're just gutter rats looking for a quick score. Show 'em you're not scared, and they'll back down."

Doug swallows hard. "You better be right."

He steps forward slowly, turns to face the group, and raises the laser prod like he's done it a thousand times— though his trembling hands betray the truth.

"Back off. Or I swear, I'll light up every one of you," Doug says. The voice wavers, but the eyes are trying their best to glare.

The lead scavenger laughs. "Ya gotta pay us a tax to get in."

Doug turns to face the one who is speaking. "And what's the tax?" Doug waivers between fear and a desire to be confident for a change. Sweat seeps from every pour. His heart races.

The man grins, teeth yellow and crooked. "Credits if preferrable. Or… maybe some time with your girl." His tongue runs across his lips, eyes landing on Clutch.

A flash of fury overtakes Doug's hesitation. He fires the prod into the man's chest. The scavenger convulses violently, smoke curling from the impact points. Doug grits his teeth and cranks the voltage higher, the man jerking like a broken marionette until he collapses, twitching and silent.

The rest of the group freezes. Eyes wide. Hands inching toward weapons… and then stopping.

Doug breathes hard. "Anyone else want to collect taxes?"

Before they can answer, Clutch raises her arm and fires a fan of tranque darts. The remaining thugs drop in a synchronized thud, one of them staggering a few steps before collapsing.

Clutch walks past Doug, calm as ever. "Dat was sweet'a ya."

Doug stares at her back, then slowly smiles.

Pranz walks up beside him, claps a hand on his shoulder, and leans in. "See?"

A short while later, as they cut through the mess of broken corridors and jerry-rigged stalls that make up Fun Town, Pranz reminds everyone, "Remember, we need a ship."

Doug sighs. "We know. But that's all I know. I didn't know this place existed let alone where to go or how to find one."

"I usually just throw credits at people until something shakes loose. Half the time it gets me captured, the other half I lose the credits in a scam," Pranz shrugs. "The good news is that my father refuses to come down here or be part of anything going on in this area."

"Well, lucky ya got me," Clutch says, eyes scanning the shadows.

She jerks her head to the side and takes a sharp turn down a narrow corridor that smells like grease, ozone, and bad decisions.

"Follow me," she says, already vanishing into the crowd.

They weave through the grime-slicked arteries of Fun Town, a chaotic sprawl of smoke, shouts, and old flickering signs. Street vendors hawk greasy skewers and questionable tech scraps from foldout crates. Brawls spark and fizzle out like static. Watchful eyes track them from shadowed alcoves—smugglers, gamblers, and worse sizing them up.

Clutch walks like she owns the place. Chin high, shoulders loose, every step a statement: *Don't fuck with me.* Doug and Pranz flank her, trying their best to match the swagger, like they're just bodyguards to anyone watching—and the locals are definitely watching.

Eventually, Clutch veers into a side door. A simple flickering sign overhead reads BAR. Inside, it's darker than expected, thick with the scent of old liquor and sweat-stained desperation.

"Ya two don't wander," Clutch mutters, then glances at Doug. "Spesh'ly ya."

"Yeah, no," Doug mutters, falling into step behind her. "Learned that lesson. Definitely sticking with you."

Clutch smirks and then strides straight to the bar.

The bartender's voice blasts through the din. "Ain't seen you three around. What's your business?"

Clutch doesn't flinch. "Can't a girl git a drink wif her fella?" she replies coolly, tilting her head toward Doug.

Doug's face ignites in crimson. The sudden attention in the room turns to them. He stares at the floor, but a stupid grin pulls at his lips.

The bartender snorts. "Ya got two fellas with you."

"Dat's jus' my bruder," Clutch shoots back, eyes deadpan, voice unbothered.

They reach the bar. Clutch takes the center seat, Doug on one side, Pranz on the other—wedged beside a human oil spill of a man, drooping sideways in a drunk slump, reeking of years of spilled drink and zero hygiene. Gratitude overtakes Doug when he glances nervously to his left and sees an empty seat next to him.

Three glasses clink down in front of them. The bartender starts pouring a colorless liquid into each.

"We didn't ord—" Doug starts.

Clutch's hand lands firmly on his thigh. She gives him a look that says shut up or die.

Doug goes silent.

She downs the shot in a single practiced motion. Pranz doesn't hesitate and knocks his back too. Doug lifts his glass slowly, sniffs, instantly regrets it, and finally throws it back. It hits like liquefied fire and battery acid—a moonshine so raw it could power a small ship. His throat lights up like someone took sandpaper to his esophagus.

"Smooth," Doug chokes.

The bartender smirks and clears the glasses. "What'll it be?"

Before they can answer, a massive figure looms beside Doug.

"So this lil' fella snatched you up?" The man's voice is like gravel over a speaker. He's massive—seven feet tall, muscle packed like crates under stretched skin. His eyes leer at Clutch.

Doug turns, slowly.

"Nah," the man continues, leaning over Doug like a predator sizing up prey. "You need a real man."

"If ya see one," Clutch says, still not looking up, "point 'em out."

The man laughs and grabs Doug by the collar, flinging him off the stool like an afterthought. He slides in beside Clutch, practically pressing against her. "C'mon, iron ant. You don't get to say no."

The breath from the man reeks—hot, sour, and thick with rot. Doug starts to rise, shaking with fury.

"I wouldn't do that," Clutch and Doug say in eerie unison.

Pranz tilts his head, amused. "Ooh. They're in sync now."

He nudges the slumped drunk next to him. "You're gonna wanna see this."

The drunk topples sideways off his stool, landing in a heap. Pranz just shrugs and props his chin in his palms.

"I get what I want," the brute snarls.

"Yeti," the bartender says sharply. "Back off."

"Go fuck yourself, Ondo," Yeti snarls. "She's comin' with me."

He grabs Clutch's arm.

Doug reacts first—jamming his laser prod into Yeti's ribs. The charge surges. The man flinches, but doesn't release.

Doug cranks the voltage.

Still nothing. Yeti snarls and starts turning toward him.

Clutch moves with surgical calm. She pulls a baton-like tool from her side and shoves it just above Yeti's knee. With a thumb press, the baton unfolds—wrapping straps whip around the leg and knee, a powered twist sends torque screaming through the joint.

SNAP.

Yeti roars and collapses, his leg folding in an unnatural angle, slamming his head into the edge of the bar as he falls.

"You bitch!" he screams.

Doug steps in behind him, presses the prod to the base of Yeti's neck, and fires. The man seizes violently—arching, spasming—before slumping into silence.

Clutch releases the straps and holsters her baton without a word.

"Where was we?" she asks, turning back to the bartender like nothing happened.

"I think Ondo was about to help us out," Pranz shares, the smile on his face now from ear to ear.

Doug stands behind Clutch, breathing hard. His stool lies in ruins beneath Yeti's limp, three hundred pound twitching mass.

"Help you out with what?" Ondo asks, a tremble in his voice, half smiling and half afraid.

Chapter 38

"Thanks, Ondo," Pranz says with a lazy salute as the three companions exit the bar, leaving a trail of whispers behind them.

"Okay," Doug says, exhaling as they push into the chaos of Fun Town's main artery. "We have a lead on a ship… just had to take down a behemoth to get it." He smiles, the adrenaline still buzzing through him.

"Doug, ya need ta learn sum udder weapons, like da gun," Clutch says beside him, adjusting the new rig on her belt. "Ya only eva use dat one." She points to the laser prod.

"I like this one," Doug says, patting his favored weapon. "It doesn't kill. Just hurts. I'm… not ready to take someone's life."

"Ya ain't need ta kill," Clutch replies. "Jus' make it hard fer dem ta move."

Doug considers this, then nods. "Alright. Next time someone disrespects you, I'll get creative."

Clutch grins, turning her face slightly as if hiding it, and Doug catches the softness in her eyes. Pranz notices, raising his brows in silent approval. Doug's making progress, and Pranz knows it.

The corridor ahead is different now. Energy shifts. Whispers grow like a rising tide. Eyes track them—wary, curious, even respectful. Word spreads fast down here. Yeti's defeat was already legend, and somehow the tale seemed to be outpacing them.

As they pass, a few people nod or mutter, "Thank you," in hushed tones. Clutch returns the nods without stopping. Pranz gives a little wave. Doug just keeps walking, uncertain what to make of the strange celebrity.

But the atmosphere shifts again—suddenly colder. A tall figure steps out from a shadowed archway, halting their path.

He's wrapped in a long, dusty coat, his wide-brimmed hat tilted forward, hiding everything but the smirk on his lips. Weapons bulge subtly beneath the coat—too many to count.

He tilts his head, just enough for his voice to slither out like smoke. "We don't got room for the likes of you three."

Pranz folds his arms. "And you are?"

"Most would call me the mayor of Fun Town," the man says. He doesn't speak to any of them directly. His words drift forward, ambient and ominous. "Those who don't, well, let's just say I don't like being disrespected."

"Well, Mr. Mayor," Pranz replies, "we're just passing through. Headed to a ship. We'll be out of your decaying hair in no time."

The mayor's smirk doesn't waver. "You think that. But you haven't paid your taxes."

"We paid someone taxes," Doug says with a confident smile.

"I don't think they liked the delivery of said taxes," Pranz adds, a smile on his face as well. A small chuckle shared between the two of them.

"I don't care who you paid. You didn't pay me," the mayor repeats. His hands move—slowly, deliberately—toward the inside of his jacket.

Clutch tenses. "I wouldn't," she warns without her accent.

The mayor turns his chin slightly, enough to glimpse her more fully. "An iron ant, huh?" he muses. "You'll do. As payment."

"The fuck she will!" Doug says taking a step forward, a new device in his hand. It's small, the size of a deck of cards. He holds it out in front of him.

"Oh. You already have claim over her?" The mayor asks, still not lifting his head.

"Take it," Doug says, holding the device out, his finger pressed hard into the corner.

"Why?" The mayor asks.

"Tax payment," Doug shares, holding it out a little further.

The mayor hesitates.

"Take it," Doug says. "Tax paid."

The mayor reaches out, his body fully facing Doug rather than a neutral position. As his fingers close around the device, Doug releases his finger.

A quiet click. Then—

SHHHNK.

Spikes erupt from every micron-sized hole in the device, driving deep into the mayor's palm and fingers with a sickening squelch. He doesn't scream—just inhales sharply through his teeth, the pain contained behind grit and fury. Blood trickles down his wrist as he fumbles backward.

Clutch moves. A magfire pistol appears in her hand as if conjured. She fires.

Metal discs whistle toward the mayor's chest—fast, precise, quiet, and deadly. But the mayor slaps a reverse magnetic disruptor patch on his chest. The discs stop mid-air, vibrating millimeters from his skin before falling to the floor.

Pranz lunges with a heavy metal baton. The mayor dodges, the weapon slamming into the wall with a resonating clang. Sparks fly. The mayor slams his elbow into Pranz's side as he goes by. Pranz lands on the ground, stunned, grabbing his ribs.

Doug pulls out his trusty laser prod and fires. Nothing. Dead battery.

"Fuck!" he yells, tossing it aside.

The mayor finally draws a weapon—sleek, short-barreled, glowing faintly red at the muzzle. He raises it at Pranz.

But Clutch is already pulling out something bigger.

A long-barreled laser rifle slides off her back and locks into her hands. The mayor hesitates, shifting his weapon toward her.

Doug doesn't hesitate.

He draws the one weapon he never wanted to use—the kinetic pistol. Heavy. Lethal.

BANG.

The sound echoes like a punch through steel.

The mayor stumbles. For a heartbeat, nothing happens.

Then blood oozes from a neat, dark hole through the center of his wide-brimmed hat.

The mayor's body sways. The hat falls. His eyes—cold, inhuman, cybernetic—flicker briefly before dimming.

He collapses.

Silence.

Everyone in the corridor stares. Dozens of eyes fixed on the trio. Doug's arm is still extended. His hand trembles.

"Taxes paid," Pranz says, voice high with false cheer as he stands, but his eyes lock on to Doug.

Doug doesn't move. His hand remains raised in the mayor's direction. His breathing wavers between fast and not at all. A cold sweat takes over his body. His eyes looking at the space where the mayor stood.

"Doug?" Clutch steps forward. She gently places her hand on his arm. "Ya okay."

He blinks. But his gaze remains forward. Lost.

Clutch eases the gun from his hand. Helps him lower his arm.

All around them, the eyes of Fun Town watch silently. Waiting. Judging.

"We need to go," Pranz says, scanning the crowd. "Either they'll worship us or hang us upside down for this."

"Doug," Clutch says softly, stepping in front of him.

He meets her eyes—confused, broken, unsure what just happened.

"Thank you. You did nothing wrong," Clutch says in her best and most normal accent possible. She leans in and kisses Doug on his cheek. "Let's go.

The kiss grounds him. He breathes. Nods.

She pulls him forward, and this time, Doug doesn't resist.

The crowd surges forward, but not in anger—curiosity and cautious excitement drive their steps. They gather around the fallen mayor's body, whispering, pointing, murmuring. For a few tense seconds, Pranz watches over his shoulder, ready to run, his hand hovering near a concealed weapon.

Then the applause starts.

First from a woman. Then a second. Then the whole corridor erupts.

Cheers. Clapping. A sudden, almost surreal wave of celebration.

Pranz halts mid-step. "Wasn't expecting that," he mutters, half-turning. He gestures for Clutch and Doug to stop as well.

Doug barely registers it. His mind still loops the moment— gun raised, finger pulled, the echo of death still bouncing inside his head.

Out of nowhere, an old man shuffles up to Doug, face worn by decades, eyes shining with something between reverence and relief.

"What's your name, young man?" the elder asks softly.

Doug hesitates. His voice catches in his throat. "Doug."

The old man's eyes light up. He straightens slightly and turns to the crowd. "To Doug!" he roars, with surprising strength for someone his age.

Clutch and Pranz whip around at the sound. They watch as the crowd's mood shifts again—this time to a unified chant, rising in tempo and volume.

"DOUG! DOUG! DOUG!"

Doug stares, stunned.

"I guess you're the new mayor," Pranz says with a smirk, clapping a hand on Doug's back as he strolls by. "You might want to start working on your victory speech."

Clutch chuckles and keeps walking, shaking her head.

Doug remains frozen, overwhelmed by the noise, the attention, the blood on his hands still metaphorical but very real to him.

A tall man in dark, worn leathers steps out of the crowd and approaches with calm precision. Doug tenses immediately. His eyes dart—Pranz and Clutch are already several paces ahead.

Shit. Not now. Not another one.

The man halts, hands visible. "Doug, right?"

Doug nods, stiff. "Yes."

"We are in your debt. Take this. If you need anything from us in the future, just name it," the man hands Doug a data chip. "And my name is Remo. I've been leading a resistance movement against the mayor and his thugs for years. We can make real progress now that he is dead."

Doug takes the chip without a word.

Doug's throat tightens. "I... I didn't mean to..."

"I know." Remo's eyes soften. "That's why it matters. You did it because it had to be done, not because you wanted to. The best revolutions start with men like you."

Doug's fingers curl around the chip.

Remo steps closer, lowering his voice. "Don't you worry about this mess. We'll clean it up. Nobody will ever know you were here."

Doug slowly nods.

"Oh—and one more thing." Remo turns, walks back toward the body, now slumped on a makeshift cart. He bends, rolls up the mayor's sleeve, and cuts into the flesh. With a wet sound, he extracts a blood-slick implant from the man's semi-bionic forearm.

He tosses it to Doug. "Key to his ship. Big, fast, and untraceable. He's not going to need it anymore, and I've heard a rumor you're looking for a ship."

Doug stares at the two chips in his hand. One promise. One key.

"Thank you," he finally whispers, but Remo is already fading into the crowd.

Doug turns and bolts after Pranz and Clutch, weaving through onlookers who part like water. As he runs, the chanting fades behind him—but the weight of what he's done, and what it's given them, clings tightly to his chest.

Chapter 39

"It was so nice of the mayor to donate his ship," Pranz says dryly as the three step aboard, their boots echoing softly against the polished deck.

"Yeah… I guess it was," Doug replies, voice distant. He glances down at his hands, still holding both data chips. The dried blood on the mayor's chip feels like it's burning into his palm. Without a word, he hands it to Clutch.

She takes it gently and slides it into the console. The ship hums to life—sleek, fast, and fully powered. "Where my ship?" Clutch asks, fingers already dancing across the console.

Pranz steps forward, wiping the exhaustion from his face with a breath. He enters coordinates into the nav panel. "Hidden station. All our gear, and your ride, should be waiting."

Clutch locks the nav and angles the ship out of dock. With a subtle flick of controls, the vessel vanishes into warp.

Moments later, space warps and snaps open again— Pranz's hidden station materializes out of the dark. Orbiting in silence, safe from the world. Among the other ships, one stands out immediately: Clutch's. Sleek. Familiar. Hers.

A rare smile flickers across her lips.

She guides the ship in and docks it without a word. Systems shut down. Lights dim. Still silence.

The door opens and the three step out into the station's main section.

They don't speak. The weight of what they've survived presses on all sides.

"I don't know what lies ahead," Pranz finally says, voice low and tired. "I don't know what we should do next. But I do know this—I'm running on fumes. And Doug... you look like you could use some rest."

Doug doesn't argue. He looks like he's still floating between worlds.

"Food. Sleep. Then we plan," Pranz says, eyes scanning the station as if to remind himself it's still here.

"I could use some sleep," Doug mumbles, rubbing his eyes.

"I got sleep at da station," Clutch says, her voice light but focused. "Ya two git some sleep, I'ill check on my ship 'n git tings ready."

Doug nods silently. Pranz places a reassuring hand on his shoulder and gestures him toward the hallway. "Come on. I've got rooms set up with actual beds, not steel slabs. You'll like it."

The two of them disappear down the corridor, their footsteps fading.

Clutch remains.

Alone now, she wanders the station, moving from room to room, fingers gliding across old consoles and half-forgotten tools. She finds a tablet and starts making notes—

inventory, status updates, what needs fixing, what needs scrapping.

She boards her ship, checking systems, recalibrating old mods, pulling crates from storage and dragging parts between rooms. Her face remains unreadable, but the rhythm of her work is fierce, steady—like she's racing a clock only she can hear.

Doug jerks awake, his breath catching. The room is dimly lit by the soft ambient glow from the control panel on the wall. Something's different—someone's here.

He blinks.

Clutch sits at the edge of his bed, her silhouette barely outlined in the faint light. Her elbows rest on her knees, her shoulders slumped—not from defeat, but exhaustion.

"Clutch?" Doug sits up slowly, rubbing the sleep from his eyes. "What's wrong?"

"I'm tired," she says, her voice quieter than usual. "Didn't tink I was. But I am. 'N der ain't nowhere else ta sleep."

Doug straightens, instinctively wanting to reach for her but catching himself. "You can have the bed. I'll take the floor. I don't mind."

Clutch turns her head just enough for her eyes to meet his in the dark. "Nah. Ya can stay. Jus'... don't try nutin'."

He smiles softly. "Wouldn't dream of it. I like my ribs unbroken."

Clutch smirks and climbs into the bed beside him, rolling to face the ceiling. Doug lies back, stiff for a moment, unsure what to do with his arms, his breath, his thoughts.

The silence stretches, not uncomfortable, just full.

She's here. In his bed. Her ship is docked just outside this room, ready and waiting, and yet... she chose to be here.

A small smile sneaks across Doug's face. He tries to hide it, but Clutch notices.

"Whatcha smilin' at?" she asks, eyes still on the ceiling.

Doug swallows and shrugs. "Nothing," he says, voice soft. "Just... sleep well, Clutch."

She closes her eyes but doesn't turn away. "Night, Doug."

The air stills. The hum of the station lulls them both. And in the space between heartbeat and breath, two people who've been through hell share the only calm they've had in days—no plans, no danger, just proximity and possibility.

"Isn't this the best thing I've seen since Doug prodded my father in the ribs?" Pranz's voice cuts through the quiet, leaning casually against the doorframe, arms crossed and grinning like a kid who just caught his friends doing something secret.

Doug and Clutch both jolt awake. Doug blinks rapidly, realizing his arm is draped over Clutch's waist, her fingers still laced around his wrist. She doesn't pull away.

Doug begins to withdraw instinctively, embarrassment rising like a tide. But then—Clutch tightens her grip.

He pauses. Takes a breath. Relaxes.

Pranz's grin widens. "Should I give you two some more time? Maybe breakfast in bed? A formal announcement to the galactic feed?"

"We didn't do anything," Doug blurts, a little too quickly, a little too earnestly—like a teenager caught sneaking out after curfew.

Clutch's lips curl into a smirk. "Yeah... git out."

Pranz puts his hands up in mock surrender and backs out of the room. "No rush. Just... don't name your first kid after me or anything." He closes the door behind him, the grin still stretching across his face.

Silence settles in, soft and a little awkward.

Doug stares at the ceiling.

"Doug?" Clutch says quietly, her voice uncharacteristically vulnerable.

"Yes?" he says, turning his head slightly toward her.

"I ain't one ta be likin' nobody. Ain't never seen what a healfy 'lationship look like." Her voice wavers slightly. "But I find myself likin' ya. It ain't a feelin' I'm use ta."

Doug shifts, just enough to hold her closer. "Clutch... I have feelings for you too. And I don't need to understand everything to know that I care about you. I've seen pieces of what Fornokey did to you—and your people. And I'll never be okay with that. I just want you to know... I'll never push you into something you don't want. You have my respect. Always."

Clutch lets the words settle. Then she murmurs, "Like I said… ya sweet."

She pulls his arm tighter around her waist, curling into him, drawing comfort from the warmth of his body. Doug leans in and presses a soft kiss to the back of her head, letting his breath drift through her hair.

"Do dat again," she says, her voice a whisper.

He kisses her again, more slowly this time. Then a third, closer to her ear. She tilts her head slightly, inviting more.

"Again," she says even softer.

Doug trails a feather-light kiss along the ridge of her ear, then down to her cheek, where a strand of hair veils her skin. He gently tucks it back behind her ear, fingers grazing her skin.

She lets out a soft sound—half sigh, half moan.

"Again," she breathes.

Doug leans in, this time to her cheek—but before he lands it, Clutch shifts. Their lips meet.

It's a kiss of invitation and surprise, heat and affection, a joining of two people who've fought for air, for safety, for survival—and now, for connection.

Doug melts into it, heart pounding, hand moving to the back of her head, fingers tangling in her hair. She pulls him closer, her hand pressing into his back. They kiss like it matters. Like it's the one thing that feels real after everything they've been through.

They don't rush. Their hands explore gently, learning each other's shapes and reactions. Every kiss is slow and intentional. Between kisses, they share small glances, little smiles, as if neither one can believe the moment is happening.

Clutch breaks a kiss and rests her forehead against his. "Told ya. Ya sweet," she whispers, her breath warm against his lips.

Doug smiles, his thumb brushing her jaw. "Only for you."

A while later, Clutch and Doug emerge from their room. They walk in step, quiet but visibly lighter—like some unspoken tension has finally slipped from their shoulders. They make their way to the galley, where Pranz is lounging in a chair with a tablet in hand.

Pranz barely glances up. "Called it!"

Doug freezes mid-step. "Called what?" he asks, too quickly—his voice shooting a full octave higher in faux innocence.

"That you two would become an item." Pranz grins like he's just won a bet with himself.

Clutch doesn't flinch. She breezes past and grabs a ration pack from the warmer. "We gotta find dat news lady ya spoke 'bout," she says flatly, not giving Pranz the satisfaction.

Pranz raises an eyebrow at the pivot, then nods. "Sora. Her name's Sora."

Doug stops short, eyes going wide. "Wait—what? Sora Volt? The Sora Volt?"

"The very one," Pranz replies, trying to sound nonchalant but clearly pleased with the reaction.

"She's like... the most famous investigative journalist in the galaxy," Doug says, turning to Clutch with genuine awe. "If she reports something, it spreads across the comm grid in seconds."

"She famous 'nough?" Clutch asks between bites.

Doug nods emphatically. "She's trusted by almost everyone who doesn't already work for the people she's exposing. If she says it, people believe her."

"Unless the execs get to her first," Pranz mutters, tapping his tablet. "That's why she streams everything she can live. No post-editing, no spin, just raw footage. Execs tolerate her because she pulls in ridiculous ratings... and that means profit."

"But I've seen her get shut down mid-broadcast before," Doug adds. "Then there's always some generic excuse. 'Comm relay failure,' 'power grid overload'... classic cover-ups. Remember that story she started on unauthorized post-mortem experimentation? We never found out who was behind it."

"Yeah." Pranz's voice turns bitter. "That was the one that ended... everything. She blamed me. Thought I was feeding info to my father, or at least covering for him. His reach is just too vast."

He looks down, the grin long gone now.

Clutch sets down her fork. "Ain't got time fer 'grets. We need her help. We bring her da biggest story in hooman his'ory, 'n we'ill see if she da real deal."

"I'll do what I can to track her down," Pranz says, snapping himself out of it. "She's always on the move, usually chasing a story. If we can figure out where she'll be next, maybe we can intercept before the execs catch wind."

"If she still trusts you," Doug says gently.

Pranz doesn't answer. He just nods, eyes locked on the screen, already searching.

Chapter 40

"How did you find me?" Sora Volt snaps as she strides through the crowded corridors of Yult Station, not breaking pace.

Her heels click like gunshots against the deck plating. Tall and lean, she glides through the chaos with a presence that commands attention. Her straight black hair shifts gently across her face, always in motion, like she herself cuts against the background. Her features are inviting—warm eyes, a disarming smile—the kind that could put any mind at ease, yet steal the truth from your lips before you realized you'd spoken. She wears her signature blazer, one that is tailor made to make eyes turn as she enters the room.

"You're kind of famous, Sora. Not exactly subtle," Pranz says, keeping step with her. "Plus, you're always chasing the next big story."

"Right. And that story always vanishes when you're around. Leave me alone, Pranz—I don't need you screwing me over again."

"I've apologized a hundred times. It wasn't my fault—my father is just a giant, galaxy-sized asshole," he says, exasperation bleeding through.

"And somehow, being your proximity bomb means every story I touch turns to ash. Just knowing you ruins my credibility," Sora hisses, barely glancing at him.

"Please, just stop and listen," Pranz pleads, reaching for her shoulder.

She jerks away and keeps moving. Until—

"Proof of aliens," Pranz says, loudly enough to cut through the buzz of the corridor.

Sora stops. She doesn't turn around.

Doug and Clutch jog up, short of breath. Doug steps forward. "It's true."

"I ain't tus' 'em at firs' eidder," Clutch says. "He help'd free me from his daddy's chains."

Sora turns slowly, her sharp gaze darting from one face to the next. "You three might be the weirdest trio I've ever encountered," she says, eyes narrowing at Clutch. "Especially you."

"I ain't into diggin' fer no corp'ration," Clutch shrugs.

"And you," Sora says to Doug, "I genuinely can't figure you out."

"I used to be unlucky," Doug says with a smile. "Then I met Clutch."

Sora rolls her eyes. "How cliché."

"We found something," Pranz says, stepping in. "A structure or station. Alien in origin. It links to other structures, we think. My father wants it, and we don't want him to have it. The only way they will give us credit is to have you do a live story about it."

"Why not just file a salvage claim?" Sora asks.

"He owns the office," Pranz replies flatly. "Any claim of interest mysteriously gets 'predated' by a different claim. A new entity created that takes credit. One that is owned by Fornokey in some way."

Sora's expression shifts. That strikes a nerve. "Now that's a story," she says. "And I want exclusive rights to it."

"You can have that and more," Pranz says. "You break this story—live—and you'll be too valuable for the execs to silence. Even with my father threatening them."

"But I won't get authorization. Not for something this big. They always want to know what the story is about before they give me the go ahead. The news execs are already in his pocket," Sora says.

"What about your underground channels?" Doug asks.

"Won't work. I'd get labeled as another conspiracy peddler. Deepfaked. Discredited before it even spreads," she replies, matter-of-fact.

"We could hack da feeds. Force a full tra'mission," Clutch offers.

Sora laughs sharply. "Those networks are locked down tighter than the Regy's black vaults."

"But you've got access to the building, right?" Pranz presses.

"I have access to my studio. Not to the full broadcast suite. I don't even get near the core systems. That's guarded like a treasury."

"What if someone got inside disguised as an engineer?" Pranz asks, casting a look toward Doug.

Doug gulps but says nothing.

"He might look the part but won't have access. Won't have biometrics in the system. Again, won't get close," Sora replies. "Not even Regy goons have access."

"Okay, smarty pants. What will work? What can we all do to come out ahead? For all of us to get what we want?" Pranz asks.

"And what do you want, traitor?" Sora asks in an accusatory tone.

"Freedom from my father. If I'm untouchable, he will lose his power over me," Pranz declares.

"Untouchable because you found existence of aliens?" Sora asks to make sure she understands.

"That's the idea," Pranz replies. "And with that fame, I can help you bury him with story after story. The execs will turn on him because you will be giving them the viewership they want. You'll make them more money than my father could ever just give them. Freedom for me comes at a cost to my father."

She watches him for a long beat, weighing his words.

"I want to see it," she finally says. "Before I agree to anything. If I'm sticking my neck out, I need to know it's worth it."

"Let's go then. We can jump there now," Pranz replies.

Sora tilts her head. "You assume I can just walk away from my assignments?"

Pranz grins. "I assume you want the biggest scoop in human history."

Clutch crosses her arms. "Ya ain't gonna be dis'pointed."

Sora sighs and runs a hand through her hair.

"Just make sure you leave any trackable devices behind. Anything that your company would have given you," Pranz shares. "I don't trust my father or anyone he knows. They probably gave you a tracking device, or a lot of them, just to keep tabs on you. Especially when…" Pranz doesn't finish his thought, but instead looks down, regretting what happened between him and Sora and her biggest story flushed away because of greed and deceit.

"Yeah, you are going to owe me big time for this. I want all of the stories on your dad," Sora says, removing everything she is carrying and moving toward a nearby set of lockers to strip down even more.

"I'll give you more than you can process. You'll be busy for many cycles," Pranz replies with a grin.

Chapter 41

After returning to Pranz's hidden shipyard, the group transfers over to Clutch's sleek, battle-worn vessel. The moment Sora steps aboard, her reporter's instincts kick in.

"I don't want to sound rude, but... how are you not locked up in the mines?" Sora asks, scanning the dimly lit corridor with a curious eye.

Clutch shrugs. "I got my ways."

"You're... rare," Sora says, stepping carefully. "So rare, actually, it's almost myth. No one sees iron—uh—your people... out here. Not free. Not flying their own ship."

"You can say 'humans," Clutch says dryly. Then she tilts her head, slipping back into her accent with a sharp grin. "Or red-head hoomans, if ya wanna get spe'fic."

Sora chuckles awkwardly. "You know what I mean. The ones who've been forced into labor or worse. Mining. Sex slavery. I've heard the rumors, but proof? That's another story. And here you are."

"I ain't wanna be part'a needer," Clutch replies, her voice turning cold.

"And I'm glad she is free," Doug adds, stepping into the cockpit beside her. "She's saved my life several times over."

Clutch flashes Doug a soft smile, then settles into the pilot's chair. Her fingers dance over the controls. The ship hums awake beneath them, systems lighting up one by one. With a smooth jolt, the ship detaches from its cradle and eases into open space, its nose angling toward the jump coordinates.

Doug watches the stars drift, then says, "We also need to do something about those mines. About what's happening on the rocks. We saw it. We were there. It's—"

"Horrific?" Sora cuts in, her voice low, almost excited about the prospect of reporting the atrocities.

"Needs to be exposed," Doug finishes. "Publicly. Permanently."

Sora leans back, the edge in her posture sharpening. "Good. That's my specialty."

"You're about to break the biggest story in human history," Pranz says, turning from a side console. "And once you do, you'll be untouchable. I'll give you everything. Every dirty little secret I've got—on my father, on Fornokey, on the mines. You'll become the most famous journalist ever."

Sora tilts her head, studying him. "And what's in it for you, golden boy?"

Pranz starts to speak.

"And don't give me that 'freedom from your daddy' bullshit," Sora adds.

Pranz lowers his gaze, jaw tightening. For a moment, silence stretches across the ship.

"Oh. I have a feeling it's of a personal matter," Doug says. "One I can get behind."

Pranz lifts his eyes, meeting Doug's. Something wordless passes between them—shared pain, shared understanding.

Clutch glances back from the controls, watching them both. Sora sits in silence for a beat longer, then folds her arms and exhales.

The ship lurches from its position in space to the alien structure.

Sora turns from the console as they arrive, her gaze drawn to the enormous object outside the main viewport. The sight hits her like a gut punch.

"What the fuck is that?" she breathes, a rush of excitement rising in her voice.

"That," Pranz says, stepping forward like a ringmaster unveiling his prized spectacle, "is our discovery."

"Eight seconds," Clutch announces from the pilot's seat, eyes locked on a glowing countdown.

"Eight seconds until what?" Sora asks, stepping closer to the window.

"Just watch," Doug says, calm but tense.

Time drips forward, thick with anticipation. Then it happens.

A beam of pure light zips past the port side of the ship, slicing through the blackness of space like a razor. It connects with one corner of the massive alien pyramid.

The entire structure responds.

Other beams converge from the surrounding void, each targeting a separate corner of the pyramid. Then the structure flares to life—lines and channels of blue-white energy racing across its surface like veins igniting.

A massive central beam shoots from its apex, aimed into the void. It pulses once. Then flickers.

And just like before—silence. The light dies. The beams vanish. The pyramid slumps back into stillness.

"What did I just witness?" Sora asks, blinking hard, her voice hushed now. Not fear. Awe.

"We'll show you what we've seen," Pranz says, smiling. "Clutch, dock us."

Without a word, Clutch swings the ship toward the makeshift docking bay nestled into the edge of the alien station.

Sora glances around. "I wish I had my recording gear."

"I got sum," Clutch replies, already on her feet as the new docking clamps Clutch built for the structure engage. Doug follows her to the supply hold.

"Ya ain't need ta come wif me," Clutch says, rummaging through a crate.

"But then I couldn't kiss you," he says, standing hopeful with a small smile on his face.

She turns and gives him a quick kiss, then back to finding the recording equipment.

Doug smiles but was also hoping for more. *Now isn't ideal, I get it. But I really like kissing Clutch,* Doug says to himself as Clutch stands with a crate and heads back to the bridge.

Clutch hands Sora the gear—head-mounted recorder synced to her ocular movement, a chest rig, and a sleek handheld cam.

"These are... incredible," Sora says, already adjusting the straps. "This is professional-grade—where'd you even get this?"

"Long story," Clutch says with a sly grin. "Les' jus' say smugglas was 'volved."

Sora eyes her, half amused, half impressed. "You're hard to understand. Are all of you that way?"

Clutch's smile turns sharp. "Maybe ta ya. But we 'stand each udder fine."

"She grows on you fast," Doug adds. "You'll be fluent in no time."

"Pop speeders?" Pranz asks, checking a side panel.

"You have pop speeders?" Sora gawks. "Those are rarer than—"

"Don't say it," Pranz warns with a wink.

Clutch steps to the side console. "Got tree workin'. I'ill stay back. Da ship need more fixin'. Ya'll go."

"You sure you don't want me to stay and help?" Doug asks.

Clutch kisses him softly on the lips. "Yeah. We ain't get nutin' done if ya stay."

Doug smiles. "Good point."

Pranz is already at the hatch. "Let's move."

Moments later, Doug, Pranz, and Sora launch into the core corridor of the alien station, mounted on the sleek pop speeders. The structure unfurls before them—its scale impossible, humbling.

Sora records everything. Her eyes are wide. "This is... this is remarkable!"

They reach the pyramid's end of the structure. The chamber is still and cavernous. The rippling membrane of the wall, the pulsing orb—everything seems alive.

Sora steps in, stunned. "It's so beautiful..."

Then the room changes.

Doug and Pranz brace instinctively against the wall. Sora drifts forward, lost in the alien glow.

The orb pulses. The waves intensify across the wall's surface. The high-pitched whine builds—fast. Familiar to Doug and Pranz. Foreign and disorienting to Sora.

Then it hits.

The orb erupts with energy. Blinding light floods the room. The walls seem to buckle as if caught in an invisible storm.

BOOM.

The sound crushes the air. Sora is thrown off her feet. Doug winces but holds steady. Pranz barely flinches, already covering his ears and averting his eyes.

A second later, silence returns. The orb dims. The chamber stills.

Sora rises slowly, stunned and breathless. Her head-mounted camera still active, capturing everything.

Sora stands up and shouts, "That was awesome!!! How long until it goes again?"

Doug and Pranz glance at each other—and smile. She's in.

She's all in.

Chapter 42

"How do we stake our claim, get word out, and keep greedy hands off this?" Pranz asks, pacing just behind Sora as she scans the horizon of alien tech pulsing in quiet rhythm.

"It will definitely have to be a live feed," Sora replies, eyes darting, calculating. "That's the only way to keep the story from being buried. But that's going to take serious convincing. Execs aren't going to greenlight that without knowing what they're getting. And I'm sure your father already has them in his pocket for this very thing."

"That's what we figured," Pranz mutters, jaw clenched.

"Prox'mity 'lert," ClutchAI interrupts, its tone calm but cold.

Everyone's attention snaps to Clutch. She just grins.

"Ship sound good, huh?" she says, pride slipping into her tone—until the weight of the situation hits them all.

A cold silence washes over the room.

Clutch bolts to her controls. "Mult'ple ships," she reports, eyes narrowing on the incoming signatures.

"What do we do?" Doug asks, already at her side.

"I ain't tink dey know we's here," Clutch replies, leaning closer to the screen. Her tone shifts—calculating, cautious.

"Who are they?" Sora asks. "Can you tell without giving away our location?"

"Not wifout pingin' 'em back," Clutch replies. "Dey ain't need ta know hoomans is lurkin' dough."

On the display, three ships slide into view—dark silhouettes against the eerie backdrop of the alien pyramid.

Two of the vessels break off, heading directly toward the points at the pyramid's edge.

"Dat ain't gonna be good for dem," Clutch murmurs with a wicked little smirk.

Time ticks. The tension grows.

Warning: energy surge detected. An alert appears on the screen.

"At least there will be two less ships," Pranz mutters.

The beams of light strike as expected. Incoming beams disintegrate the two ships. The final beam shooting out from the tip toward the center of this alien made system.

"Incomin' tran'mission," ClutchAI announces.

"Listen only," Pranz orders. "No response."

"Ain't gonna 'spond," Clutch confirms, fingers hovering over the comm interface.

The room fills with static—then his voice.

"Jason. I know you're there. Show yourself."

Pranz's face goes pale. His breath catches.

"How the fuck did my father find us?" he whispers.

"You're probably wondering how I found you," Gabe Fornokey says, voice dripping arrogance. *"Just know—I'm smarter than you."*

"Egotistical fuck," Doug mutters.

"You'll never get credit for this. Show yourselves."

Sora's face twists in frustration. "He's already sent a claims packet, I'd bet my life on it."

"He ain't," Clutch says, not even looking up. "Ain't no subs out dis far."

"Subs?" Sora asks.

"Subspace relays," Doug explains. "This far out? No direct lines. Sending anything from here would take decades to reach a relay."

"And he knows that," Pranz growls. "Which means he didn't come to file a claim."

"Let's keep it that way. Prevent him from leaving," Sora shares. "You have to act quickly."

"Pranz?" Clutch asks.

She doesn't say what she's asking. But everyone knows. Her hand rests near the weapons console.

Before Pranz can respond, Gabe's voice returns, sharper, colder.

"It's time to show yourselves and face the consequences of your actions."

"You've destabilized our home. Thousands are dead because of you."

"Lies," Doug growls. "All of it. Don't let it in, Pranz."

"You are a disappointment to me," Gabe spits. *"I thought you could become something. But just like your mother, you were never cut out for this life."*

Pranz flinches.

"Don't listen to him," Sora says, putting a hand on his arm. "He's baiting you. Stay focused."

But Gabe's voice won't stop.

"You never knew the truth about your mother, did you?"

Pranz stiffens.

"She didn't die of sickness. She was sick of me. She wanted to expose me. Just like you."

"And I couldn't have that."

The silence that follows is heavy. Unbreathable.

"You killed her..." Pranz whispers.

His fists curl at his sides, nails digging into his palms.

Sora steps forward. "Pranz. Look at me."

He doesn't move.

"Listen to me," she says more firmly. "This is what he does. He doesn't control you anymore."

Clutch stands still, waiting. Doug watches, fists clenched.

"Either turn yourself over and face the consequences or you'll have to meet the same end as her."

Gabe's ultimatum is set. It's clear.

"Too bad that monster didn't kill you too!" Pranz shouts, slamming his hand down on the comm panel. "Fuck you!"

"Got you," Gabe replies smugly.

An instant later, a missile streaks from Gabe's ship toward Clutch's, still attached to the structure.

Clutch is already moving, hands flying across the console. The ship detaches from the alien structure in a sharp jolt, veering away as her fingers tap out a precision firing sequence. A single pulse-laser shoots across the void—boom—detonating the missile mid-flight in a fiery blossom of light.

"Ya ain't gonna fuck up dat structure," Clutch snarls, eyes hard.

"Ah… the iron ant lives," Gabe replies, his voice like oil over gravel. *"You'll have a special place in my personal office when this is all over."*

"The hell you will!" Doug snaps, stepping forward, fury in his voice.

"Shut up, you worthless little sidekick," Gabe bites back. *"You're not even worth the air you breathe."*

Another missile fires—then four more, flanking like teeth in a mechanical snarl.

Clutch launches her own ordinance. A scatter of glowing red decoys tumble into space. The missiles adjust mid-flight, chasing the false heat signatures.

BOOM. BOOM. BOOM. Each one explodes harmlessly, far from the ship.

"Ain't waitin' fer yer permission, Pranz," Clutch growls—
and fires.

Her laser lances toward Gabe's hull. The beam does
nothing. It dissipates better than Patrick's pirate ship.

"Nice try," Gabe hisses over the comm. *"But not good
enough."*

A railgun system roars to life.

A thousand tungsten needles shred the void, too fast to
dodge. They riddle Clutch's ship, piercing through walls,
slicing through metal. Sparks fly. Atmosphere hisses.
Miraculously, no one's hit.

"Ship decompressin'," ClutchAI warns coldly.

Clutch slams her hand down on a red trigger beneath the
console. Emergency seals clamp down, locking the bridge
in a vacuum-safe cocoon.

Then she pushes the throttle to max.

The ship jerks forward—directly at Gabe's vessel.

"What are you doing?!" Pranz yells, grabbing a support
strut.

"Trus' me," Clutch says calmly, her eyes locked on the
approaching target.

Gabe's voice returns, strained now. *"Are you seriously
going to kill us all?"*

His ship tries to veer away. Clutch mirrors the move
perfectly.

"Is this real? Are we—?" Sora starts to ask, clutching her seat. Doug says nothing, eyes fixed on Clutch, trusting.

Gabe fires railgun bursts again—too late, too wide. They scream past harmlessly.

He launches missiles but quickly realizes that they are missing Clutch's ship, circling back, and following Clutch's momentum toward Gabe's ship. He sees that they might miss and hit him instead. He self-destructs them before that can happen.

They're nearly nose-to-nose now. Gabe tries to do everything he can short of fleeing.

At the last possible second, Clutch throws the ship into a barrel roll, veering sharply off the collision path.

THUMP-THUMP-THUMP.

Small magnetic canisters eject from hidden launchers and slam onto Gabe's hull. They glow bright, drilling instantly into the plating. When they breach the interior oxygen ignites with explosive force—

BOOM.

Chain reactions erupt across the ship. Explosions ripple along its body, shredding decks, melting armor, cracking the spine of the vessel.

Clutch spins the ship around to watch the carnage. Her eyes narrow.

She fires again—laser slicing through floating debris, severing large chunks before they can tumble free. She turns the laser toward anything big enough to house a survivor and obliterates it.

Only one large chunk remains.

She lines up the shot—when it suddenly vanishes.

A blip.

Gone.

"Fuck!" Pranz shouts, slamming the console. "We were so close! He always escapes!"

Clutch exhales through her nose. "Not ness'sarly… ya know where dat migh' go?"

Pranz looks up, realization dawning. "Yeah. Gervantion Station. His fortress."

"Home turf," Sora mutters.

"Back where he's protected. Where we can't touch him," Pranz growls, pacing now, fire in his eyes.

Clutch punches in the coordinates and lurches the ship across the galaxy to Gervantion Station.

Chapter 43

"Why are we here? We're exposed!" Pranz says, panic cracking through his voice as he leans over Clutch's shoulder to scan the incoming telemetry. "This place is crawling with defense systems!"

"He ain't got a good drive," Clutch replies, calm but focused. Her fingers dance across the console. "We beat 'em here."

"Maybe by a few minutes!" Pranz snaps. "Just enough time for the station to tag us, ID us, and turn us into dust."

"We jus' gonna have ta chance it," Clutch says, her eyes fixed on the nav grid. "Ain't lettin' 'em win 'gain."

'Incomin' ships,' ClutchAI intones with mechanical precision.

"That didn't take long at all," Doug mutters, eyes widening as small blips appear and multiply across the radar.

"Put me through," Sora commands, stepping forward like she owns the ship.

"To which uns?" Clutch asks without looking.

"All of them!" Sora insists, urgency rippling through her voice as the display floods with converging ships. "Everyone who's listening."

Clutch flicks a switch. "Go 'head."

Sora straightens. Her voice comes out crisp, commanding, weaponized:

"Stand down or you all go down."

The signal echoes across every comm frequency.

"We have proof of what you've done. Of what this station, your leaders, and some of you have been part of. Crimes against humanity. Forced labor. Mass exploitation. You shoot us down, and every ounce of it goes public."

A beat. Then—

Chatter. Frantic, garbled, overlapping. Voices from different command decks flood the airwaves.

'—Is she bluffing?'

'—I didn't know anything about—'

'—Shut up, don't say another word—'

'—What crimes? I am just a pilot—'

Sora steps closer to the mic, her tone turning razor-sharp:

"Some of you are innocent. Many of you are complicit. That line will be drawn soon. Don't put yourselves on the wrong side of it. We're not here for you. We're here for someone else. Let us do what we came to do, and you can all walk away exonerated."

Silence falls for a moment. Just long enough for the tension to stretch taut.

Then the chatter spikes again. Some voices call for surrender. Others for caution. Some still want to open fire.

It's chaos. A volatile mix of uncertainty, fear, and suppressed guilt.

Clutch reaches over and taps a button. The comms fall silent on their end.

"Why did you do that?" Doug asks.

"Da noise ain't helpin' us none," Clutch says. Her fingers stay ready over the controls, eyes glued to the screen.

"Da 'scape pod jus' 'rived," ClutchAI reports, calm despite the tension hanging in the room.

"'Bout time," Clutch mutters, switching the display. She locks onto the pod's signature and without hesitation, opens fire. The laser slices through the pod's hull in a clean, surgical motion—then again, and again, until the entire pod is little more than drifting scrap metal.

Clutch leans forward, squinting at the aftermath. "Dat's odd."

"What's odd?" Doug asks, already bracing for another curveball.

"I ain't seein' no body parts drif'in in da void," Clutch says, her tone flat but tinged with suspicion. She zooms in on the wreckage—empty. No limbs. No blood. No sign of Gabe.

"Fuck!" Pranz shouts, spinning away from the console and pacing the room. "It was a decoy of some kind. He's still out there."

"We need to go live. Now," Sora snaps, urgency surging in her voice. "We don't have time for permissions or authorizations."

"So what's the play?" Pranz asks, turning back to the group.

"Anyone here know how to hack the feeds?" Sora asks, half-sarcastic, half-desperate.

"I ain't eva tried," Clutch says, shrugging. "But I bet da ship can."

"Affirmative," ClutchAI replies.

"Where's our best shot at pulling this off?" Pranz asks.

"We'll need one of the main feed hubs," Sora replies. "Hub 121 is the largest and has feeds into every major system. But it's a fortress."

"Aren't those places heavily guarded?" Doug asks, glancing nervously at the map. "Like, wouldn't it be easier to walk into a Regy black vault?"

"Yeah. Nobody wants to fuck with their defenses," Sora admits. "Just come at it from a mil and that will buy us time."

"A million kilometers will make communication with the hub slow. Response time won't be adequate," ClutchAI states without the accent. "One hundred thousand kilometers would be better while still maintaining enough distance from incoming trouble."

"We won't last long at that range," Sora replies.

"It won't take long to hack the feed at that range," ClutchAI replies.

"Should we be concerned about this whole AI thing?" Doug asks.

"No time to argue," Pranz cuts in. "We move now. My father's probably already en route to bury this. If we don't beat him to it, we lose."

Clutch is already one step ahead—she launches the ship into motion, veering away from the incoming ships that have now made their decision. A barrage of fire trails them as they lurch into jump space. Destination: Hub 121. One hundred thousand klicks.

"Taking control," ClutchAI states.

"We don't need control," Sora barks. "Just shadow-access. Let us press the button when we're ready. If they detect intrusion, it's game over."

"Confirmed. Ghost mode enabled."

Before Clutch can even finish confirming the course, warning lights erupt across Doug's console.

"Uh… guys?" he calls out, staring at the screen.

"Not now, Doug," Pranz replies, eyes glued to the hacking process.

"We're almost in," Sora adds.

Doug's eyes go wide. He turns to Clutch—she's deep in sync with the AI. No help there. The radar screams as missile after missile arcs toward them.

Doug clenches his jaw, flips up the override panel, and takes command of the defensive systems. Without waiting for approval, he fires off a rapid salvo of heat blocks. Glowing red decoys streak away from the ship.

Seconds later, explosions light up the black.

He's fast—but not fast enough.

One missile is still coming.

Doug pulls the ship hard sideways, aligning the front-mounted laser. The sudden jolt throws everyone off their rhythm. Clutch looks up in surprise. Pranz nearly topples out of his seat.

Doug fires.

The missile explodes just before impact. Shrapnel peppers the ship, rattling across its hull like hail.

"YES!" Doug shouts, breathless. His knuckles still white on the controls.

Clutch taps her screen, reviews the playback, and then— smiles. A real one. She glances back at Doug. He beams, sweat on his brow, heart still racing.

She nods and gets back to work.

"Package delivered. Feed available on your command," ClutchAI says, perfectly calm.

"We go live from the alien station," Sora says, already standing. "The visuals will be undeniable."

"Stop at Barnight Station. I know a guy who will give us a portable sub, for a price," Pranz interrupts. "We'll need it before we can go live."

A second wave of missiles registers.

"And I will need drone cameras!" Sora shouts.

The missiles barrel closer at remarkable speed.

"Barnight and then my hub. I have plenty of drone cameras there," Pranz replies quickly.

"Wan' me ta stop fer groceries to?" Clutch asks, working frantically on the controls.

"Better be quick about something. Pick a place. Anywhere!" Doug calls out, already seeing the next swarm close in. "We're out of blocks!"

The missiles ever closer, hit inevitable.

Clutch spins the ship and slams the jump control. The stars stretch—and the black swallows them.

Doug finally exhales, sinking back into his seat.

"That…" he breathes, "was too close."

Chapter 44

Sora stands poised on Clutch's ship, the colossal structure looming behind her, like a sleeping giant. She adjusts her mic, rolls her shoulders, and runs through rapid vocal warmups—sharp consonants and stretched vowels echoing off the hull's metal walls. Every camera is locked in place: one focused on her face, another on the crew, and a slew of drone cameras hover in the black catching the eerie beauty of the structure. Lights hum to life, casting a glow that's more dramatic than staged.

Above them, a floating subspace relay hovers—freshly bribed into existence. The tech who handed it over, off the books, is already counting his credits somewhere quiet on Barnight Station, knowing his little crime will be forgotten the moment the feed goes live. After all, with a discovery like this, a relay would've been installed anyway. They just skipped the paperwork.

Pranz watches Sora from a few steps back, arms crossed, his face lit by the feed monitor's glow. There's admiration in his eyes—but also a hint of apprehension.

Sora glances over her shoulder at him. "You know I'll have to interview you," she says, her tone half-serious, half-warning. "You'll have to go on record. You'll have to expose your father."

The light in Pranz's eyes dims. The smile fades. He doesn't respond immediately. He just nods once, slow and heavy, as the weight of the moment settles onto his shoulders. His expression twists—conflict, pain, clarity. The truth isn't just a report anymore. It's personal.

"That is," Sora adds gently, "unless you want to let Clutch and Doug take the spotlight. Make them the ones who discovered alien life. You'd just be the background investor. The anonymous funder. No exposure. No glory. No freedom from your father."

Pranz's jaw tightens.

"But…" Sora's voice shifts to something softer, more genuine. "If you do speak up, if you help bring this to light—no matter what happens to your father—you'll have your name carved into the foundation of human history. You'll be untouchable. The son who ended an empire and helped bring truth to the stars."

Clutch leans against a support beam, arms crossed. "'Member," she says plainly, "it's his 'n yers karma."

Doug nods in agreement beside her, nudging Clutch with his elbow. "And around here, we don't fuck with karma."

Pranz takes a slow breath. He looks from Clutch to Doug, then to Sora. His eyes linger on the feed display one more time. "I understand," he says at last. "I'm ready."

"Great. Since we don't know where your dad is, we best get this show rolling before he shows up with an army," Sora says with confidence.

Clutch spins her seat around to her terminal. Her fingers dance across the console. "Start'n da hack," she announces with her usual ease.

The ship groans softly as systems come alive—data pulses humming through panels and conduits. The relay connection bursts online, flooding the feeds, trickling into every stream-fed node tied to every screen. The signal spreads like wildfire, beyond reach, beyond redaction.

"Connec'ed," Clutch confirms. The feed is live. The universe is listening.

"Alien existence? Yes. The answer is finally yes. We have proof and I am here with the three individuals who discovered alien existence because gravity whispered in their ear. This crew found signals radiating from a section of space that pointed the way," Sora starts.

The camera feeds change automatically from Sora to the crew as she speaks, then to the structure itself.

"As you can see, this structure is massive. And shortly, you will see a light show unlike anything we have ever seen," Sora continues. "In fact, the time displayed on the wall says we have about ten seconds. Just know this is the beginning of something new. We don't know what this structure is, why it was put here, and what else lies in this mapping of the stars that Clutch, Doug, and Pranz discovered. And here we go!"

The cameras point toward the alien structure's pyramid shape. The beams of light come in from multiple areas of space, all hitting the pyramid corners. A final beam shoots out from the tip of the pyramid. It last mere seconds, just like every time before.

"Our next feed will be from inside the structure, right at the heart of that same anomaly," Sora shares. "But first, we need to make sure you aren't lied to by greedy assholes who would do and have done everything to stop these three from making the claim to this discovery. Gabe Fornokey and the Fornokey Corporation would be the primary greed monger. Proof you ask? Of course you want proof. I do too. And that's where Pranz comes in. His mom made sure he kept her maiden name. Pranz is actually Fornokey's son."

The camera feed puts Pranz's face in the full frame of the feed.

"Pranz, tell us who your dad really is," Sora demands.

Pranz stares at the camera, at Sora, then looks over to Doug and Clutch. He gulps. There's no turning back once he opens his mouth. He can screw over his companions to curry favor and earn his father's respect. He can take this as his chance to stand up to his father in a way where Gabe can't fight back. What will come out is anyone's guess, especially Pranz's.

Doug's stomach tugs at him.
Is this where Pranz fucks us or helps us?

The silence lasts too long for comfort.

"My father prefers money over family." Pranz finally gets out the hardest part. The point of no return.

"He is greedy and ruthless. He even tried to interrogate me, his own son to gain the upper hand. We would have gone to salvage claims with this finding, but my father admitted that he owns it. Maybe not directly, but in a way where they can deny a claim just so they can have it as their own. I recommend anyone who has been denied, start a lawsuit. I'm sure he will be busy with those after this," Pranz says, then takes a deep breath.

"I owe my life to Clutch," Pranz says, turning toward her. The camera does the same. "Those looking at the feed, you'll probably immediately think that she is an 'iron ant' and you would be wrong. There is no such thing."

Clutch's eyes look at Pranz's. Confusion setting in. 'What does he mean by that?'

"There are only human slaves. My father is a slaver. He keeps people who look similar to Clutch as slaves in his mining operations. They don't get to leave. You probably have never heard of anyone getting one of those lucrative jobs that are all over the feed. That's because they want people to believe they are so coveted that nobody leaves. The reality is that nobody leaves because they are born, raised, work, and then die without ever knowing life elsewhere."

Pranz looks at Clutch, tears forming in his eyes.

"It's wrong and it needs to be stopped," Pranz declares.

"But a few people have seen people like Clutch in various stations. Care to explain that phenomenon?" Sora asks. "Why aren't they on asteroids?"

"Slaves. Sex slaves. If you see them, they are being moved from a ship to somewhere else. Always with a guard as an escort. Always when very few people are around. And unless you have the money, that's all you see," Pranz shares. "Again, it needs to stop. Clutch and anyone like her are decent human beings. They have been discriminated against for far too long. They deserve real lives."

"You are saying that your dad is behind all of this?" Sora asks, just to hit it home.

"My father. Yes. He isn't much of a dad and I would never call him that," Pranz replies. "He has a secret R&D department with some really messed up experiments going on. You probably saw the result of one of those getting out in Gervantion. If not, it's because the feed was edited to not show it. But the destruction there and the death toll is real. My father is responsible for it."

"There is a lot to explore with these accusations, but the main thing here today is this proof of alien existence!" Sora declares. "We are going to head inside so we can see the anomaly again. This time from the most amazing view ever."

The feed continues, the ship docks, and crew heads inside. Sora, Pranz, and Doug head down the corridor on pop speeders to the main show. The feed continues.

"Da feed 'bout ta be pulled," ClutchAI says to Clutch a little while later.

"Dat 'll make em look guilty," Clutch replies. "How much time dey got?"

"Dey should get da 'nomaly 'fore dey complete da pull," ClutchAI declares. "Dey are trying ta figua out if dey can cut jus' our feed er if dey have ta down da 'tire hub."

"Ha!" Clutch laughs, then sits back and watches the crew heading through the structure.

She continues watching the feed, the anomaly, and Sora spouting her excitement for the event.

Sora speeds down the path again with Doug and Pranz flanking her sides. She continues to report the experience as they go through the featureless halls of the structure. They finally make it to the orb, just in time to have it's brilliance recorded.

"Event 'cessfully sent true da feed," ClutchAI declares. "Da hub has been taken offline, howeva."

Clutch nods and then sits up.

"Ya'll can come back. De feed is gone," Clutch says to the crew.

Chapter 45

"What's our next move?" Doug asks, breaking the momentary silence as the group settles into the galley aboard Pranz's hideout. His eyes flick from face to face, searching for direction.

"The accusations alone—and the fact that they came from his own son—should keep Gabe busy for a while," Sora replies, her voice calm but tinged with amusement.

"Maybe his army of lawyers will be buried in paperwork," Pranz says, crossing his arms. "But my father? He won't slow down. He'll come after us with everything he's got."

"I disagree," Sora says, flashing a confident smile as she leans back in her seat.

"You don't know my father," Pranz scoffs, shaking his head. "You think he plays by the rules?"

"I know greedy people who don't like to lose. He has nothing going for him on this. Any alliances will be tested. People don't want to stick around and be part of the implications that may come of this. Others will see more profit in siding with this new revelation. Gabe will lose friends and gain enemies," Sora suggests. "Just look at history. It happens every time."

Pranz doesn't respond, but his clenched jaw says plenty.

Doug leans forward, folding his hands on the table. "That's great. But it still doesn't answer my question—what's our next move?"

"I tink we should free da rocks," Clutch says, standing up as if the decision is already made.

Doug straightens, nodding eagerly. "I'm in."

"I ensured the hub broadcast included the code needed to access nearby relay systems," ClutchAI interjects, her voice neutral and confident. "We can hack a hub near the asteroid mines and stream another live feed. Unfiltered. Unstoppable."

"More fuel for the fire!" Sora grins, energized by the momentum. "Let's go. There won't be a better time. They'll never expect a second hack so soon."

"Might as well hit them while they're still dizzy," Pranz says, pushing his chair back. "Expose the truth, strip Gabe down to bone. If he's got nowhere to hide, even the scum who owe him favors will scatter."

Before anyone can say another word, Clutch pivots toward her ship, her voice steady as steel. "We got work ta do."

Doug jumps up and follows, his steps quick and eager, eyes fixed on her like a magnet.

"Do we need any more defensive upgrades before we head into the lion's den?" Pranz asks, already moving after them. "I don't think they're going to roll out a welcome mat when we show up with cameras."

Clutch doesn't stop walking. She veers toward a workroom and cracks her knuckles with a grin that could slice steel. "Prolly a good 'dea."

Without hesitation, she disappears through the hatch, already plotting new weapons in her mind—tools not just to survive, but to finish what they started.

"Now that we're ready," Sora says, practically vibrating with anticipation, "can we finally get there and make this happen? I've got a story begging to be told."

"Yeah," Clutch nods, her eyes locked on the nav panel, voice steely with resolve. "We 'er goin' 'n libratin' da rocks."

Before Clutch can input the final jump coordinates, Doug stands. He clears his throat awkwardly, then speaks.

"Before we go… I just have to say—if my ship hadn't broken down, if none of this happened… I never would've met Clutch. I never would've met any of you. And I honestly feel like—for the first time—I'm exactly where I'm supposed to be."

Clutch gives him a sidelong glance and smirks. "Nah. Was yer karma ta git so lucky."

Doug smiles back, the warmth in his eyes undeniable. "Whatever it was… I'm just glad I'm here."

Pranz leans back, arms crossed with a content grin. "Well, if we're doing feelings—I'm glad I met all of you, too. You're not here for my money. You're here because—somehow—we're actually making a difference."

"We are," Clutch replies with a wink. "Ya got all da stuff we need ta…"

"Funny. But you know what I mean," Pranz interjects, rolling his eyes.

Clutch nods once, silently acknowledging it. Doug mirrors the gesture.

Sora crosses her arms, watching the exchange, then speaks with a dry smirk. "I'm seeing you in a new light, Pranz. You're not as much of a jackass as I remember. But don't get ideas—we're never getting back together. It'd be a conflict of interest. And I've got too many interests. Especially now."

Pranz lifts his chin, the humor in his eyes dulled by the sting, but he takes it gracefully. "Understood."

There's a beat of quiet. The ship hums beneath them.

"We done sharin' feelin's now?" Clutch asks, half amused, half eager to move.

"You didn't share anything," Sora points out, raising an eyebrow.

Clutch shrugs, fingers dancing across the controls. "It'ill wait. We got work ta do."

"I agree," Doug says quickly, not needing a reason. Just ready to follow her lead.

With nothing else said, Clutch slams a final sequence of commands into the console. The ship hums louder, then lurches forward—space folding in on itself as they jump.

"Hack the feed! Go live—now!" Sora barks, already stepping into frame as the cameras hum to life.

The viewport floods with light as they arrive—seeing something unexpected.

Thousands of small personal ships hover around Crunch Rock, blinking and shifting around in an uncoordinated pattern.

"Connected," ClutchAI confirms.

Sora's eyes widen as her broadcast begins. "We are witnessing something unimaginable. A protest in space. Civilians—risking everything to stand for the enslaved miners of Fornokey."

Cameras shift from Sora to the ships. Their lights blink in rhythmic protest, a celestial Morse code of rebellion.

Doug glances at Clutch. Tears well in her eyes, her chest rising in silent, stunned disbelief.

"We're not the only ones who care," Doug whispers, resting a steady hand on her shoulder.

Clutch squeezes his fingers and nods, eyes locked on the glowing constellation of allies outside.

"We are going to get into the mix and move in closer. We are going to show you the injustice of these mines," Sora declares to the camera.

Clutch wipes her tears, steel returning to her gaze. She takes the controls.

The camera catches her face—human, raw, resolute—and beams it across the stars. For the first time, the galaxy sees what the 'iron ants' truly are: people.

The ship maneuvers to a side of the asteroid left out of view from the protests. There, on the rock's jagged flank, people in patched suits stagger through freezing vacuum—

no safety measures, no guards to help, just airlocks guarded like prisons.

But worse than that, are the bodies that didn't make it back. They are left out on the asteroid like garbage that fell from a trashcan. Guards preventing anyone from bringing them back in.

The zoom lens tightens. A miner holds the hole in another's suit, trying desperately to drag them back to safety. But before they reach the door, a Fornokey guard raises his weapon—and shoots the wounded one in the chest. He then motions for the miner to turn around and get back to work.

"No…" Sora breathes, her voice shaking. "I had no idea…"

"It's worse inside," Doug says, barely audible.

"Then let's go inside," Sora replies. "Let's show them everything."

Clutch guides the ship toward the main docking bay. As they approach, the protest ships part, opening a path. The recognize the ship from the feeds. But fighters—corporate enforcers—the ones keeping the protesters at bay—intercept.

"You are in violation of so many laws right now. Turn around or we will open fire," a voice snarls through comms.

"Great! And you'll be on the feed doing so," Sora replies. "This whole operation and your part in it are being fed live through the feeds. Do you really want to implicate yourself further?"

Silence. The fighters hesitate. Some shift position, unsure.

"You can bug out now and save the embarrassment for later or fight and see what happens," Sora continues. "And that goes for all ships listening. You are all going down. Best to surrender and let us in."

The pause is agonizing. Then, slowly, the fighters begin to peel away.

But one doesn't. A black ship bursts from the formation and opens fire, spinning and strafing across the protest line. It hits several civilian ships, turning the crowd into a frenzy.

Clutch doesn't flinch. She flips a switch and fires—a precise laser beam slicing through the attacker, the ship bursting apart in a brilliant chain of explosions.

The protest line breaks. Chaos ignites.

Other fighters, emboldened, take the opportunity and open fire.

"Fuck!" Pranz yells.

Clutch spins her ship into a barrage of enemy fighters, laser beams cleaving swaths through the void.

"They're flanking us!" Doug warns. He launches a spread of red-hot countermeasures. Explosions ripple behind them, but more missiles come.

"Out of blocks!" Pranz shouts.

"Laser power at five percent," Doug adds, teeth clenched.

It's not enough.

Inside the ship, a weight settles over everyone. They've fought too long. The ammo's low. The enemy's closing in.

"If we don't make it…" Doug says, turning to Clutch. "I just want you to know—I think I'm falling in love with you."

The camera captures Clutch's face, softening despite the battle. She smiles, focused but moved.

The feed continues. "The iron ants are human," Sora says, her voice tight with emotion. "They feel love. Loss. Pain. And they've been used up and thrown away. If we die, let this transmission expose the truth."

The fighter ships close in.

The crew looks at each other, trying to prepare themselves for the inevitable.

And then—the asteroid fights back.

From the mines, massive rock-crushers—machines once used to shatter ore—launch boulders into space. Precision strikes. Fighters explode on impact.

"They're doing it," Sora says, turning the feed toward the asteroid's surface. "The miners—the people—they've taken the tools meant to enslave them and turned them into weapons of freedom!"

Fighters retaliate, firing blindly into the rock. Clutch's rage flares. She fires what little remains of the laser system, targeting those firing on the surface.

"Laser 'pleted," ClutchAI says flatly.

"We're out," Pranz mutters.

"And sitting ducks," Doug says grimly.

Just then—salvation arrives.

Sleek, heavily armed Regimentary ships burst from the void, lighting up the fighters with precision. Their fire is surgical. Merciless.

"We are here to liberate this asteroid and all others enslaved under Fornokey," a commanding voice broadcasts. "We were unaware of the full extent of their illegal operations."

"Sure they didn't," Sora mutters off-mic. "Doesn't matter right now. They're saving our asses."

As the last of the fighters scatter or fall, Clutch docks the ship. The feed still rolling. The world still watching.

She stands, walks to Doug—and kisses him hard. Fierce. Triumphant.

The camera catches it all.

Chapter 46

Sora doesn't wait.

The moment the ship's doors hiss open, she bolts out—drones buzzing after her, camera rigs strapped across her chest and shoulders, another in-hand already rolling.

"We are stepping into the middle of a revolution," she reports into the feed, her voice charged with adrenaline and urgency. "This is Crunch Rock, and what we're seeing is the result of a people pushed too far. Miners, armed with nothing but their tools, rising against the system that imprisoned them."

Around her, chaos crackles in the air. Smoke coils up from ruined corridors. Guards sprint by, weapons discarded, chased down by enraged miners swinging drills and cutters once used to carve rock.

Scattered bodies mark the hallways—some slumped against bloodied walls, others lying still amid flickering debris. There is no triumph in this. Only the raw cost of a long-awaited reckoning.

Back at the ship, Doug and Clutch emerge. The hum of battle has dulled, replaced by the hollow echoes of footfalls and distant shouts. Clutch steps forward, then stops—frozen. Her eyes scan the devastation.

She's seen this place before—but never like this.

Smoke curls into the air. Alarms wail somewhere distant. And everywhere, humans move in scattered waves—

running, yelling, crying, clutching wounds, clutching each other. Shooting.

Doug watches her. The way her chest rises unevenly. The silent quiver of her lower lip.

"You okay?" he asks gently.

"Yeah… jus'…" Clutch's voice trails off, breaking before the sentence finishes. She blinks hard, sniffing, fighting.

Doug steps closer. "Too many feelings to pick just one?"

Clutch gives a small, breathless laugh. A nod. Her voice escapes in a whisper. "Yuh."

"What do you want to do?" Doug asks, quiet, steady. "Join the fight? Or just… take this all in?"

Her head shakes slowly. "I got some'em diff'ren' in mine."

Before he can ask, she takes off.

Her walk becomes a jog. Then a sprint.

"Clutch!" Doug calls, stumbling after her. He breaks into a run, pushing harder with every step, heart pounding—not just from the exertion but from fear. She's faster. He's never seen her move like this. And it terrifies him to think what might lie ahead.

She turns a corner. Disappears.

Doug curses under his breath and sprints harder, boots pounding against metal grating.

He rounds the same corner—and stops short.

Clutch is kneeling beside a crumpled body.

The hallway is quiet here, eerily removed from the noise of rebellion. The woman lying there is limp, red curls matted with blood, her breathing so faint it's almost imperceptible. Clutch's trembling hand is wrapped around hers.

Doug approaches carefully. "Did you… Did you know her?"

The look Clutch gives him could break stone.

Tears line her eyes, but don't fall—not yet. She brushes hair from the woman's face with a tenderness so unlike her usual blunt force that it steals Doug's breath.

"She s'ill warm," Clutch murmurs, then presses two fingers to the woman's neck. Her eyes flare with sudden hope. "Pulse. Slow. Real slow."

Doug doesn't hesitate. "I'll get your nanos!"

He spins and takes off down the corridor, legs burning as he pushes to run faster than he ever has before.

Behind him, Clutch stays by the woman's side, one hand holding tight, the other gently stroking her forehead.

'I can help save someone. Someone Clutch cares about.'

Doug repeats the thought like a mantra, each step pounding it into the metal floor. His lungs burn. His legs scream. But he doesn't stop. He can't stop.

He rounds the last corridor, the ship finally in sight—his salvation, her salvation. He reaches for the docking ramp—

And freezes.

A figure steps from the shadows.

Gun raised. Face obscured. Voice like poison.

"You and your little crew have cost me everything," the man growls.

Doug's chest heaves. He raises his hands, eyes locked on the weapon. The man steps forward into the light.

Gabe Fornokey.

Doug swallows hard. Rage curls in his gut.

"You cost yourself everything," Doug fires back. "That's karma. You don't get to blame me for your own corruption. I didn't ruin your empire. You did."

"I'm not here for philosophy, boy," Gabe sneers, advancing. "I'm here to make her suffer. She'll come back here and find your cold, useless body… and then I'll put her where she belongs. Strapped down. Broken. Mine."

Doug's hands tighten. His eyes narrow. He steps closer with each breath.

"Fuck you. You won't lay a finger on her."

"And you're going to stop me?" Gabe laughs, dark and hollow. "You're unarmed, and you're moving closer. Idiot."

Doug takes another step anyway. "You're the idiot," he says, tilting his chin behind Gabe. "for turning your attention from Clutch's ship."

Gabe flinches. Turns.

Behind him stands Pranz—calm, steady, rifle raised and locked on target. A sardonic smile plays across his lips.

"Hey, father."

Doug doesn't wait. He surges forward, rips the gun from Gabe's hand, and storms past them into the ship.

As he crosses the threshold, Pranz speaks:

"You don't deserve a quick death," he says coldly. "You deserve to stand trial. For every life you ruined. Every crime. Every scream that echoed in your name."

He steps closer, rifle unwavering. "You've got three options. One: I end you here. Two: I throw you to the mob, and they take you apart piece by piece. Or three… I lock you in a cage and let every planet in the system pile on the charges. Choice is yours."

Doug doesn't stop to hear the answer. He's already tearing through storage compartments, grabbing the nanos and a laser prod. The second he finds the case, he's gone—back down the ramp, sprinting like his soul's on fire.

He glances back as he clears the ship.

Gabe is on the ground. Breathing, maybe. Bleeding, probably. Pranz stands over him, eyes unreadable.

Doug doesn't have time to care.

'I'm coming, Clutch!'

His legs burn, lungs sting, but nothing will stop him now.

Not until he saves Clutch's friend.

Not until he makes good on his promise.

Doug slides to a stop, nearly collapsing from the sprint. Clutch sits hunched over the woman's body—head resting on the woman's chest, tears falling freely. She looks shattered.

Doug doesn't hesitate. He drops to one knee, yanks the cap off the nanos vial, and plunges it into the woman's neck.

Clutch jerks upright, startled. Her eyes dart to Doug, confused and red-rimmed.

"I didn't just run through this place three times and almost get shot by Gabe to fail this woman," Doug says, voice trembling but firm as the nanos begin their work. "It's not to late. Not with your tech."

"Gabe here?" Clutch's tears twist into fire, her voice cracking under the weight of grief morphing into rage.

"Yeah," Doug breathes, still winded. "Either dead or being gift-wrapped by Pranz right now. I didn't stick around to ask."

Clutch's eyes narrow. Her jaw sets.

She stands. Says something soft to the unconscious woman—words Doug can't hear but feels in his bones. Then, without a word, she bolts.

Doug starts to follow but stops. He looks down at the woman, coming back to life, her pulse just beginning to strengthen.

She matters. She matters to Clutch.

And so he stays.

Doug sinks back against the wall, guarding her. Gunfire echoes in the distance. Screams and shouting bounce off the metal halls. But somehow, a strange calm wraps around him. He glances at the woman, his voice soft.

"I don't know who you are… but you mean the world to Clutch. And she…" He pauses, lets out a breath. "I just want you to know that she is important to me too. She's changed my life. My fortune."

He smiles, emotion slipping into his voice.

"She's an angel. My angel. And I love her."

The hallway trembles slightly as a skirmish unfolds somewhere nearby. A group runs past in a panic. Doug watches them, alert but unmoved—until a guard chasing the group stops. His eyes land on Doug… and the woman.

"You," the guard growls, raising his weapon. "You're one of them."

Doug doesn't flinch. "One of who?"

"One of the assholes who caused all this."

Doug stands slowly. Calm. Collected. "No. Your karma caused this."

The guard steps forward, pressing the barrel of the weapon into Doug's chest. "You sound just like those damn iron ants. Worthless. Delusional."

Doug smiles.

"That's funny," he says. "Because it was an iron ant named Clutch who built the tech that started this revolution. She's smarter than you, me, and every bastard in this mine put together. So if you want to call someone stupid… grab a mirror."

"Fuck you!" the guard snarls and cocks the weapon—

"After you," Doug says, then sees the woman sweep her leg under the guard as Doug pushes him away, sliding sideways to avoid the muzzle of the gun.

The guard crashes down with a grunt but quickly levels his gun again—this time at the woman.

Doug doesn't think.

He pulls his laser prod and fires.

The shock hits the guard square in the face. Doug cranks the voltage. The guard thrashes violently. His neck snaps under the strain. The gun clatters to the floor. Doug lets the prod fall beside it, left there until the power drains.

Doug kneels beside the woman—now struggling to sit up. Her eyes meet his. And Doug sees it—the same steel Clutch carries. The same fire.

"We thought we lost you," he says softly. "Whoever you are."

"Dat was sweet o' ya ta say 'bout my gurl," the woman says, her voice raspy but full of warmth.

Doug's breath catches. "Clutch… she's your daughter?"

The woman nods, eyes glistening.

"Well… it was her invention that just saved your life," Doug says, offering a hand to help her up. "The nanos that are fixing you up. Clutch made them."

The woman smiles faintly. "Dat's nice. Where she at?"

"What's your name?" Doug asks as he steadies her, helping her stand.

"Dey call me Happy," her voice still weak, but positive all the same.

"Happy. I like that," Doug replies with a smile. "Happy, let's go find your daughter."

They start walking and finally round a corner. Clutch nearly slams into them as she nears the same intersection.

"Mama!" Clutch cries, her voice cracking as she rushes forward and throws her arms around the woman. Tears stream freely now, no longer tears of grief—but joy.

Doug steps back, his heart pounding, a weight lifting from his shoulders.

"You saved her," he says, watching Clutch cradle her mother.

"Ain't true," Clutch replies through tears. "Ya did it."

"Nah," Happy says, reaching out to grip Doug's hand. "Ya bof did. And ya got a good one here, baby girl."

Clutch pulls away and looks at Doug. Her eyes soften. "Yeah. He is a good one," Clutch says in a normal accent, which Doug now realizes is her playful mocking voice.

Doug can't stop smiling.

"Let's get out of here," he says. "The guards are a little pissed off at us."

Clutch wipes her eyes and grins. "Yeah. Dey is."

And together, the three of them head out—mother, daughter, and the man who finally found his place.

Epilogue

One Year Later…

The studio lights glow softly. Polished. Professional. A sleek news backdrop shimmers with Sora Volt's name, now synonymous with revolution and truth.

She smiles into the camera, then turns to face her guests.

"We're here again with Clutch and Doug—co-leaders of the most important expedition in human history," Sora begins, her trademark poise flawless. "Tell us, what have we learned since the discovery?"

Doug leans forward, his voice steady but excited. "There are twelve alien structures—each positioned at precise points across vast distances. They all pulse at the same intervals, and they all beam toward the center of this massive, hexagonal sphere."

Sora raises an eyebrow. "And what's at the center?"

"Ain't nobody know yet," Clutch chimes in, folding her arms casually. "Can't git close. Can't scan it. It's like it ain't even der."

"But we've finally cleared a new consortium to explore it all," Doug adds. "One that's trustworthy."

Sora nods, intrigued. "Tell us about the consortium."

Doug's smile widens. "Well, as you know, Fornokey has been on trial after trial for the last year. He's been exposed in so many different crimes, his life sentences might just be served in court."

"Because of the depth of that corruption," Doug continues, "it took a long time to build a team of honest researchers, scientists, engineers—people we trust with the future of humanity."

Sora smiles knowingly. "My viewers are very aware. I've been the one reporting it."

Doug chuckles. "Yeah. And Pranz—sorry—Jason Pranz, CEO of the Karma Corporation, has been a major source for your reporting."

"Indeed he has," Sora says smoothly. "Where does Jason fit in with the alien research?"

"He funds it," Doug answers. "Fully transparent. Full access. Karma Corp doesn't move a bolt without logging it somewhere public. Even the interviews, and how they are done, are transparent. With his approach, we know the consortium is trustworthy."

"I'm sure money isn't an issue for you two, now that you own the mining operations for all asteroid mines," Sora teases, grinning.

Clutch shrugs. "Yeah. Dey made rep'rations fer us. We got us a workforce of people dat wanna be der 'n make a good livin' while doze who was slaved up are now da foremen."

"But I imagine a lot of them wanted out?" Sora probes.

"Dey don't know much else. Only a few are out der learnin' somtin' new," Clutch says. "I been helpin' where I can."

"There've been reports of conflict," Sora adds. "People struggling to accept the new leadership. Different cultures clashing. Some... deeply uncomfortable with change."

Doug nods. "Change is hard for a lot of people, but if they just open their hearts and realize that nobody should have been treated that way, they will find forgiveness and become more welcoming to their new neighbors."

"Wise words," Sora says warmly. "Time will also help. It always does."

She leans forward, eyes twinkling. "But let's shift to something a little lighter. I've heard there may be... wedding bells in your future?"

Doug and Clutch glance at each other. Just one look. A smile from Clutch. A small blush from Doug.

"We'll leave it there," Sora laughs. "I respect your privacy... even if no one else does."

"You two—and Jason—are the most well-known humans in the galaxy. That level of fame changes everything. How does that sit with you?"

Clutch rolls her eyes. "I ain't like it, but dat's my karma fer findin' da aileen shit."

Doug laughs. "It's weird. I love parts of it. But it'd be nice to go for a walk with the love of my life without being stopped for alien questions every three meters."

Sora leans in again, sly. "Is that why you're building your own secret space station?"

Doug squints. "Wait... how do you know about that?"

"I'm Sora Volt. It's literally my job to know." She winks. "But don't worry. As long as I get the first exclusive tour, I won't leak the coordinates."

Doug and Clutch share another look.

"Deal," they say in unison.

Sora turns to the camera, slipping effortlessly into anchor mode. "And that's all for now. As we learn more about the alien structures and what lies at the center of the hexasphere, we'll bring you the truth, live and unfiltered."

She pauses, smile lingering.

"In the meantime—let Doug and Clutch walk in peace. Remember, they know less than the scientists still studying this thing."

Sora leans back, her closing line smooth as ever:

"I bring the shock, not the spin. This is Sora Volt. Thanks for watching."

Gravity s Whisper
By Ben Winter

ISBN: 979-8-9895476-8-5

For inquiries and other work by Ben Winter, contact:
https://mrimprov.com